The Chaucer Codex

John Conlee

Pale Horse Books

Library of Congress Control Number: 2020900011

ISBN: 978-1-939917-06-5

Cover Layout: Sally Stiles

www.PaleHorseBooks.com

Also by John Conlee:

> *THE DRAGON STONE*
> *A CUP OF KINDNESS*
> *THE KING OF MUD & GRASS*
> *IN THE SUMMER COUNTRY*
> *THE HEATER*
> *ROUNDING THIRD*
> *THE VOYAGE OF MAELDUN*
> *THE BROTHERS PENDRAGON*
> *CATACLYSM*

"By Pol, Tre, and Pen
Shall ye know Cornishmen"

– Traditional Cornish Saying

1

Charles Bascombe stepped out through the main doorway of the Bodleian Library and moved quickly across the Old Schools Quadrangle toward the quad's left-side entrance. He barely glanced at the Lord Thomas Bodley statue or the clutch of tourists gawking at it or snapping off photos.

Charles threaded his way between the Clarendon Building and the Sheldonian Theatre and passed beneath the Broad Street archway. He stopped for a moment to look to the right and then to the left before jay-walking across the Broad. He needed only a few more steps to reach his goal, the White Horse Pub, tucked neatly beneath flanking sections of Blackwell's Bookstore.

At 2:30 in the afternoon the dark, narrow pub was mostly empty. Charles paused a moment for his eyes to adjust.

"Charlie," came a familiar voice. "Back here." From the gloomy depths of the pub, he made out a hand waving to him.

"Got my message, I see," the man said, as Charles slid onto a stool across from him.

"Yeah, I did. But Professor, whatever it is you want, it had better be pretty damn good – you just interrupted a guy who was on a roll."

"A roll? Doing what?"

"Transcribing, of course. Lydgate. A stunning early 15th-century manuscript, sir. Colorful rubrics, wonderful illuminated capitals, floral marginalia, and written in a precise and consistent book hand. A joy to look at and to work with."

"Well, Charlie, had it been Chaucer I interrupted," the professor said, "then I would surely apologize. But Lydgate? No, don't think an apology's required."

The speaker, whom Charles referred to as "Professor," was a slight, bespectacled, elderly man wearing a shapeless brown sweater and threadbare corduroy trousers. He was Professor William Wentworth, Charles Bascombe's close friend and mentor. He was also one of Oxford University's most distinguished professors of English Literature and the current holder of the Bosworth Chair in Medieval Studies.

"C'mon, Professor," Charles said, "you know Lydgate can be good. Of course not always, but every now and then. Even you have to admit that the *Prologue to The Siege of Thebes* isn't half bad, so how about giving the guy some credit. Anyway, we can debate the merits of Lydgate another day. But sir, what's so urgent that you needed to interfere with serious acts of scholarship?"

"Maybe you should order a drink?" Professor Wentworth said. A half-empty pint of bitter already sat on the table in front of him.

"Well, okay. Still got several hours of work ahead of me, but a half of lager couldn't hurt."

"Maybe you still have several hours of work ahead of you and maybe you don't," Professor Wentworth said. "You can decide that after you've heard what I have to tell you." Charles raised his eyebrows at the old professor's words.

"Goodness, sir, you make this sound rather momentous.

Ominous, even."

"I don't mean to sound ominous, Charlie. Here." He handed Charles a five-pound note. "While you're getting your drink, could you bring me some beer nuts? I'll break the news when you get back."

A minute later Charles had returned with his half pint of Carlsberg. He set it down on the table and slid the packet of beer nuts and the change across to his old friend. The two men lifted their glasses to each other and drank.

"So Charlie," the professor said, "ever been to Cornwall?"

"Cornwall? Uh, no, never have."

"Well, to quote the late, great Buddy Holly, 'you don't know what you been a-missin', oh boy.' "

"Umm, you're dating yourself, Professor. Anyway, I thought that song was about love and kisses, not Cornwall. But sir, perhaps we could cut to the chase? What's all this about Cornwall?"

"The man I want you to go and see lives there. Actually, he lives on the Lizard."

"He lives with a lizard?"

"No, Charlie, not *with* a lizard, *on* the Lizard. It's an especially wonderful part of Cornwall, down near the southeastern tip. Come to think of it, though," the professor mused, "his first wife was rather a bit of a lizard." The professor grinned, and when he did, he exposed the gap in his top front teeth that made Charles think of the actor Terry Thomas, and also, inevitably, of the "gat-toothed" Wife of Bath. Charles smiled at the thought.

"Okay, so who's this man, sir, and why do I need to go and see him?" Charles took a pull on his lager while the professor pondered his response.

"I'm actually rather hesitant to tell you too much at this stage. I want you to see what he has without any preconceptions. Experience it fresh, as it were."

"What he has?"

"Yes, Charlie, what he has. It's a manuscript. Something he's recently procured, I'll say that much. The truth is, I haven't seen it myself. But I know he's terribly excited about it. And from what he's told me, it sounds like he has every reason to be. He's a fellow who tends to know his stuff."

"Wait, Professor. Let's back up just a bit. Who is this man who lives on – but not with – the Lizard?" Charles asked, "this man who's procured a mysterious manuscript he's excited about?"

The professor stared down at his beer glass while making small, damp circles on the tabletop with it. Then he looked up.

"You know, Charlie, I think he's going to quite like you, my youthful American protégé. The truth is, he's not only a bit of a curmudgeon, he's also rather a loner and a misanthrope. He rarely takes to people, and the people he especially hates are British academics. He thinks they are frauds, posers, and perverts."

"He'll get no argument from me," Charles said, smiling.

"He's also a bit strait-laced, you see. But you, Charlie, you're such a modest and self-effacing sort of chap, you just might strike a chord with him. Anyway, that's what I'm betting. You've probably never heard of him because he is a very private person, but he's actually quite well known in bibliographical circles. His name, by the way, is Rhys ap

Roberts Tremayne."

"Wow. Quite a Celtic name."

"It is. Which is one reason why he's likely to take to you – the fact that you, too, have a Celtic surname: Bascombe. Added to that is the fact that you are an American, not a Brit. That will help. But most of all, Charlie, he'll like you because you are *not* a fraud, poser, or pervert."

"Are you sure, Professor?" Charles said, again smiling.

"You can certainly be a bit of a wise-ass, no question about that, but I know for a fact you aren't a fraud. I know for a fact you are the second best philologist I've ever run into," the professor said, with a self-deprecating smile, "and that you may even be the best medieval paleographer I've ever run into."

"Even better than you?"

"Well . . . yes. It has to be acknowledged, Charlie, that you are the finest reader of medieval scripts the world has ever known."

"Ah, shucks, Professor."

"Okay, a bit of hyperbole there. But you really are a natural."

Now the professor was smiling also. He held his glass out to the one sitting on the table before Charles and clinked it. "It's true, Charlie."

"But sir, the reason we're two of the best philologists and paleographers is that we're just about the only ones left. We're well on our way to becoming an endangered species."

"Sadly, Charlie, that's pretty much true. We're a dying breed, alas."

"So, okay, this guy has come into possession of a medieval

manuscript, and he wants an expert opinion on it. That about it?"

"Quite right."

"And he asked you to give it to him, and you turned him down?"

"Quite right again."

"Why'd you turn him down, Professor?"

"Because it's you who's the right man for this, not me."

"Level with me, sir. Why *did* you turn him down?" Charles spoke forcefully, tilting his head and staring intently at his old friend.

"Because you are ready for this. It's your time. For me, it's grass time. I'm going out to pasture, Charlie, with no looking back."

Charles Bascombe took in a deep breath, then let it out slowly. "Tell me more about Rhys Tremayne," he finally said.

"Now you're talking, Charlie. That's what I like to hear. Rhys Tremayne. He's a private scholar and bibliophile. Mostly specializes in incunabula and sixteenth-century books. More Renaissance than medieval. Has a particular passion for Shakespeare's dramatic contemporaries. He was educated at Sherburne College, then went on to Oxford where he was a Merton man. He hated both places with a passion. He hated Oxford so much he's never once been back. He had only a few friends here. I was one of them."

"Because you weren't a fraud, a poser, or a pervert," a remark the professor ignored.

"He did his graduate studies at Edinburgh. That was a place he actually enjoyed. But after that he returned home to Cornwall, where he's lived ever since. He was never interested in holding an academic position. He has a spacious home on the Lizard that overlooks the sea, a few miles beyond Helston. He also keeps a small flat in St. Ives. He's an art lover as well as a bibliophile."

"His money?"

"Old family money. Which he has managed most astutely, apparently. But he hasn't contributed tuppence to Oxford University, not even to the Bodleian. He is one of Basil Blackwell's best customers, though. Does his bit to keep the old bookstore in business."

"He lives alone?"

"Oh, no. He has a beautiful and charming wife. She's his second wife – she's not the lizard. He also has a daughter from his first marriage. She's off at art school somewhere, I believe."

"So he wants an expert to come and have a look at his manuscript?"

"Yes. He wants *you*. I've sung your praises, and he's agreed."

"Hope I won't disappoint you."

"Me too, Charlie," he said with a smile. "But I'm sure you won't."

"When?"

"Soon as possible. Could you leave tomorrow?"

"Whoa! Just drop everything and go traipsing off to Cornwall?"

"Train from Paddington will get you there in five, maybe six, hours."

"Sir, I do have a life."

"You do?"

"Well . . . sort of."

"Charlie, this is big. It's possible it's much ado about nothing, but I really don't think so. Not with Rhys. If he's right, this could be a career-maker."

Charles Bascombe's eyes widened at the professor's last remark. Then he lifted his glass and downed the final inch of beer.

Charles Bascombe, his head still spinning from his little tête-à-tête with Professor Wentworth, walked back to the Duke Humfries Library in the Bodleian to collect his work and turn in the manuscript he'd been transcribing. Beside the bookstand he found a handwritten note.

"Movie on Saturday? Hope so. Sophie." The note was from a young woman named Sophia Sinclair, a Ph.D. student at a university in Michigan. She and Charles had gone for coffee a few times when taking a break from their work, and she was clearly interested in seeing their acquaintance develop. Charles was still undecided about that.

Charles glanced over at the corner where Sophie usually sat, but she wasn't there. He quickly scrawled a reply, saying he was going on a short trip but would see her when he got back. Charles really did think he was going on a *short* trip. As it turned out, he was wrong.

Charles Bascombe strode quickly up the Banbury Road, as he often did after completing an intense day of poring over medieval manuscripts. It was a two-mile walk to his little flat in North Oxford, but the physical exercise was just what he liked after all the concentrated mental exercise.

On this day, lost in his own thoughts – thoughts concerning Cornwall, the Lizard, Rhys Tremayne, and a mysterious medieval manuscript – he hardly glanced at the old, stylish, red brick structures that lined the road. Charles wondered what the manuscript could contain. He knew, of course, that there were a great many significant works that had long since disappeared. He remembered the scattering of references to a character named Wade – Wade and his boat – but that no romance or saga of Wade was extant. He thought about the discovery of the unique manuscript called Cotton Nero A.x., that contained the great Middle English romance *Sir Gawain and the Green Knight*, a manuscript discovered in the mid-nineteenth century after languishing in obscurity for nearly five centuries. He thought of the discovery of the Winchester Manuscript of Sir Thomas Malory's *Le Morte d'Arthur*, its text previously known only from Caxton's early printed book – a discovery that had radically altered Malory scholarship. Was there any chance that this manuscript might really contain something as momentous as that? Charles Bascombe knew it would be foolish to have any such expectations. And yet Professor Wentworth believed that what this manuscript contained could very possibly be a career-maker.

✠ ✠ ✠

"Home early, Charlie?" Mrs. Hawkins said as he approached the door. She was just on her way out, preparing to take her Dalmatian, Agnes, for her late afternoon stroll.

"Going to take a trip," he said. "To Cornwall."

"Oh, how lovely. Where about in Cornwall?"

"Place called the Lizard."

"Oh, how lovely. It's the Cornish Riviera, Charlie. Very scenic. You must certainly pack your swim trunks."

A bathing suit, however, wasn't an item that Charles Bascombe even possessed. "Don't know how long I'll be there, Mrs. Hawkins. Could be a very short trip."

"Oh, Charlie, you haven't forgotten that your friend is coming next week, have you?"

"Oh, yes, that's right. Thanks for the reminder. Jackson. Jackson Lockhart, my old college roommate. Gosh, it's been a couple of years since I've seen Jack. Well, I'll surely be back by then."

"Shall I pack you a lunch for the trip?"

"That would be great. Thanks so much, Mrs. Hawkins. You're a wonder."

2

Rather than send Charles Bascombe off to Cornwall on his own, Professor William Wentworth had had second thoughts. "You can be such a shy lad at times, Charlie," he said when he phoned that evening, "I've decided it might be best for me to be with you when you meet the fellow. Introduce you properly and keep you from getting cold feet, eh?"

"I'd appreciate that, Professor. But sir, I can't help feeling that you would quite like to take a peek at this manuscript yourself. Yes? Maybe I'm just the man for the job, but you, sir, can't help wanting to be right there looking over my shoulder."

"Charlie, you know me too well. Yes, I will admit to

being extremely curious. But I promise you, you'll get no kibitzing from me."

"Yeah, right."

The professor's old black Morris Minor pulled up in front of Charles' flat in North Oxford just after nine o'clock. He beeped the horn. Charles hurried out and tossed a small travel bag and his shoulder bag, which also contained his laptop computer, into the back seat. He climbed in front beside his old friend.

"Look through those CDs and pick your poison," Professor Wentworth said. "We've got a goodly drive ahead of us."

"You've had a CD player installed in this old wreck?"

"Hey, watch who you're calling an old wreck! A CD player? But of course. I've not quite reached your iPod generation, Charlie. I'm only twenty years behind."

"Better make it thirty, sir."

"I used to have a Walkman, Charlie."

"So did my grandfather."

Their drive took them south through the Vale of the White Horse, west on the M4 past Swindon and Bath, and then south on the M5 through Somerset and Devon. All the while they listened to the works of American composers like Aaron Copland and Leonard Bernstein. The professor's love for American music wasn't limited to Buddy Holly and Chuck Berry, though they were high on his list.

"What was that last short piece?" the professor asked as Charles was changing CDs.

"I think it was called 'Slaughter on the Lizard,' " Charles

replied with a straight face. The professor looked across at his companion with a bent eyebrow and pursed lips.

"No, wait a second," Charles said. "Guess I misspoke. Not 'Slaughter on the Lizard,' 'Slaughter on Tenth Avenue.' Umm, Richard Rodgers, the composer, and the Boston Pops, conducted by Arthur Fiedler."

"Charlie, Charlie, Charlie. What am I ever going to do with you?"

"Grit your teeth and take me as I am?"

"It's a wonder I have any teeth left," the professor muttered.

At a service area near Taunton, they pulled off for petrol and coffee. The car park was fairly crowded since it was nearing midday, and Charles had to avert his eyes as the professor pulled into a space so narrow their doors could barely be opened. Sucking in their stomachs, they managed to squeeze themselves out. It was a major miracle the professor hadn't scraped either of the other cars. Any fresh scrapes on his own car would have merely blended in.

As they walked toward the entrance, Charles noticed a hulking fellow one row of cars over who was eyeing them intently. As they passed through the automatic doors, Charles glanced back and saw that the man's eyes were still on them. What's *that* all about? he wondered.

"I'll nab a table for us, Charlie. You get the coffee. White please," the professor said, meaning coffee with cream.

"Large?"

"Oh yes, indeed."

There was a long line at the Costa Coffee bar, and it took

Charles ten minutes to get their croissants and coffees. As he moved back toward the table where the professor awaited him, Charles noticed the hulking fellow from the car park standing just inside the door, staring at the professor. As Charles approached the table, the man's gaze shifted to him. Charles felt a chill run down his back.

"Professor, there's a strange-looking dude over there who I'm pretty sure has been watching us," Charles said in a low voice.

"A *dude*?"

"Yeah, a strange-looking bloke. Over near the door. I spotted him out in the car park, and now he's standing over there looking at us. The guy gives me the willies. Oh, man, here he comes."

The fellow loomed up beside their table. To Charles, he was strange-looking for sure. He had a jutting brow, a simian face, and a bulky though slightly stooped physique. His wild bush of hair was matted and tangled. The guy looked like Dr. Jekyll in the act of becoming Mr. Hyde, the process having stalled about half way through.

"That be your Morris out there?" he grunted at Professor Wentworth, gesturing with a large and thickly callused thumb. "Old black 'un? Dented up good?"

"Uh, yes, that sounds about right."

"You sell it?"

"Would I *sell* it? Well . . . yes . . . I suppose I might be willing to sell it."

"How much for?"

"How much for? Hmm . . . well . . . I don't really know. You, Charlie?" Charles just shrugged. "Hmm . . . umm . . .

how does five thousand quid sound to you?"

"Five? Five?" Mr. Half-Hyde held up one hand, splaying all five sausage-like fingers. His simian face bore a look of shock.

"Too high?" the professor said.

"Erg," the man grunted, nodding in agreement.

"Well, umm, how does thirty-five hundred sound?" It was obvious to Charles that the professor had no idea what the car might be worth and had never had any such previous dealings.

The fellow rubbed his massive jaw, apparently giving the professor's offer some thought. "Erg, gettin' warmer," he finally grunted, moving his head back and forth.

"Tell you what. Why don't you give me your contact information and I'll get back to you quite soon. You see, my friend and I will need to have use of the car for the next few days, so I can't be selling it right off anyway. We're on our way to Cornwall and probably won't be back until next week."

"Cornwall? Why'n ya wantin' to go there? Nothin' good in Cornwall."

"Oh no, my friend, I really have to say that you are quite wrong about that. There are many good things in Cornwall."

"Can't think o' none myself," the man said.

"Take my word for it, there are," the professor replied.

The man looked over at Charles, who just shrugged.

"Never been there," he said. "Don't have an opinion. But the professor usually knows what he's talking about."

The ape-like fellow shook his head in dismay. He obviously couldn't understand why anyone would want to go to Cornwall. The professor handed him a small piece of paper and a pen. The fellow stared at the pen for a while, then gripped it in his massive paw and scrawled something on the paper.

"Well, sir, thank you for your interest in the car," the professor said. "I'll be back in touch with you as soon as I can."

"Sure do like that car," the man mumbled. "Sure could do some good with it." He stood there a moment longer, then finally turned about and shambled away, mumbling to himself all the while. Charles thought he heard the man saying "Five thousand quid" and shaking his head as if in disbelief.

"Sir," Charles said to Professor Wentworth, "I had no idea you were the proud possessor of a collector's item."

"Nor did I, Charlie. But I'll let you in on a little secret. That collector's item out there? It doesn't belong to me. It isn't my car."

"What?"

"The car's not mine, Charlie. It belongs to my wife. And here's the thing. She doesn't know we've borrowed it."

"That *we've* borrowed it? What do you mean by *we*?"

✢✢✢

3

Just beyond Exeter the professor said, "Why don't we take the A30 rather than the A38. It's only a bit longer and far more scenic. It'll take us 'round the western side of Dartmoor and later through the middle of Bodmin Moor. Okay by you?"

"It's your car, sir, and you're the driver. Well, actually, it isn't your car, but you know what I mean."

"Charlie, dig around in the CD box and see if you can't find 'Rhapsody in Blue.' Been having a yen to hear it. Oh, and here." The professor extracted a scrap of paper from his pocket and handed it to his young friend and protégé. "What's it say, Charlie? What *was* that chap's name, anyway?"

"Wow. What a horrible scrawl. Is this a test of my paleographical skills, Professor? Hmm. Okay, looks like his surname is probably Stevenson. And his first name – "

"Adlai?" said Professor Wentworth, unhelpfully.

"Har. Now let's see. Hmm. No, definitely not Adlai. Looks like it might be something like Robbie." Then, because of the thought that suddenly popped into his head, Charles couldn't help laughing out loud. "That's a good one, Professor. Makes my day."

"Eh? What's the big joke?"

"It's not a big joke, sir, maybe a very small one. Best keep it to myself." The professor gave Charlie a dubious glance.

"So, Charlie, what's happened to 'Rhapsody in Blue'? Dun is in the mire, Charlie."

Charles, who was familiar with the professor's fondness

for obscure Chaucerian allusions, went back to digging through the professor's CDs, in hopes of getting Dun out of the mire. "Aha, found it." He removed it from its plastic case and pushed it through the CD slot.

They listened in silence as the piece began with a solo clarinet playing a smooth and haunting sequence of rising notes.

"Ah, Charlie, that sinuous opening melodic line is a balm to the soul," the professor said with a sigh.

"With apologies, sir, I believe it's called a glissando," Charles said.

The professor looked over at his young friend and grinned. "Oh, Charlie, I feel certain that Rhys is really going to take to you," he said. "At the same time, though, it might be wise to refrain from correcting him in the way you just did me. He'll admire your strange and eclectic lumber room of a mind, since it will mirror his own. But a word to the wise: don't *ever* correct him. Got that?"

"I got it, sir. I'll be sure to remember that bit of advice. And in the future I'll limit all my corrections to just you." The professor made a rude sound.

For the next several minutes they drove without speaking, both of them absorbed in the music. But the professor finally broke the quiet by saying, "Back there at the service area, you didn't happen to notice a tow truck in the car park, did you?"

"A tow lorry?"

"Charlie, in this country we call them 'tow trucks.' "

"No, sir, I didn't notice a tow truck. Or a tow lorry."

"As we were pulling out of the service area, I'm pretty

sure I saw one come out not far behind us. And right at this moment there's another one a-trundling maybe half a mile back. The blighter's been cruising along back there keeping the same distance for the last ten minutes. Looks quite a bit like the very same one."

"Tow trucks on major highways aren't exactly rare sights, sir."

"Yes, that's true. But if it is the same one, that would be quite odd. Those blighters tend to service fairly limited areas. We're a hundred miles from Taunton by now. If it is the same one, that bloke's wandered a good bit off his patch, I should think."

"Well, sir, maybe it's that Adlai Stevenson fellow again," Charles said.

"Just be quiet, Charlie" the professor grumped. "Some of us are trying to listen to Gershwin."

✢✢✢

They drove over the bridge crossing the River Tamar and passed the "Duchy of Cornwall" sign.

"Welcome to Cornwall, Charlie," the professor said brightly. "This is going to be an experience you will never forget, I can feel it in my bones. And don't go telling me there aren't any nerves in bones. It's just an expression."

"To tell you the truth, sir, I'm pretty excited also." The professor, his eyes glued to the road, smiled at Charles' words.

For a good while they drove on in silence, for the moment without music or conversation. Finally Professor Wentworth said, "That young woman in the library, Charlie, how are things going with her?"

"Young woman?"

"Brunette? About five foot six or five-seven? Slender-ish? Shining dark eyes? From her conversation, seems to be working on Malory? Goes with you for your elevenses every second or third morning?"

"Oh, you mean Sophie."

"Sophia. Good name for a scholar. So how are things going with her?"

"There are no things, sir. Sophie's just an acquaintance. Someone to share a coffee with, right?"

"A very pleasant and attractive someone, no doubt."

"Well, yes. But don't go reading too much into that, Professor."

"You live too abstemious a life, Charlie. Maybe on this trip we'll have to make an effort to change that."

"Professor, I thought we were on this outing in order to provide an opinion on a medieval manuscript. You haven't lured me down here on some false pretext, have you sir?"

"Not a bit of it. But dear boy, there *is* more to life than medieval manuscripts."

"Yes, I'm sure there is." To shut the professor up, Charles shoved Buddy Holly's *Greatest Hits* into the CD player.

"Rather bleak terrain," Charles said, staring out at the dry, brown countryside about them.

"Yes, it is. Not at all like the lush rolling hills and wet bogs of Dartmoor. But filled with secret wonders. Megalithic tombs, ancient stone circles, beautiful late medieval churches tucked away in tiny villages. Not to mention the spectacular cliffs and tiny harbors of the North Cornwall coast.

"Up ahead to our left, do you see that rugged-looking

tor? That high, rocky eminence? That's Brown Willy, the highest point in Cornwall. Just a bit higher than Rough Tor, a couple of miles from here."

"Brown Willy? Rather strange name."

"Not for Cornwall. Lots of strange names in Cornwall. It's likely to be a corruption of two Cornish words, one meaning 'hill' – like the Welsh word *bryn*, as in your American college Bryn Mawr – and one probably meaning 'highest.'"

"Why don't we stop and climb Brown Willy? Give our legs a middle-of-the-afternoon stretch. Do you think I could pick up a T-shirt that says 'I climbed Brown Willy'?"

The professor gave Charles a stern look. "Thou shalt not make fun of Brown Willy. There are ancient deities up there you'd be well advised not to stir up, ancient deities known for their ingenious and painful revenges. As for stopping and climbing Brown Willy . . . *I think not.*"

"Well, okay then," Charles said. "Just an innocent suggestion."

"You can keep your innocent suggestions to yourself. Anyway, Charlie, right now we've come to the heart of Bodmin Moor. Daphne du Maurier country. Ever read any of her works?"

"Actually, no."

"Not even *Castle Dor?* Kind of a re-telling of the Tristan and Iseult story. Your sort of thing, Charlie."

"I'll put it on my list."

"Yes, you must. And up here just a few more miles and we'll pass Jamaica Inn. When we get to Rhys's place, it will almost be like walking onto the set of *Rebecca.* Do you know the Hitchcock film?"

"Rings a bell."

"As well it should, my boy. And here's a little known fact for you. The Hitchcock film *The Birds* was actually adapted from a du Maurier short story. How about that?"

"Yikes. What have you got me into, Professor? Mrs. Hawkins had me looking forward to a few languorous days of lolling on the Cornish Riviera. And now you've got me worried that we're about to step into some gothic nightmare world."

"Well, it could be rather a mixture of both, dear boy. But seriously, I rather doubt that we're likely to have much gothic nightmare stuff in our future."

"No. All you want to do is break me of my abstemious habits."

"One can always hope, Charlie. One can always try."

"Anyway, sir," Charles said, turning and staring through the little car's back window, "the good news is that I don't see any tow lorries a-motoring away in our wake. We must've ditched that blighter."

"Tow *trucks*, Charlie, they're called tow *trucks*."

After another forty-five minutes they passed the turnoff to Carbis Bay and St. Ives, and in just a few more miles reached the junction where they would turn left toward the Lizard. To their right lay the town and harbor of Penzance and, nine or ten miles beyond Penzance, Land's End.

"Wow," Charles Bascombe suddenly exclaimed.

"Yes, Charlie, quite a sight, isn't it. Definitely worth a 'wow.'"

The professor pulled the old Morris into a mostly empty,

sandy parking area and stopped so the two of them could gaze across the waters of Mount's Bay at St. Michael's Mount, which loomed up dramatically half a mile away.

"Not quite Mont Saint Michel, perhaps, but quite impressive nonetheless. Part castle, part church, part manor house."

Charles pulled his camera from his backpack and took a couple of photos.

"From up on the hill above Marazion, the views will be even more striking. This is a good time of day for photography, too. If you'd like, perhaps you can come back and have a proper visit sometime in the next day or two. When the tide is out, you can walk across the causeway to the island. When it's in, you can hire a small boat to take you across. Well worth a look, Charlie."

They set off again and drove up the steep, winding main street of Marazion, whose buildings to Charles seemed a bit gray and grim.

"Yes," the professor said, as if reading the young man's thoughts, "rather a dour and depressing little town, isn't it. Not at all typical of Cornwall."

When the road had taken them higher above the town, Charles craned his neck in order to look back and take in a final sight of the little island and its impressive castle.

"Welcome to the Lizard," the professor said. "And this is just the beginning."

A few minutes later they skirted the bustling market town of Helston and then drove on toward their final destination, the home of Rhys ap Roberts Tremayne, perched high on the cliffs overlooking the western end of the English Channel.

Two tall, plain, stone pillars flanked the entrance to the manor house. No sign, no gate, and beyond the entrance a long stretch of graveled driveway. Charles noticed a pair of large stone birds atop the pillars.

"Crows?" he asked.

"Very like crows, Charlie. Cornish choughs, actually, birds that hold special significance to Cornwall and its inhabitants."

"Choughs? Well, you could've fooled me," Charles said.

"We'll have to add all the myths and legends about choughs to your lumber room of a mind, Charlie. Actually, it might be best for Rhys to be the one to do that. Ask him about choughs and you'll surely endear yourself to him. But be prepared for an hour's lecture."

"An hour?"

"Rhys is not always a man of few words – not like you, Charlie."

The gravel crunched noisily beneath the tires of the Morris as the pair of medieval scholars traveled the last four hundred yards of their journey.

"Well, here we are, my boy," Professor Wentworth announced as the car pulled to a stop just short of a broad set of steps leading to a covered entryway. "Journey's end. Will it be a profitable journey? If I were a betting man, I'd say the odds are about seven to five in favor."

"Only seven to five? That's terribly reassuring, Professor," Charles said. "I'm so glad you aren't a betting man. And I'm even gladder that the odds you're offering aren't a hundred to one."

✛✛✛

A very short, elderly woman opened the door, and after a moment's hesitation, her wizened face cracked into a wide smile. "Oh, Professor," she said in a distinctive croak, "it's so nice to see you again."

"And you, too, Maria. This lad is Charles Bascombe. It's Charles that Rhys especially wants to see, not me."

"Oh, Professor, he always wants to see you. Please come in. I shall just go and track down the master." She closed the door behind them, then scurried off through a large sitting room to their left.

"Maria's their sole domestic," the professor said to Charles. "Been with the family since the time of Rhys's father. I've known her for thirty years. She's looked exactly the same the entire time."

Charles heard rapid footsteps, and then a lean and vigorous-looking gray-haired man who appeared to Charles to be in his late sixties approached them with extended hand.

"Greetings, greetings, my old friend," he said. "And you must be Charles, Charles Bascombe. So very delighted you could come." He reached out and took Charles' hand, his grip as firm and vigorous as the man himself looked. No limp-wristed English handshake for Rhys Tremayne.

"When Professor Wentworth told me about the manuscript, sir, I could hardly stay away."

"Two men after my own heart," Rhys replied, smiling at both of them. "Yes, it hasn't escaped my notice that the professor, in the end, couldn't stay away either." The two old friends grinned at each other.

"Well, Charles, why don't you and the professor take a

few moments to stash your things away in your rooms, and then we can all sit down and have a chat. And perhaps a drop of something as well. Maria will show you where to go. Charles, we've got you all the way up at the top. It will give you greater privacy up there, not to mention an excellent sea view. Hope you don't mind all the stair steps. But you look to be rather a fit young chap. There's a storm expected tonight, so when you settle down for the night, you'd best pull in the wooden shutters."

"That sounds great, sir. I appreciate all your hospitality."

Maria led the two of them up a winding, ornate staircase, directing the professor to a second-floor bedroom and then leading Charles up another fight to the top floor, which consisted of just two small bedrooms and a connecting bath.

"You'll have this floor to yourself, Mr. Bascombe. Sorry to make you climb all those steep steps," she said in her ancient-sounding voice, "but there's just the one extra guest bedroom on the second floor where the professor will be. The master's daughter's room is there too, and we always keep it ready for her since we never know when she might decide to pop in. The master thinks she may be stopping 'round in another day or two, since she's just finished her year at art school. With Ally, one can never be quite sure of her comings and goings."

"Ally?"

"Alwyn. Such a delightful young woman. I think you'll like her, Mr. Bascombe, though one must admit, she's every bit as unpredictable as she is talented. There's a good few of her paintings in the master's study. Not quite to my taste, though highly thought of by people who understand such things." Maria, Charles realized, was proving a valuable source of information. "Come down to the sitting room when you've had a moment to unpack your things. Oh, there's just a duvet on the bed, but lots of extra blankets on the top shelf of the wardrobe. Washroom right through that door," she said, pointing.

"Thank you, Maria. It all looks very cozy."

Finally left to himself, Charles took a moment to look over the room: a rather smallish double bed, a night stand and a reading lamp, a chest of drawers, a large wardrobe in lieu of a closet, and a small wooden table close to the window. Charles placed his travel bag on the floor inside the wardrobe and his backpack beside the nightstand. Then he stepped over to the window and stared out.

His room faced the back of the house, and beneath him a landscaped garden of three levels marched down toward the sea cliff maybe a quarter of a mile distant. The gray, choppy sea drew his eyes. On the far horizon loomed a steep bank of dark clouds, probably the leading edge of the coming storm Rhys Tremayne had mentioned. It was an impressive tableau. Welcome to Manderley, Charles said to himself. Welcome to the world of Alfred Hitchcock.

4

Three small sofas graced the sitting room, one facing the fireplace and two facing each other at right angles to the fireplace. An ancient Persian carpet, well-worn and faded but still quite exquisite in an intricate pattern of pinks and reds and blues, lay between them. As Charles came in, Rhys

Tremayne and Professor William Wentworth were sitting across from each other, deep in conversation. Without missing a conversational beat, Rhys motioned Charles to the sofa facing the fireplace.

"It's an outrage," he was saying, "a total outrage. How could Parliament ever allow such a thing?"

"Politics?" Charles said. "Maybe I'd better excuse myself."

"No, no, dear boy," Rhys said, "we'll be good. Just had to get a few things off my chest, you know. William and I don't often agree on politics, but I can't resist trying to set him straight now and then – though it's rather like talking to a pile of stones."

"Sir, I believe the professor is quite set in his liberal views."

"Sadly, yes. But fortunately, one of my dear friend's few faults. Anyway, Charles, what about you? Tell me all about yourself. William is obviously very fond of you, which is good enough for me. But let's hear you tell your own story, eh?"

"My own story. Golly. Well, I've just completed my third year as an assistant professor in a small college in Virginia. They've granted me a research year to finish the book I've been working on. That's what's allowed me the chance to come and work in Oxford and to renew my friendship with my old mentor."

"You're at Waverly College?"

"Yes, that's right. So you've heard of it?"

"The Harvard of the South, I believe they call it," Rhys Tremayne said, smiling.

"Yes, I've heard people say that," Charles agreed, "though

I'm not sure I consider it a compliment."

"Ha, ha. Maybe your attitude toward the Ivy League schools is similar to mine toward Oxford and Cambridge. Pompous, pretentious, self-important snobs, the lot of them. That about right?"

"Well, I don't know that I would go quite that far," Charles replied, with a lift of his shoulders. "It's just that I don't like comparisons of that kind. Seems to me it's better to be proud of what you are and not try to pass yourself off as something you aren't."

The professor was beaming. Rhys caught his eye and chuckled. "William, have you coached this young man? How else would he know to say the kind of things I would wish him to say?"

"No, Rhys, not a bit of it. Charlie is entirely his own man – sometimes to a fault. But if there was ever a person who was the antithesis of a pretentious and self-important snob, it's young Charlie Bascombe."

"Umm, Mr. Tremayne," Charles said, "maybe we could talk a little bit about why you've asked us to come? I'm very eager to hear more about this manuscript the professor says you have. Hard for me to contain my curiosity, sir."

"Trying to change the subject, eh?" Rhys said. "Makes you uncomfortable to talk about yourself, I dare say. Well, fair enough. I don't need to hear your full autobiography, but I have to say that I quite like what I've seen and heard thus far. And my initial judgments are usually spot on."

Maria came in carrying a drinks tray, and Rhys motioned for her to leave it on the sideboard. "Half eight for our meal, Maria?" he asked.

"Oh, yes indeed, sir," she croaked. "And sir, will Ailish be joining us?"

"Why don't you assume that she will. That's my best guess. Thank you, Maria." Turning back to Charles he said, "Ailish is my wife. I expect she'll be driving back from Truro this evening."

"She works for BBC Radio Cornwall," the professor said. "She's a media star."

"She is, actually," Rhys Tremayne agreed. "She's done wonders with that outfit in just a very few years' time. Well, chaps, what would you like to drink?"

"The manuscript, sir?" Charles said, when each of them had poured himself a glass of wine – claret for Charles, sherry for the two older men.

Rhys Tremayne laughed. "You are quite the eager beaver, aren't you? I quite like that, my lad. Well, for tonight I'll share just a few things with you. Then tomorrow, the manuscript will be entirely at your disposal. William and I shall go sloping off for a few hours and leave you to your solitary toils. Later, you can give us an initial progress report.

"As to the manuscript, of course it has no official name, since none of the famous repositories such as the British Library or the Bodleian Library have ever seen it, have ever had it in their grubby little paws. So its owner – *me* – is free to call it whatever he wishes. The name I've given it is the Polminster Manuscript. There's a reason for that which I won't go into now."

"Pol- ? Ha, ha. Charlie, about half the names in Cornwall start with Pol-."

"And most of the rest with Tre-, so I've heard," Charles

replied.

"But Polminster?" the professor asked, giving their host a questioning look. "Isn't there some little bitty place up on the north coast named something like that? Rings a faint bell with me."

"Hush!" Rhys said forcefully, flinging his arms out to his sides and looking daggers at Professor Wentworth. The startled, wide-eyed professor held his hands up before his chest in apology.

"Sir," Charles said, taken aback by the little flareup but sensing it was best to ignore it, "I have to admit that you've got me quite excited. Being one of the first to see a medieval manuscript that's completely unknown to the entire academic establishment – sir, that is truly an honor."

"Charles, all of those people in the academic establishment . . . well, maybe I shouldn't say what I think they should go and do to themselves. You, Charles, are not like them. The professor here says you are entirely your own person. I sense that, too. You must stay that way, dear boy. You must never become like them."

"I'm honored, Mr. Tremayne, that you would entrust this endeavor to me."

"If William Wentworth says *he* is not the man for the job, that *you* are the man for the job, then that's exactly how this thing is going to go. Prove us right, Charles, prove us right."

"Well," Charles said, " 'a man can but assay.' "

"That's a line from *Sir Gawain & and Green Knight*," the professor said.

"Yes, Bill, I got the allusion," Rhys replied, sourly. "I do know a few things myself, you know."

Rapid footsteps sounded from somewhere in the back of the house. Then a woman, a very stunning woman in a stylish, dark blue suit – tall and slender, with shoulder-length auburn hair – stood framed in the doorway. She paused there for just a moment, then gave the three men in the sitting room a quick wave and a bright smile before quickly withdrawing from sight. "Hello! I'll be back in three shakes," her voice came trailing after her as she hurried off. She'd left faint traces of her perfume behind her.

Charles took a deep breath and mouthed a silent "wow."

The professor, looking across at his young protégé, nodded in agreement. Charles read the professor's lips as he said, "Wow is right, Charlie."

For Charles Bascombe, sleep didn't come easily that night. The storm had hit, and the wind moaned and whistled through the heavy shutters and beneath the eaves. But the sounds of the wind and the storm were the least of his problems. There were two other things he couldn't get out of his mind. One of them was the lovely Ailish Tremayne. Her conversation had been animated and intelligent, her demeanor elegant and refined, and Charles had been totally charmed. It seemed to him that Professor Wentworth was as taken by her as he was. Rhys Tremayne obviously doted on his wife, and Charles couldn't help wondering about what had brought such a mismatched couple together.

Weighing even more heavily on his mind was this unknown manuscript which Rhys Tremayne was calling the Polminster Manuscript. Charles wondered why Rhys had seemed so miffed when the professor alluded to the place for which the manuscript had apparently been named. Something kind of strange going on there, he thought. But even more, he wondered what the manuscript could possibly contain that led Rhys Tremayne to believe it was so remarkable. Charles had said, truthfully, that he felt honored to be asked to examine it ahead of the greatest scholars from Britain's finest universities or libraries. He really did feel honored. But now, too, he was starting to feel more than a little bit anxious. Charles Bascombe rarely had doubts about his own capabilities, but right now a few had begun to creep in. The pressure was really going to be on, no doubt about it. Could he actually do this? William Wentworth said he had complete confidence in Charles. And yet the professor had decided to come along. Was that because he was unable to contain his own curiosity? Or might it be because he really wasn't sure that his young protégé was up to the task?

Charles tossed and turned for several hours. At one point he got up, opened the bedroom window, threw back the sodden shutters. A heavy gust of cold rain came crashing in against his face and chest. He ran his fingers through his wet hair and stared off into the dark, stormy night.

"Well, which shall it be?" their host was saying to the professor, "beach walk, cliff walk, or moors?"

"Could we walk down past the Loe and then out across Loe Bar? That be all right?"

"That would be splendid. Excellent choice. Let's just get Charles situated, shall we, and then we can be off."

Rhys Tremayne led Charles Bascombe and Professor

Wentworth into his library, a room Charles hadn't yet been in. Two walls were filled with towering bookcases, and on a third, lower, glass-fronted cases filled a deep recess. Charles guessed those cases held some of their host's most cherished possessions. On the wall above the cases hung several large banners displaying various coats of arms. The one that immediately caught Charles' attention displayed three black birds with red beaks and red legs against a field of white. Choughs, no doubt, though he had no idea what the banner might represent. High above one of the taller bookcases was a pair of narrow, rectangular windows, but the room's primary illumination came from a central chandelier.

"This will be your work place, dear boy," Rhys said, pointing to a spacious library table. Beside it was a solid oak chair with ornately carved arms, a brown cushion on the seat. The table was bare except for two widely spaced reading lamps. "Let me set up a book stand for you, Charles, and then I'll go and fetch the manuscript. If you don't mind, please don't use an ink pen." At those words, Charles held up a retractable pencil. "Ah, splendid. Of course you already know the drill."

Then Rhys Tremayne padded from the room to retrieve the manuscript. Their host, Charles surmised, must have another special place, perhaps in his study, where he kept his most cherished items. While he waited, Charles pulled a thick pad of lined paper from his shoulder bag and placed it on the table, alongside a trio of retractable pencils. Always a good idea to have a spare or two.

"Well, here we are." Their host was clutching a sizeable tome bound in brown leather. He hoisted it up and placed the thick volume carefully on the sturdy bookstand. "You shouldn't have any need to remove it from the stand, Charles. And if for some reason you should, please don't lay it flat on the table. But you know that. And of course no eating or drinking." Charles nodded his understanding. He'd long become accustomed to observing these basic rules.

"Are you good, then?" Rhys Tremayne finally asked.

"I'm good, sir. Thank you."

"Splendid, splendid. Well, my boy, the professor and I shall be off."

William Wentworth reached out and placed his hand on Charles' shoulder. The eyes of the younger man and the older man met, and then the professor shot Charles a very faint wink.

When he was finally alone, Charles sat there for a moment, staring at the large volume on the stand before him. The butterflies in his stomach were every bit as active as they'd always been just before the opening tipoff, back when he'd played high school basketball.

He straightened the pad of paper and fiddled with one of the pencils. He reached out and pulled each of the two desk lamps just a little bit closer. Then for the better part of a minute he just sat there, staring at the brown leather cover of the manuscript.

Finally Charles extended his right arm and began fingering the lower right corner of the cover. He knew that physical contact with the manuscript should be kept to a bare minimum, ideally nothing more than his fingers turning the pages. But he couldn't help himself. He loved to luxuriate in the physical presence, the solid reality, of the object he was working with. To him, this thing that now sat before him was a very, very palpable thing. Nothing in a digital world, Charles believed, could ever come close to that feeling of realness. So for another few seconds Charles fingered the lower corner of the manuscript's cover. "It's just you and me," he whispered. "Let's get to know each other."

Slowly, he lifted the cover and opened the book.

5

It was 12:15, and Charles had had enough. It had been a grueling three hours, especially with no coffee. But he felt he'd achieved quite a bit during those three hours; indeed, he felt that he now had a pretty good handle on Rhys Tremayne's manuscript. During that time he had answered a lot of questions. Still, one very big question remained. Perhaps in the next day or two he might know the answer to that question, too. It was possible, of course, that he might never know the answer. But a notion had already begun to form in his mind. Though it was far from a certainty, Charles Bascombe had an inkling of what might be so special about this manuscript. Oh, man, he said to himself, if only it would prove to be so.

He stepped over to the small bathroom just off the library and splashed his face with cold water. His reflection in the mirror showed a pair of bleary eyes – no surprise after such a long period of intense concentration.

He walked back through the library, pausing by his work area and looking down at the thick manuscript, now closed, sitting upright on the bookstand, a small notecard just sticking up where he'd marked his place. As always happened, he had begun to bond with it, developing with it a special sense of intimacy. It was a unique thing in his experience, forming such a bond with a difficult and challenging manuscript. That manuscript was the work of other men, perhaps men not greatly unlike him, men who had labored over this same object hundreds of years ago. Oddly, though, the bond Charles felt wasn't so much with those men, it was with the object itself. For Charles, the object seemed to exude its own spiritual essence. It was the soul of the physical volume that spoke to him.

Noises coming from the kitchen area toward the rear of the house startled him from his reverie. Probably Maria, he thought, or maybe the two men had already returned from their walk. No, now he heard a woman's voice singing, a voice that sounded far younger than Maria's ancient croak.

When Charles stepped into the kitchen, he saw the back of a woman who was peering into an open refrigerator.

"Good morning, Mrs. Tremayne," he announced cheerfully.

"*Mrs.* Tremayne?" The woman whirled about, and she certainly wasn't Ailish Tremayne. "I'm hardly *Mrs.* Tremayne," the young woman said, her words tinged with acerbity. "And I'd appreciate it if you didn't start calling me Ms. Tremayne. That "Ms." business always sounds dumb to me. And speaking of dumb things, who the hell are you?"

"Oh . . . umm . . . I guess I'm Charles. Charles Bascombe."

"You mean you aren't quite sure?"

"No, no, I'm quite sure. That I'm Charles, that is."

The young woman stood there and scrutinized Charles for a long moment. "An American, I suppose. Come to help Daddy with his precious manuscript. Is that about it?"

"Uh, yes, I guess that's about it."

"Well, Charles Bascombe, would you like a sandwich?"

"Uh, sure. That would be great. Thanks."

"Roast beef? Cheddar cheese? Horse radish? English mustard? Lettuce? Tomato? Pickle? Slice of onion?"

"Sure. Give me the works."

"The works it is, Charles Bascombe. But would it be all right with you if I just call you Charlie? Charles seems so frightfully formal."

"Charlie's fine. That's what the professor calls me. And what should I call you?"

"Just Ally, please. Daddy gave me a Celtic name, of course, but I'm quite happy just being Ally."

As the young woman busied herself with the sandwiches, Charles took his turn at studying her. In contrast to her elegant stepmother, Ally was an inch or two shorter, a bit rounder, and she certainly exuded energy and vivaciousness. Her honey-blond hair, cut short, seemed to fly in all directions. Charles had read somewhere in some old mystery novel that women had three kinds of faces: mouse face, horse face, and apple cheeks (each of which, the novelist averred, could be quite lovely). Ally was definitely apple cheeks.

Charles noticed that she was slicing the bread from a long loaf of French bread. He could smell its freshness from across the room. She must've just bought it at a local bakery.

"When did you arrive?" he asked.

She glanced at her watch. "About twenty minutes ago.

How 'bout you?"

"Late yesterday afternoon. The professor and I drove down from Oxford."

"Oxford?"

"Doing research there. Working on a book."

"And now you're here helping dear old Dad. Quite a sport, Charlie. Though maybe it will make you a famous scholar. Is that the plan?"

"There's no plan. But yes, perhaps it will. One can always hope."

"Maybe my paintings will hang in the Tate Modern one day. One can always hope."

"Could I see some of them?"

"My word, Charlie, you really are a sport. Daddy has a few of them hanging in his private study. He probably hasn't let you in there. He's very guarded about letting others into his inner sanctum. But maybe we can sneak in when he isn't looking."

"Maybe you can do *what*?" came the voice of Rhys Tremayne. He and the professor were just coming in through the back entrance.

"Maybe Charlie and I can sneak off and do what young lovers do, Daddy," she said. "That's something you can understand, isn't it?"

"And just how long have you known Charlie?"

"Going on maybe ten minutes, Daddy."

"I told you so, William. That daughter of mine is a devilish little minx." Rhys Tremayne stepped across the floor and enveloped his daughter in a vigorous hug. "If you and this little minx have already become lovers, Charles," he said, still holding her in his firm embrace, "this must be your lucky day. Maybe," he said, pointing toward the library, "your doubly lucky day?"

"I think I've done okay with the manuscript, sir, though of course only in a preliminary way."

"Well, let's all of us have a bite, eh? Then we'll want to hear all about your discoveries. Alwyn, could you make two more of those sandwiches? One for William and one for your old father?" Looking rather put upon, Ally nodded that she could.

"And what to drink, William? What to drink, Charles?"

"Daddy, I'm off to town and shall abandon you fine fellows to your boring academic discussion. I've brewed a fresh pot of coffee. Charlie needs to keep his strength up. Is there anything any of you might wish me to bring back?" They all shook their heads. "All right, then. Charlie, I'm thinking that we should take our beach walk around five. Okay? I'll show you some of the glorious Cornish sights. In the meantime, try to keep your strength up."

"Sounds great," Charles began to say, but before he could even get the words out, she'd left the room. Charles glanced over at the two older men. Having a beach walk with Ally was news to him, though after a long day of scholarship, might be just the ticket.

"She won't corrupt you *too* much, Charles," their host said. "It's just her way."

"Charlie could stand a little bit of corrupting," the professor said. All three of them laughed.

"So, Charles," their host said, once their mirth had

subsided, "what have you to tell us? And please don't make it boring."

"I think it's all relative, sir. Anyway, I don't think you or the professor will find it boring."

"So please carry on, dear boy."

"Actually, might I just pour myself a cup of the coffee before plunging in? Need to keep up my strength.

"Okay," Charles said, coffee cup in hand, "here goes.

"As I'm sure you know, sir, your manuscript is a miscellany, both in the usual meaning of the word and in another sense as well. It's a diverse collection of medieval works, fairly typical of what you'd find in other well-known miscellanies, though with not quite as many works as is usually the case. Just seven items in this one. One is a portion of a moral treatise on the Seven Deadly Sins; one's a comic animal fable; one is an exemplum taken from Robert Mannyng of Brunne's *Handlyng Synne*; one's a short extract from a lapidary; one's a medical treatise in Latin; and one's a selection of Middle English crucifixion lyrics. Lastly, there's a longish narrative work in Middle English verse which I have yet to identify.

"It's a miscellany also in the sense that it isn't just one manuscript, it's actually portions of seven different manuscripts bound together as a single volume. At some time in the past, someone trimmed all the leaves to give the pages a uniform appearance. Maybe they wanted to give the impression that it's a discrete manuscript, but it doesn't take much expertise to see that it isn't. For a couple of the items, it's obvious that their original leaves were larger, because after the trimming, there's hardly any margin space. No text material has been lost, but the esthetic effect isn't pleasing."

Charles glanced over at the two men. "Too boring?"

"Not a bit of it," Rhys Tremayne replied. "So carry on."

Charles drank deeply from his coffee cup and sighed before continuing.

"Also, if you examine the leaves closely, you can see real qualitative differences in the vellum. In two cases, the works are written on parchment, not vellum. That's pretty clear evidence that the volume incorporates material from disparate manuscripts. Two of the works, the animal fable and the unknown Middle English poem, are written on high quality vellum with which a lot of care has been taken. At the other end of the spectrum are the pages with Middle English lyrics. Those have been recorded on pretty inferior parchment, maybe even recycled parchment. The roughness of their surfaces suggests they've undergone a good bit of scraping."

"The animal fable, Charlie?" the professor asked. "Did you recognize it?"

"It's the story about the fox and the wolf in the well, the one from the Reynard the Fox cycle."

"Oh, splendid, Charlie. If memory serves, that tale only survives in a single text in English. In Digby 86. This would make two."

"Yes, I think that's right."

"Go on and tell us about the rest of these works, dear boy," their host said.

"Not too boring?"

"For normal mortals, certainly. The three of us are far from normal mortals."

"Speak for yourself," said the professor. "Anyway, I'll need to pop into the bathroom for just a moment. Charlie, don't say anything earth-shattering till I get back."

"Are those choughs?" Charles asked their host, to fill in the time while the professor was away. Charles was pointing at the banner with the three black birds on the wall above the lower cases.

"Quite right. Do you know about our famous birds, then?"

"William said I should ask you about them. They are very striking looking."

"Wondrous creatures, my boy. I would love to tell you about them. Curiously enough, that banner is one of the coats of arms of Thomas Becket: 'the holy blissful martyr for to seeke,' to quote the father of English poetry."

"Your Chaucerian pronunciation, sir," the professor said, as he was coming back, "leaves a great deal to be desired."

"William, you should be applauding me just for remembering the bloody line."

The professor offered a single clap of his hands.

"That's it?"

"That's it. So Charlie, go on with your disquisition."

"You sure?"

"We're sure," their host said. "Though I think quoting that line should have merited at least another clap or two."

"As do I," Charles said. "Anyway, the moral exemplum taken from Robert Mannyng is quite well known – 'The Cursed Dancers of Colbeck.' There are several texts of that around, so nothing earthshaking there. The excerpt from the treatise on the Seven Deadly Sins only deals with *gula* and *luxuria*."

"Gluttony and Lechery, everyone's favorites," the professor said. "The sins of the flesh, always more interesting than the sins of the spirit."

"I have no idea what it's from," Charles went on, "but it isn't from 'The Parson's Tale,' in case you were wondering. I didn't spend any time on the medical treatise in Latin, though it has a few pretty wild illustrations. The lapidary excerpt looks to be the usual stuff – the nature of the stones, their medical uses, their connections to the planets, their symbolic values, that sort of thing. I did look to see if there was an entry on *margarita*, and there is. I'd like to read it closely."

"Margarita?" Rhys asked.

"Latin word for 'pearl,' " Professor Wentworth said. "Hence Margaret as a given name, and hence the drink with a white ring of salt around the top of the glass."

"Goodness. You learn something every day," their host declared. "Well, please go on, dear boy."

"The group of Middle English lyrics should hold a good bit of interest for scholars who study the lyrics. I recognized most of them, but not all. It's possible, sir, you have a few poems here that have never been recorded in the *Index of Middle English Verse*."

"That would be lovely. But Charles, I kind of suspect that you have kept the best for last."

"Maybe so. And sir, I kind of suspect that it's this last work that prompted you to invite us down here."

Rhys Tremayne was smiling as he rubbed his hands vigorously together, as if he were thinking, now we're getting to the good stuff.

He glanced over at the professor. The professor tilted his head and his eyes met those of his friend. Then he looked over at his young protégé and said, "Okay, Charlie, let's have it."

6

"The long narrative poem occupies some nine folios. That is, thirty-six manuscript pages. It was once longer, since one or more leaves are missing at the beginning."

"An acephalous text," the professor said.

"You don't need to tell us what it's called," their host grumped, "we know the word."

"Not having the beginning makes identifying it a lot harder. The end of the poem is missing also."

"Bummer," the professor said. "That word okay with you?" he said, looking at their host.

"Written in rhyming couplets," Charles continued, "about fifteen to a page. Down the right hand margin of each page are square brackets connecting the lines in each couplet. Makes it easy to count them. So, about thirty verses to a manuscript page and thirty-six pages. Do the math and it comes out to a work of more than 1,000 lines. Factor in the missing pages at the beginning and end, and it's probably a poem of between 1,100 and 1,400 lines."

"So Charles," Rhys Tremayne said, "time for the sixty-four shilling question. What is this work?"

"No, please hang on," Charles said. "How 'bout we don't go jumping ahead? Let's do this properly, one step at a time, okay?" At Charles' slightly sharpish tone, their host looked somewhat abashed.

"Anyway, the verses are written in what look to be eight-syllable lines."

"Octosyllabic couplets," the professor said.

"Octosyllabic couplets? Is that an important clue?" Rhys asked. "Are there particular poets who used them?"

"Just everybody and his brother," the professor replied sourly.

"Bummer," their host said. The professor gave him a squinty-eyed look, wondering if his friend was making fun of him.

"Yes," Charles said, "from the late twelfth century on, that was one of the most common verse forms in English."

"So it tells us nothing?"

Charles paused to reflect on that question. "No, not necessarily," he said after a moment. "There are a lot of reasons for suspecting that this work was written in the second half of the fourteenth century, and that it was recorded in this manuscript not much later than its date of composition. If so, that would narrow the field considerably."

Charles stopped speaking, and the three men sat in silence the better part of a minute.

Charles finished off his coffee and took a deep breath. He was about to take the plunge.

"Sir," Charles said sternly, staring pointedly at their host, "I have a feeling that all the things I've told you in the last few minutes are things you already knew." He continued to look Rhys Tremayne straight in the eye. The man showed no reaction. Professor Wentworth sat still as a stone.

"You told the professor," Charles went on, "that this manuscript of yours could be a career-maker. If you didn't already know quite a bit about it, why would you say that? It's begun to dawn on me that this whole thing has been nothing but a charade, that you've just been putting me through my paces to see if I really have the goods. Is that right? Well, if that's the case, what do you think now?"

Rhys Tremayne scowled at the young man. But then a smile began creeping slowly across his face. He glanced over at the professor, his head tilted to one side. The professor also tilted his head to one side. Charles crossed his arms on his chest. He looked from one man to the other. His ire was rising.

"Umm," said the professor, "I think perhaps I'll just be popping into the loo one more time. That happens to us oldsters." He stood up and scurried away.

Charles and Rhys Tremayne sat across from each other without speaking, Charles' anger continuing to grow. He deeply resented the possibility that these men had simply been testing him. In the case of the professor, that even seemed a little like a betrayal.

Finally Charles said, knowing that he might be courting trouble and not caring, "Sir, what can you tell me about the provenance of this manuscript? Knowing about its history could be quite important."

The professor, just returning, stopped short behind the sofa in which their host was sitting and began moving his arms rapidly back and forth, signaling to Charles that he should cease and desist. It didn't work.

"Young man," Rhys Tremayne spat out, "that's *not*

an issue here. What we are concerned with here is the manuscript and nothing else. You must stick to what is your business, and you must keep your nose out of what isn't your business."

"I'm sorry, sir, but I don't agree. Where this manuscript comes from and how it was obtained is certainly an issue here."

"What are you implying, young sir? Illegality? I can assure you that this manuscript was *not* obtained illegally. And that, sir, is an end of it."

The professor came over and sat down again. "Hello, chaps," he said brightly. "All good here? All friends here? I certainly hope so."

The other two men still glared at each other.

"This poem, Charles," their host finally said, "what do you think? Could it really be what I think it might be?"

"What am I, a mind reader?" Charles said. "How do I know what you think it might be?"

"Oh, come on now, Charles. I believe that your thoughts about this poem are quite similar to my own. Are they not?"

"I'm not given to idle speculations, sir. What I would need to do is transcribe the whole thing, have a readable text of it typed up, and then study it carefully. That would take several days. Probably at least a week. Sir, I have work in Oxford that I would like to get back to."

"There's nothing for you in Oxford that comes close to being as important as this manuscript. You solve this riddle, dear boy, and you will surely make a name for yourself. Stay here, Charles. My house and library are entirely at your disposal. Take all the time you need."

Rhys Tremayne breathed a big sigh. "Charles, I'm sorry I snapped at you. Quite unmannerly of me. But, my boy, there are certain things that I'm touchy about. The professor, I'm sure, knows that all too well."

"Indeed," said the professor. "*All* too well."

Charles shrugged his shoulders, feeling slightly more mollified. "So tell me the truth," he said at last. "Were you really just giving me a tryout. Is that what this was all about?"

"Oh, well, I wouldn't quite put it that way. I knew what this looked like to me, but I hoped someone with greater expertise might come to much the same conclusion. I wanted an independent confirmation. And that, dear boy, is what I believe you have done. Am I right?"

"Hmm," Charles said. "Well, I will admit that the three hours I spent with the manuscript this morning were three of the most exhilarating I've had since coming to the U.K."

"That's the spirit, Charlie," the professor said. "I knew you weren't a spoilsport."

"Well, sir," Charles said to their host, "if this poem turns out to be what you and I both hope it turns out to be, that would be truly phenomenal."

"And what would that be?" asked the professor.

"As if you didn't know. But okay, I'll say it. That's what you both want, isn't it? For me to say it? What we're all hoping is this: that lurking within the pages of this so-called Polminster Manuscript is an unknown poem that will prove to be of great consequence to the scholarly world – an unknown poem that was written by Geoffrey Chaucer."

7

"I must say, Charlie, you seem to have won over my father in record time," Alwen said, as the two of them strode down through the garden behind the manor house, starting off for their beach walk. "Given his loathing toward all you academic chaps, that's quite a neat feat."

"Ally, I'm not your typical academic."

"You can say that again."

"Ally, I'm not your —"

"Okay, okay!" The two of them couldn't help laughing at the corny joke.

A few minutes later they stood close together looking down at the surging sea and listening to the surf as it broke fiercely against black rocks at the foot of the cliff. The stiff breeze that blew against their faces brought color to their cheeks. Charles watched the ebb and flow of the water in the tide pools beneath them, then looked up at the swirl of seagulls above their heads.

"It's heavenly," he said softly.

"Yes, most of the time. But it can be quite hellish when the mood comes upon it."

They lingered there for another minute before Ally said, "If we head off to the left, there are nice stretches of sandy beach. And in only a ten-minute walk there's quite a scenic lake. Any takers?"

"For sure," Charles said.

They set off along the path, passing deep clefts in the rocky cliff and rugged little coves. "This path," she said, "is the Cornish Coastal Path. It goes all the way around the perimeter of Cornwall. It's quite popular with hikers, usually taking them a couple of weeks. I've never done it, but someday I will."

Then they came to a halt, and there before them was the lake Ally had mentioned.

"That's your lake, hmm?" Charles said. "I'm surprised at how large it is. What's it called?"

"The Loe," she said. "Largest lake in Cornwall."

"The Loe?"

"Or Loe Pool. 'Loe' is an old Cornish word that means – ta da – 'lake'! In Scotland they call them lochs, in Ireland loughs, in Cornwall loes. Actually, Charlie, it's King Arthur's lake. Now that's something that you, as a medieval scholar, should certainly want to know."

"King's Arthur's lake? And how is it King Arthur's lake?"

"The famous sword. You know, Excalibur. This is from whence it came and to whence it had to be returned. Returned to the Lady of the Lake. She'd only lent it to Arthur."

"Is that so?"

"It is surely so. That's the local legend, anyway. Don't tell me you don't believe the legend?"

"If you say it's true, Ally, then it must be true."

"It's not just me who says it's true. Everyone says it's true."

"Well, far be it from me to contradict everyone."

Ally threaded her arm through Charles'. "You are a most delightful skeptic," she said. "An American pragmatist. 'Just the facts, ma'am,' " she said in her deepest voice. "Is that the kind of guy you are?"

"I hope I'm a little bit more freewheeling than that."

"Good, Charlie. I hope you are a little bit more free-wheeling than that as well."

"I suppose we should be starting back," Ally said after another half an hour.

"I suppose, though I'm not really in any hurry."

"Good."

As they started retracing their steps Charles said, "I met your stepmother the other night. Impressive woman."

"Isn't she? And she's been wonderful for Daddy. She and Daddy make quite a contrast, and people often wonder how he was able to land her."

"What draws people together is often inexplicable," Charles said.

"Yes," Ally replied, and gave his arm a little squeeze. "But Ailish is much better for him than my mother ever was. My mother was, and is, a most difficult woman."

"So you get along well with Ailish?"

"Oh yes, pretty well. For the most part we stay out of each other's way. Since they've been married, I've been away at school a good bit of the time, or else working in St. Ives. In recent years, I think, Daddy's been much happier than before he and my mum split up. Ailish isn't a person who bears ill-will, not like Mum. Mum's been known to have a vindictive streak."

"What ill-will do you mean?"

"Well, for one thing, Mother placed a lot of the blame for the death of her dearest friend on Daddy. Blamed him most unfairly."

"How did her friend die?"

"Brain cancer."

"Yikes. Hard to blame someone for someone getting brain cancer."

"Yes, that's what I mean by unfair. But Mum believed that if Daddy hadn't insisted on their traipsing off to Italy when Emmeline was first getting sick, her cancer would have been diagnosed earlier and then might not have been fatal. Emmie had been getting bad headaches for a while at that point, and Mum wanted to delay their trip. Daddy was insistent, so off they went. When they got back, it was too late. The cancer had become inoperable."

"That sucks."

"It really does. Anyway, I'm pretty sure that was a big factor in my parents splitting up. But, honestly, their splitting up was for the best. My mother had become a massive pain in the rear, both to my father and to me, which caused unhappiness all around.

"Emmeline and my mother were lifelong friends. They'd grown up together. But in their twenties, Mum married above her and Emmie below her. But to Mum's credit, she never looked down on Emmie and her husband. He was a fisherman, and one night he and five of his mates met a sad demise at sea."

"Oh, man."

"Yeah, it was really tragic. But for Cornwall, not all that unusual. Anyway, before Emmie died, she got Mum to promise her that she'd look after her daughter. And Mum always has, to such an extent that sometimes it's made me a trifle jealous. But the truth is that I was always closer to

Daddy than to Mum. When I was little, he was the one who taught me how to ride a bike and to play table tennis and toss darts; he was the one who read to me; he was the one who taught me about all the great illustrators – Tenniel, Caldecott, Rackham, Greenaway, Shepard. That's when I first began to develop my love of art."

"All of them favorites of mine," Charles said.

"Of course they are," Ally said. "I wouldn't expect anything else."

The long evening's light was fading as they walked up through the back garden toward the manor house.

"Such a perfect evening, Charles Bascombe," she said, "a perfect evening with my lovely and laconic American friend."

"You were chatty enough for both of us," he said. She poked him in the ribs with her finger.

"So, Charlie, how about breakfast at eight? I'd like to see you before I take off, and before you put that cute little nose of yours back onto that horrid grindstone."

"Take off?"

"Off to St. Ives. Summer job in an art gallery. Daddy keeps a small flat there year-round. Works out quite well for me. When I'm not in school, I spend more time there than here."

"Sure, breakfast at eight. And hey, thanks for showing me around. Our walk this evening has been wonderful fun. I even got to see King Arthur's lake."

"I sense you are a fella who needs a little more fun in his life, Charlie. Listen, why not come and visit me in St. Ives?"

"Oh gosh, thanks. But I suspect I'm going to have my hands full around here for the next several days."

"You could come and have your hands full in St. Ives," she said, giving him an arch look. "You know what they say, Charlie, all work and no play."

"Maybe so, Ally. Let me see how it goes."

In the morning, Charles did breakfast with Ally and did see her off.

"There's a standing invitation for you in St. Ives, Charlie. You won't forget, right?"

"My memory hasn't failed me yet."

"It better not." She hugged him and then lowered herself into her little red Triumph. Seeing her snazzy little car parked next to the professor's beat-up Morris made him smile at the incongruity.

Charles stood and watched the wheels of her car kick up gravel as she shot down the long drive. When she was gone, he breathed out a deep sigh.

Charles spent the day working in the library, transcribing the unidentified Middle English poem. He took a brief, late-morning coffee break and a short lunch break at one. That was it. He kept at it steadily until nearly six. By then his head was spinning, but he was pleased with all he'd done. He'd transcribed over five hundred verses, nearly half the work.

But Charles had also done something on his own volition, something for which he had not asked permission. Using his phone, he photographed each manuscript page of the poem. He planned to download those photos to his laptop and send the files back to Waverly College where they would be stored safely on the college's mainframe computer. He wasn't sure if Rhys Tremayne would have approved, so he did it without asking. If the man didn't like it, too bad. Charles still felt some lingering resentment about how he'd been manipulated the day before. But more important than that, having ready access to a digital version of the text would make it a lot easier for him to double check his work. Also, as usually happened, Charles had begun to feel possessive about this text. He would miss the physical manuscript once he no longer had it to work with. Having a digital copy would be better than nothing.

As he packed his work into his shoulder bag, he heard music. Piano and cello. It was coming from a small room just off the sitting room, Mrs. Tremayne's personal study. Charles found himself drawn toward the room. Since the door was partially open, he couldn't stop himself from peeking in.

"Oh, Charles, do come in," she said, smiling. "I'm just unwinding. Come and unwind with me."

Charles stepped through the door, and Ailish Tremayne motioned him toward a high-backed wing chair across from the small desk behind which she was sitting. Charles couldn't help noticing her long legs propped up on top of the desk.

"Mendelssohn?" Charles said. "Lied ohne Wörter?"

"Well done, Charles."

"I love it when it's scored for piano and cello. That opening always gives me chills."

"That's the legendary Jacqueline du Pré on the cello," she said. Then using a handheld remote, she turned the music down a little.

Charles saw that Mrs. Tremayne was now dressed much more casually than she'd been two days before. An oversized mauve sweater, a stylish pair of designer blue jeans, and bare feet. Her lustrous auburn hair was tied back, displaying her graceful neck to full advantage.

"Have you ever heard it played by piano and French horn? It's quite wonderful."

"No, I never have."

"I might have a CD I could lend you. Charles, I was just about to treat myself to a little nip of Talisker single malt. Join me?"

"Yes, thanks. But for me, just a *very* little nip. I've had almost nothing to eat since breakfast." His eyes followed her as she got up and went to an old oaken escritoire and poured two drinks from a decanter.

"I'm so glad that you and the professor have come," she said, handing him a glass. "It does wonders for Rhys. With Ally and me away so much of the time, he sadly lacks for company. He so loves his dry old books, but they aren't any real substitute for human companionship, are they?" She handed him a glass with more whisky in it than he would have wished. She didn't ask him if he wanted water.

He held the glass up to his nose, inhaled the peaty fragrance, and then took a very small sip. He felt a burning sensation as the liquid passed down his throat.

"Tell me about your work for the BBC," he said. And for the next half hour she did. And Charles, no surprise, found this woman's conversation about her work quite enthralling.

✠ ✠ ✠

The two older men, now in their customary places on facing sofas in the sitting room, were sipping postprandial glasses of port. Charles, declining the offer, clutched a tall glass of ginger ale. A few minutes earlier, Ailish had said goodnight and left the men to the academic discourse she knew they'd want to be having.

Suddenly Professor Wentworth slapped his knee. "Charlie, I got it!" he declared.

"Got it, sir?"

"Your joke. Robbie Stevenson. Ha, ha, ha. How droll, my boy, how droll."

Rhys Tremayne looked back and forth at the two other men, completely nonplussed.

"Robbie Stevenson," the professor said. "Ha, ha. Robert Louis Stevenson! Dr. Jekyl and Mr. Hyde! Quite good, my boy, quite delightful."

Charles had to laugh also. "It was one of those strange coincidences life sometimes offers up, sir. But I agree, sir, I find it pretty amusing, too."

"Indeed, indeed."

"Sir," Charles said to their host, who still looked all at sea, "we're talking about an odd little incident that occurred on our way down here. In a service area we were briefly accosted by a very strange-looking fellow. He made me think of Mr. Hyde, and I guess the professor must've thought the same. His name, as it turned out, was Robbie Stevenson."

"Ah. Good old RLS, one of our northern brethren. I'm quite a fan of him as well. But Charles, perhaps we could leave good old RLS until later, hmm? Don't keep us on tenterhooks, laddy, tell us everything you've discovered about the poem. You labored long and hard today, so fill us in, my boy, fill us in."

"Happy to, sir. Okay, then, first off the poem is a dream-vision. And like we talked about yesterday, written in octosyllabic couplets. It doesn't appear that much is missing from the beginning of the poem. Maybe only a single manuscript leaf. If so, then maybe sixty lines. Sir, if you would like, I could show you the first verses. I have them right here in my shoulder bag."

Charles extracted a pad of lined paper. "In these lines the first-person narrator is nodding off over his book. He falls asleep and moves into his visionary experience. The passage is quite reminiscent of verses that occur near the beginning of Chaucer's *Book of the Duchess.*"

"Ah, splendid," their host said.

"Yes, let's hear it, " the professor said. "Read it, Charlie."

"Sure thing. Okay, here we go:

> *Whan that I thys tale had rede,*
> *Feir fantasies fylled my hede.*
> *A wonder thing, me thoght, to se*
> *A knight so bold, so worthy he.*
> *Than sodeynly, I wyst nat how,*
>
> . . . .
>
> *My ene drooped, my chin yfell,*
> *And into a slomber, trouthe to telle,*
> *Depe I glode, my book on my lappe,*
> *A-slepe right ther, right wher I sat.*
> *Than com to me a wondrous dreme,*
> *A swevene pure as golde so shene.*

"Hmm," the professor said. "It does sound a *little* like

Chaucer. Perhaps rather half-baked Chaucer. Rather like some of those weakish fifteenth-century imitators – Hoccleve, Clanvowe, Lydgate. But of course it could also be very early Chaucer – a pre-*Book of the Duchess* poem, say. Or maybe a youthful warm-up for things to come."

"Sounds like Chaucer to me," Rhys Tremayne declared. "You, Charles?"

"It's what comes later that sounds like Chaucer to me," he said. "As the tale develops, it becomes apparent that it's an occasional poem, one eulogizing a noble person, very likely a noble patron who's recently died. Here's the thing that most intrigues me. Of course you both remember that young Chaucer, still probably a teenager, had served as a page in the household of Prince Lionel, the third son of King Edward III. Lionel died young – in 1368 – and at that time Chaucer would have still been in his twenties. We don't know when Chaucer first began to write poetry, though we know that by the early 1370s he was. Might this poem be his very first serious effort? Could it be an elegy he wrote in the late 1360s, following the death of Lionel? Maybe specifically written for a memorial service, just like *The Book of the Duchess*?"

"My word, Charlie," the professor said, "what a notion. So besides the immaturity of the verse, what else might suggest that?"

"For one thing, the likely play on words. The clever pun on Lionel's name, which is just the sort of thing Chaucer liked to do. Portraying the prince as a lion, in life generally but also on the battlefield. The kind of thing Chaucer did with Blanche of Lancaster's name in *The Book of the Duchess*, allegorizing her as the White Queen. As for depicting Lionel as a lion on the battlefield, we know that Chaucer, still just a teenager, went with him to fight in France in the late 1350s."

"So what you're suggesting, Charlie, is that this might actually be the famous lost poem?" the professor said.

"Chaucer's *Book of the Lion*," their host declared, "his notorious lost work!"

"Anything else that suggests that possibility, Charlie?"

"In the poem the speaker is clearly glorifying the royal family, and Lionel in particular. And don't forget that the lion was one of the heraldic symbols that stood for England."

"And still is," the professor said. "So, it appears that he was attempting to curry favor with them to enhance his own standing at court. Yes, that seems quite possible, Charlie. Old Geoffrey – or in this case *young* Geoffrey – was never one to miss an opportunity."

"Sir, this is all highly conjectural. But wouldn't it be wonderful if true? If it really is true, what we would have in our hands is something no one has seen in hundreds of years. We would possess the only surviving copy of Chaucer's infamous lost poem."

"Oh, my boy," Rhys said, "you must prove it to be true."

"Lots of work ahead of us before we'd be close to doing that," Charles said.

"You can do it, my boy. William was right. You are the man to do this."

The two older men were beaming at each other.

Inside his own head Charles was saying, "I don't plan on 'proving' it to be true unless it really *is* true. And I haven't yet discounted the possibility that the whole thing could be nothing more than a masterful forgery, an elaborate fraud."

And why, Charles couldn't help wondering, had Rhys Tremayne been so guarded about divulging any information about where this manuscript came from? That fact, in itself, he found highly suspicious.

Charles Bascombe thought those things – but he didn't dare give voice to them.

After the two older men had departed for their beds, Charles remained in the sitting room perusing a coffee-table book on Cornwall. Lots of gorgeous photographs of beaches, cliffs, and stately homes and gardens. The few photos of castle ruins and ancient churches were more his cup of tea than the stately homes and gardens. He could hear Maria bustling about in the kitchen and elsewhere, but paid her little attention.

At one point he thought he heard the front door opening. He got up and moved toward the front entrance to have a look. Maria had just come in.

"Only doing a final lock up, sir," she said, when she saw him looking at her. For a second Charles wondered why she needed to be outside to do a lock up, but figured she knew what she was about.

"Good night, Maria, I'm going up now," he said.

"Good night to you, sir. Any particular time you'd prefer for breakfast?"

"Not really. How about half-past eight?"

"That's right about when the master likes it," she said.

"Okay. See you in the morning. Good night, Maria."

"Good night, sir."

And Charles climbed the stairs to his bedroom.

8

Charles Bascombe was awakened very early by the dawn chorus. He lay there for a while listening to the joyous singing of the birds, but after a few minutes his urgent desire for coffee got the better of him. Not wanting to disturb the sleep of others, he moved quietly down the stairs thinking he might brew up some coffee and take it out to a bench he'd seen in the back garden.

Just as he was pouring himself his coffee, he heard the footsteps of someone rushing in through a rear entrance. Could Ally be back? No, it wasn't her. The out-of-breath person who rushed in through the kitchen door was Maria.

"Oh, Mr. Bascombe," she panted when she saw him, "I smelled your fresh coffee. But sir, your car. What's happened to your car? Was there some reason you needed to move it?"

"Move it? I'm not quite sure what you mean? I haven't done anything with it, and I don't think the professor has."

"Then where could it be? It's not out on the drive, sir. It was sitting right there last night when I did my rounds before locking up at twelve. But it tain't there now, sir. The master nor the professor's been up as yet, and I don't reckon you've been out o' doors just yet yourself. I don't understand it, sir."

"Gosh, Maria, I'll go and have a look. Thank you."

Still carrying his coffee, Charles went out to have a look. Maria was certainly correct. The old Morris was nowhere to be seen. He stood in the spot where the car had been parked and studied the ground, but there wasn't much of anything to see. Just a couple of dark spots in the gravel where the old car had dripped some oil.

Feeling baffled, Charles slowly worked his way back down along the curving driveway, looking for any kind of clue. It wasn't until he was nearly a hundred yards farther down the drive, just around a sharp bend and out of sight of the house, that he saw it – a set of deep tread marks in the gravel, tread marks obviously made by a large vehicle. Oh man, he thought, a tow truck. Had they rolled the car silently down to that point and then hoisted it onto the truck bed? Apparently so. "Bastards," he muttered aloud.

Charles hurried back up the drive to the house and dashed inside. He knew there was a telephone in the central hallway. He quickly punched in the 999 number, the U.K. equivalent of 911.

"Yes," he said into the phone, "I'd like to report the theft of an automobile . . . . At the home of Rhys Tremayne. I'm a guest there . . . . You know the house? Great . . . . So the police will be coming soon? That's perfect . . . . Well, we think sometime between midnight and six in the morning . . . . Yes, an old black Morris Minor. No, I don't know the year or the plate number."

"Charlie, what are you doing? What's going on?" The professor, in robe and slippers, had just come down from his bedroom.

"Reporting your car, sir."

"My car? What about it, Charlie?"

"It's gone, sir. Thieves in the night."

The professor looked stunned. "Stolen? My *car*?"

Charles hung up the phone, and the two of them went

out to the driveway. The professor followed behind Charles down to the spot where they could see the scuff marks made by hauling the car up onto the tow truck.

"Well, shit!" the professor said, using an expletive Charles had never heard him use.

"My sentiments exactly, sir. And I expect your wife won't be too happy when she hears what's happened to her car."

"Damn and blast. This is *not* how I wanted to start my day."

"Nor me. The police will be here soon. Let's hope they'll be able to track down the thieves."

"Well, I'm certainly sorry about the bloody car. No doubt about that. But Charlie, that's not the real disaster here. The *real* disaster is that all my CDs, the whole kit and caboodle, were still inside the bloody car!"

As Charles and the crestfallen professor were re-entering the house, Rhys Tremayne came rushing toward them from the direction of his private study. "It's gone!" he exclaimed. "Stolen!"

"Yes," Charles said, "we've already reported it to the police. They're on their way now."

"The police?" their host said. "On their way now? How did you know it was gone?"

"They rolled it down the driveway and took it away on a tow truck. We could see the marks in the gravel where they did it."

"On a tow truck? The *manuscript*?"

"The manuscript? No, the professor's car. Sir, are you saying the manuscript is gone as well?"

Rhys Tremayne slumped down into an overstuffed chair, his face in his hands. It seemed to Charles that he was as close to crying as one can get and not be crying.

Finally he looked up. "So, the police don't know about the manuscript as yet?"

"Sir, we didn't know about the manuscript ourselves until this very moment."

"Well," their host said, rubbing his chin with his right hand, "then perhaps it's best we not tell them. Yes, I really think it would be best not to tell them."

"Rhys," the professor said, "what in the world are you going on about? Why wouldn't we want the police to know?"

"William, listen to me for once will you? We mustn't tell them. We mustn't, I say, we just mustn't. Do you hear me?"

✢ ✢ ✢

The police, now fully informed about the theft of the car, had come and gone. Since it had been several hours since the car's disappearance, they didn't seem hugely optimistic about the chances of recovering it. It could easily have been hidden away by now, they said, or even be hundreds of miles away. Still, they would get the word out and do all they could. Perhaps they'd be in luck. And if not, there was always the insurance money. That last point didn't do much to brighten the professor's mood. "Oh, Charlie," he said, "I can't tell you how bummed I truly am." The man was in deep mourning for the loss of his precious CD collection.

"If Mr. Tremayne could run us into Helston," Charles said, hoping to buck up his dear old friend, "after we find a car rental place and get us a fresh set of wheels, we could find some shops where they sell CDs and get started re-creating your collection. I would be honored, sir, if you'd grant me the privilege of buying the very first CDs for your new and even more glorious collection. How about Harry Nilsson? Or maybe The Allman Brothers?"

At Charlie's encouraging words, the professor showed signs of cheering up. He managed a broad smile, his eyes gleaming like a child preparing to blow out the candles on his birthday cake. "You'll do that, Charlie? Booker T and the MGs? Wilson Pickett? Charlie, I won't say no. Umm, and maybe Aretha Franklin?"

"And Sam Cooke," their host said, adding his tuppence worth. "And Otis Redding. But there's no need for you to rent a car, William. My wife's old Jag still runs like a top. You'd be welcome to use it. These days, it's hardly used at all. She prefers her hybrid."

"Another wife's car, hmm?" Charles said, grinning at the professor. "Well, maybe we'll have better luck this time." Their host looked back and forth at the other two men, not understanding Charles' remark.

"Now, Rhys," the professor said before the three had had a chance to sit down to breakfast, "before Charlie and I go rushing off to town, perhaps we could do a bit of sleuthing in regard to that blessed missing manuscript, eh? To start with, why don't you show us where you put it for safe keeping?"

"Don't think it's likely to do much good, William. But if you really want to, then come on and follow me."

Charles and the professor traipsed along behind their host as he led them through the corridors of the large house back to his personal study, tucked away in a far corner of the first floor. He fished a set of keys from his pocket, unlocked the heavy door, and snapped on an overhead light. "I keep this door locked at all times," he said. "And I'm certain it was locked last night. I made sure to check it before I went to bed."

"So the manuscript, Rhys, where was it?" the professor asked, glancing about the room.

"In the wall safe." He pointed across the room to where a brightly colored painting covered a large portion of the wall. He stepped over and removed the painting. Even then it took a keen eye to make out the faint outlines of the safe door, for they blended subtly into the complex pattern of the wallpaper. "I put it in here yesterday afternoon, just after Charles was finished with his transcribing."

"Are you sure? Maybe you forgot and set it down on your desk," the professor suggested.

"I most certainly did not. I would never be so careless."

The professor began examining the safe's keypad. "Rhys, who else knows how to open this contraption?"

"Only Ailish and Alwyn. No one else. Neither of them was here last night. Ailish stayed over in Truro and Ally was still in St. Ives. Just the three of us know the combination, and yet somehow someone managed to get into this carefully locked room and break into this safe. Whoever it was, it wasn't any of us."

"Open it now, would you?" the professor said. "Let's have a little peek inside, eh?"

Rhys Tremayne stood there quietly for a moment. He was actually wringing his hands, a gesture Charles had often read about but never seen anyone do.

"Come on, come on," the professor said, "we're all friends here. We won't tell anyone about your private pornography collection."

Their host made an ugly face at the professor. Then he sighed and began to punch in a sequence of numbers.

While he was doing that, Charles glanced about the man's inner sanctum, remembering Ally's little joke about it from a couple of days back just after they'd first met.

It wasn't a large room. A beautiful old desk and a high-backed desk chair took up about a third of it. A pair of antique-looking standing lamps flanked the desk, and two waist-high, glass-fronted bookcases ran along two of the walls. Paintings graced all three walls, including a couple of very colorful daubs Charlie guessed were Ally's. If so, they seemed as full of vitality as the young woman herself.

"Okay, here we are, then," their host finally said. He swung the door open to view. "I placed the manuscript right there on the top. When I went to get it out this morning, it wasn't there."

"What other goodies do you keep in there?" the professor asked. Then seeing the offended look on their host's face, he said, "Rhys, I'm not trying to pry. I only ask because I want to know if there were other valuables in the safe, and if there were, if they're still there. If they're there, the thief must've targeted the manuscript specifically."

"Ah, yes. Well, nearly all the other items in the safe are legal or financial documents. I'd have to go through them carefully to be sure, but as far as I can tell without doing that, they appear to be untouched."

"*Nearly* all the other items in the safe?" the professor said.

"Okay, there is one other item of great value I keep in there. It's still there, in that small box beneath all the documents."

"Did you check it?"

"I did. It's fine."

"And what, pray tell, is it?" When Rhys knitted his brow the professor went on, "Just from one book-lover to another, my dear old friend."

Their host sighed. "Well, okay then, just from one book-lover to another. I've got an original copy of *Tottel's Miscellany*. I prize it above everything else in the world – after my wife."

"A copy of *Songs & Sonnets*?" Charles said, his eyes wide.

"Rhys," the professor said, "there's only three or four copies of that book known to exist! How on earth did you get one?"

"My little secret, William."

"Well, goodness. Anyway, since it's still in its box, it seems clear that whoever broke in was after just one thing: the manuscript." The three of them stood silently for a moment, contemplating that conclusion.

"The room was locked. The manuscript was in a safe to which only three people knew the combination. Two of them weren't here, and the third, the owner, wouldn't have stolen his own manuscript. Goodness," the professor said again, "it's a locked room mystery, Charlie! Like something out of those old detective novels by Rex Stout or John Dickson Carr." The look on Rhys Tremayne's face said he didn't share the professor's amusement. "Well, okay then," the professor went on, "who else knew that you had the manuscript?"

The man hesitated, and Charles saw that the question discomfited him and that he was struggling to think of a way to avoid answering it.

"Well . . . ," he finally said, "no one. No one other than the man who arranged for me to get it."

"Ah, the man who procured it for you," the professor declared. "And so the plot ripens."

"Thickens," Charles said.

"And do you know who else *that* person might have mentioned the manuscript to?" the professor went on, ignoring Charles.

Their host sighed. "How could I? But I have always found him to be a man of impeccable discretion." Charles pondered the possible implications of that last statement.

"You've had previous dealings with him?"

"Only a few. But they've always worked out most satisfactorily."

"Yes. Until now."

"William, there's no reason to think he could have been involved in this in any way. I'm sure he wasn't."

"Then, my dear old friend, that leaves just your wife and daughter."

"Sir," Rhys Tremayne said stiffly, "you are my dear old friend, and you have always been a welcome guest in my home. But sir, I have to say that I deeply resent the insinuation."

"Fair enough. But Rhys, that takes us back to the chap who sold you the manuscript, doesn't it?"

Rhys Tremayne sighed deeply, then nodded his agreement. "Maybe so, maybe so."

Yes, Charles Bascombe thought, it would seem to. But perhaps there's another possibility – one much closer to home; one that didn't involve Ally or Ailish. Charles was happy not to be involved in this discussion. But he couldn't help thinking that Rhys Tremayne himself might have been a bit more involved in the "disappearance" of the manuscript than he was letting on.

And for a moment, too, Charles found himself wondering if the theft of the manuscript might be connected to the theft of the professor's car. Then he scotched that notion, for it was highly improbable.

9

Jackson Lockhart strode casually across Russell Square in the direction of the British Museum. He was in no hurry on this bright morning in early June. Yesterday evening he'd endured the last of the tedious business meetings for which he'd come to London. Now he had two free days to enjoy the city before going to Oxford to track down his old college roommate, Charles Bascombe. Jack was eager to see Charlie again – had it really been two years since they'd last been together? – but London was new to him, and he looked forward to getting acquainted with the city in the brief time he'd have here. London, no surprise, made quite a dramatic and refreshing change from Charlotte, North Carolina.

Jackson stopped for a moment to watch the squealing children as they chased after soccer balls and Frisbees in the grassy areas of the square. An old woman on a park bench took bread crumbs from a brown paper bag and tossed them to the pigeons. Couples, young and old, walked past him hand in hand or arm in arm. A young and frisky black Lab romped after a tennis ball. Jack stopped and examined one of the several clusters of ornamental flowers. He had no idea what they were, but they were certainly lovely. Raising his eyes, he looked across the square toward the looming gray tower of the University of London, which lay just to the north of the British Museum complex. Then he looked back towards the hotel where he was staying, the Russell Square Hotel, which the guidebooks called "a Victorian pile." An apt description, he thought, though he found staying in the quaint old edifice a lot of fun.

Jackson stepped up his pace down Montague Street toward Great Russell Street and the main entrance to the British Museum. He walked alongside the complex's high outer fence, then passed through the small entranceway flanked by uniformed guards who took a good look at him. The large forecourt to the museum now teemed with tourists and school groups. Jackson couldn't refrain from pausing to a take a photo of the great façade of the building, with its many huge pillars and the Union Jack floating high above the massive structure.

He climbed the steps to the entrance and was surprised to discover there was no entry fee, just a suggested donation. He shoved a five-pound note through the slot, then moved past the bag checkers who hardly glanced at him. He was also surprised by the absence of metal detectors.

Jackson stepped into the dark, people-filled lobby. He moved to one side, doing what he could to get free of the bustling throng so he could get his bearings. He hoped there would be a map or a brochure to tell him where he could find the Rosetta Stone and the Elgin Marbles.

He felt a little tug at his sleeve and turned to see a young woman with a huge smile on her face and a package under her arm.

"I *thought* that was you, Jack," she said. It took him a moment to recognize her. After all, it must've been ten years since he'd last seen her.

"Clare? Is that really who I see standing right next to me? My gosh, look at you!"

"Been a while, hasn't it?" she said. "But other than your spiffy clothes and your neatly trimmed hair, Jack, you look pretty much like the Jackson Lockhart we knew back in college."

"What brings you to London, Clare?"

"Work. Been working here for six months now. Two and a half more years to go, maybe, before the firm ships me off someplace else. And you?"

"Work, I guess. Just got through three days of really boring meetings. You won't believe this, Clare, but I'm just about to go and see Charlie."

For a fleeting moment a startled look passed across the woman's face. "Charlie?" she said.

"He's in Oxford doing research. Quite the scholar, our old Charlie. I'm going to spend a few days with him, see the sights, take in a play or two, maybe even make a run up to Stratford. Charlie's going to get me all cultured up."

The woman still seemed a bit shocked by this news. Collecting herself she said, "Do you have time for a coffee, Jack? Take a few minutes for us to get caught up some?"

"'If you got the money, honey, I got the time.'" Sorry about that. Banking hasn't completely rid me of my cornball sense of humor. I've got both the money and the time. Clare, it's wonderful to see you."

Jackson followed her out of the gloomy entrance area and into the Great Court, the most glorious part of the museum, an area that once housed its famous reading room, before the British Library separated from the museum and moved to its new facility on Marlebone Road. Then he followed her up a lovely curving staircase to the upper-levels of the museum.

"They completely renovated and redesigned this entire section a few years ago," she said. "Isn't it spectacular?"

"Look at that ceiling," he said, in awe.

"That blue you see is the sky. That's all glass up there. You got a perfect day for it."

They took a small table and ordered two coffees and Danishes. Jack smiled across at this very professional-looking young woman whom he still thought of as wearing baggy T-shirts and jeans with holes in the knees. Her hair, once nearly black, seemed a lighter shade now. No hints of gray, though, as had just begun to appear in his own hair.

Jack eyed the package she'd placed on the table by her elbow. "What's that you've got there?" he asked.

"Oh, well let me show you. You'll like it. It's a set of chessmen I'm going to send to my nephew for his birthday. Medieval chessmen. Quite wonderful. It's a replica of a famous set here in the museum. They sell them in the gift shop, which is why I'm here. I just popped in to do that one thing. And then as I was leaving I spotted a fellow coming in through the museum door who looked quite a bit like

Jackson Lockhart. Rather a shock, actually. "

"Medieval chess pieces. Sounds like Charlie's kind of thing." At that, the two of them gazed at each other for several long beats without speaking.

"When's the last time you saw him, Clare?" Jack finally asked.

Clare took several deep breaths before answering. "I haven't seen him since graduation. Haven't seen him, haven't heard from him, haven't tried to contact him."

"Two proud and stubborn knuckleheads," Jackson said. "You were so tight, too. I never would have imagined you two just going off on your separate ways, with no apparent regrets."

Again she was silent. "No regrets?" she finally said. Then she shook her head. "There were regrets," she said, "at least on my part. But I threw myself into my law school studies and tried to put Charlie out of my mind. I couldn't, of course, but eventually the hurt began to wear away. Anyway, Jack, you and Charlie drifted away too, didn't you?"

"Charlie followed his heart and went to graduate school in medieval studies. I followed the money, got my MBA, and landed a sweet job in finance. We've kind of stayed in touch, though we rarely see each other. Man, how I've envied him, doing exactly what he always wanted to do. I make three times the annual salary he makes, and I'm very good at what I do. But job satisfaction? Aye, there's the rub."

"You two guys roomed together for what, three years?"

"Yep. Roomed together, took classes together, played intramural sports together, chased girls together – until Charlie took up with you, that is. Actually, Charlie was never really much of a girl chaser. Not like me."

"I knew him about as well as you, I think," she said. "No, he was never a girl chaser, not even before me. Charlie Bascombe was one of the most morally upright and principled people I've ever known, maybe the *most* principled."

"Well yeah, but you're a lawyer. You don't *know* any principled people."

They both laughed.

"Jack, it's really nice to see you," she said.

"And you," he said. It was at that moment that his cell phone beeped for a text message. "Sorry," he said. "Excuse me while I have a look."

Jack read through the message twice before looking up. "Well, speak of the devil," he said. "Guess who that was?"

"Charlie?"

"He isn't in Oxford after all. Seems that our Charlie is stuck in some place called the Lizard. He wonders if I might be able to come and visit him there. Apparently it's in Cornwall."

10

"They didn't take your most cherished book," the professor mused. "Rather a clear indication it was only the manuscript they wanted. That little book of poetry, Rhys, I suppose it must be worth quite a bundle?"

The three men now sat around the breakfast table, Maria scurrying about them, serving up coffee, toast and a full English breakfast of eggs, sausages, bacon, and baked beans.

"Oh, yes," Rhys Tremayne muttered. "Worth quite a *big* bundle. You would be astonished at what the Huntington Library in California offered for it. Very tempting, but I just couldn't bear to part with the precious little thing." The professor lifted his eyebrows.

"Maybe the thief overlooked it," Charles suggested. "You keep it in a nondescript and unlabeled box."

"Well, I suppose that's a possibility," the professor mused. "But it seems much more likely that it was just the manuscript they were after."

"A locked room, a hidden wall safe, and a mysterious and now missing manuscript. I say, where's old Philo Vance when we need him?" the professor said with a smile.

"Philo who?" Charles said.

"Before your time, lad, before your time," the professor replied. "Well, Rhys, it seems to me that someone was either very, very good; or else someone was completely in the know."

Charles glanced at their host's face to see what reaction

he might have to the professor's comment. But he saw nothing out of the ordinary.

"Well," Charles said, "if it's money they want, maybe they'll contact you in a day or two and try to sell it back to you."

"The thought's crossed my mind," Rhys Tremayne replied glumly.

"Not too likely they'd try to sell it to any of the big museums or libraries," the professor said, "at least not directly. That would be far too risky."

"No," Rhys muttered, "but there's plenty of buyers out there, unscrupulous dealers and private collectors. And people who steal manuscripts would know how to find 'em."

Again Charles glanced over at the man. To Charles, it seemed likely that their host knew of what he spoke, that he was a man who'd had experiences with such people.

"At least we're not completely empty-handed," their host said at last.

"What do you mean?" the professor asked.

"William, we still have Charles' transcript of the Middle English poem. What a good thing that he finished it before the theft. Excellent work, my boy. So glad you were able to work so swiftly."

"I wish I'd had more time to double check it," Charles said.

"Well," their host said, "when you and William run into town today on your CD-buying spree, you must take Charles' transcription and get it photocopied. We'd better make multiple copies, just to be on the safe side. Can't take a chance on having *that* disappear."

"Excellent idea," the professor said. "But Rhys, are you sure we shouldn't be notifying the authorities about this theft? Might not do any good, but where's the harm in it?"

"William, I said we *weren't* going to do that. So just drop it, all right? That could be awkward for a dear friend of mine, a friend," he added hastily, "who has not done, and never would do, never could do, anything improper or illegal."

"Yes," Charles thought. "And it might be awkward for you as well." But he kept his own counsel.

And there was another matter about which Charles Bascombe kept his own counsel. For upstairs in his bedroom, on his laptop and also on a flash drive, were computer files that he alone knew about; files he'd already sent off to be stored on the mainframe computer at Waverly College. If the theft of the manuscript had been designed to make it impossible for anyone to ever see the original text of those pages, they hadn't totally succeeded. Charles might no longer have access to the physical pages of the manuscript, but he still had copies of them. That was his secret. For now, he planned to keep it that way. To Charles Bascombe, this whole situation had a very odd smell.

As the three men were just finishing their breakfasts, they heard noisy footsteps coming from the back entrance to the house. Then Ally rushed into the room, rosy-cheeked and out of breath.

"Oh good," she panted, "you're still here. When I didn't see your car, I was afraid you'd flown the coop."

"The car's flown the coop," the professor said, "but not us. As you can see, Charlie and I are still here." A confused look on her face, Ally glanced first at Charles and then at the professor.

"Alwyn," her father said, "I didn't expect to see you back so soon. Had to come and continue your conquest of young Charles?"

"Charlie Bascombe, I fear, may be unconquerable," she said wistfully. "But Daddy, guess what? I've sold a painting!"

"That's wonderful, lass. I knew that would happen. So which one did you sell?"

"Oh, Daddy, I'm afraid it's the large one over the bookcase across from your desk. It's one of the ones you said you quite liked."

"You've sold one of *mine*?"

"Daddy, they aren't really yours. But if you especially fancy that one, I can paint you a near duplicate – only I'll make it even better!"

"The one with all those swatches of orange and red?" the professor asked. Ally nodded. "Well, I have to say that I rather fancy that one myself," he said.

"That's one of *your* paintings?" Charles said, his words suggesting disbelief. "Wow. I'd assumed it was an original Kandinsky."

"Oh, Charlie," Ally said, "what a sweet, sweet man you are – even if you are a very poor liar." She stepped over to Charles, bent down, and kissed him on the cheek. The young woman was beaming.

"But I don't understand how you could sell someone a painting they haven't even seen," her father said.

"Daddy, surely you've heard of the Internet. They saw it on my website, of course. All of my paintings are on my website."

"Website?" he said.

"It's how the world is these days, Rhys," the professor said. "So it's not *quite* like buying a pig in a poke. Lots of things are up to date in Kansas City, even if that's not quite true here at Manderley."

"Manderley?" their host said, a puzzled look on his face. The professor winked at Charles. Ally, seeing the wink and getting the joke, laughed her joyful laugh.

Ally poured herself a cup of coffee and sat down in the fourth chair at the little breakfast table. Always a ball of energy, to Charles right now she looked so excited she couldn't help twitching. Caffeine was the last thing she needed.

"How many paintings have you sold?" Charles asked her.

"This makes two."

"The other was to Ally's mother," Rhys Tremayne said, "my former spouse."

The lizard, Charles thought. He wondered where the woman was now. "Ally, this could be the start of some really big things for you," he said. "Would you mind if I joined the queue for buying them? I'd like one too. Go great in my apartment living room."

"You're so transparent, Charlie," the professor said. "You just want to impress your friends with your original Kandinsky."

"Sir, don't be giving away my secrets. But actually, sir, this time you're quite wrong. I want to impress my friends by owning an original Alwyn Tremayne. I'll be able to say I got in on it before everyone else." Ally's apple cheeks were all aglow.

"Well, I'll need to pack the painting up and then get myself back to St. Ives. Anyone else interested in coming along?" She looked hopefully at Charles.

"How's the shopping for CDs in St. Ives?" Charles asked. "Better than in Helston?"

"CD shopping in Helston? You're joking, right? You're not likely to find much of anything in Helston. Not many places sell CDs these days. But why would anyone want to buy CDs when you can easily create an iTunes library or just download digital versions to an iPod?"

"You'll have to ask the professor that."

"Lots of things you can do, sir, instead of buying actual CDs. No disrespect, but times have changed."

"Yes, they bloody well have," the professor murmured. "I'll admit that I'm hopelessly old-school, Ally. You know the adage about old dogs."

"Well, if you really want CDs, there are a couple of places in St. Ives we could check out, if you want to come along."

"Charlie, let's do that."

"Professor," Charles said, "I don't think we should just up and abandon Mr. Tremayne right now, what with disappearing cars and manuscripts."

"Oh, tosh. I'll be perfectly all right. You two go on now with Alwyn."

"Charlie, as long as Rhys feels safe, and as long as Alwyn doesn't mind an old wet blanket like me tagging along, why don't we do it?"

"Please go ahead, the both of you," their host said. "But William, I'm counting on you to keep that daughter of mine from *totally* corrupting the lad, eh what?"

"My goal," Ally said, "is to corrupt the lad only a *little* bit." Three of them laughed, and one blushed.

Half an hour later Ally, Charles, and the professor walked out to the front drive where Ally's little red Triumph sat all bright and shiny. She opened the boot so Charles and the professor could toss in their travel bags. The professor hopped in back, alongside the large wrapped painting. Charles opened the right-side door before remembering that that was the driver's side.

"You have a hankering to drive?" Ally said.

"Uh, no, maybe not," he replied. "Just opening a door for a lady as a gent should do."

"Ha. I'm no lady, and you, sir, are no gent." Charles shrugged.

Ally pulled out slowly, trying not to spin her wheels and kick up the gravel. "Daddy always acts like he thinks I'm a wild child," she said. "Truth is, I'm really not."

"Well," the professor said from the back seat, "maybe just a little bit?"

"Oh, okay, maybe just a little bit," she replied.

They moved down the long driveway at a stately pace, and when they neared the gateway, Charles raised his eyes and gazed up at the two gray stone birds perched atop their flanking pillars. "Cornish choughs," he said beneath his breath, drawing a sidelong glance from Ally.

"So, Professor," she asked when they'd begun to whip along on the main road, "what exactly *did* happen to your car?"

"It seems to have up and vanished," he replied.

"Up and vanished? Are you saying someone pinched it?"

"Appears to be the case, yes."

"Good golly, I wonder why."

"Apparently it was a collector's item," Charles said. "Who would've guessed it?"

"No accounting for taste," the professor added.

"Well, it did have a good bit of character," she said. "It was like something out of another era."

"Just like me," the professor said. "Yes, it had character. But, alas, it also had my personal collection of CDs."

"And it wasn't even the professor's car," Charles added. "It's his wife's."

"Uh oh," Ally said.

"Well, Charlie and I will just have to figure something out, that's all," the professor replied. "Anyway, she only drives it about twice a year. Maybe Charlie and I can find her another one, and if we do, she probably won't know the difference."

En route to St. Ives, Ally said, "I'm just going to pull off up here for a moment beside the graveyard so Charlie can take photos of St. Michael's Mount. That be okay?"

"Ah, Ally, well done. Just the perfect place to do it," the professor said. "Grab your camera, Charlie, and follow Ally's lead."

"You going to wait here?"

"No, I think I'll come as well," the professor said. "I always love seeing that sight. It's quite a perfect day for it."

They stepped through an archway into an extensive

and well-kept graveyard high above the sea. A host of gravestones, many in the style of Celtic crosses, spread across the downward sloping grass. Charles was surprised to see several small palm trees in amongst the gravestones. The Cornish Riviera, he reflected.

It was indeed a perfect day, clear and bright, the sunlight glinting off the sea. Charles took several shots, some using the telephoto lens. Then he stood still for several minutes and just gazed down to the west at the splendid castle perched on the small island. Out behind it, across Mounts Bay, he could see the town of Penzance. Many small boats were to-ing or fro-ing across the harbor.

Five minutes later they were back in the car. "Fabulous sight," Charles said. "I'd like to see it up close, too. I know we don't have time right now, but maybe before we head back to Oxford?"

"Stay for two more days in St. Ives," she said. "Saturday is our busiest day at the gallery. Then on Sunday we can go and visit it on our way back to Manderley. Yes?"

"Okay with you, Professor?"

"Sounds like a plan," he said. "Manderley," he mumbled. "Good one, Ally."

They drove on down through the little gray town of Marazion and then at the crossroads turned to the right, away from Penzance, and toward St. Ives.

"As I was going to St. Ives," Charles began chanting in a sing-song voice, "I met a man with seven wives. Each wife had seven sacks. Each sack had seven cats. Each cat had seven kits. So, Professor, how many were going to St. Ives?"

"Goodness," the professor mused, "seven wives. Fellow

must've been a Mormon. Either that or he was Mickey Rooney. Hmm. So seven wives times seven sacks times seven cats times seven kits . . . . I've never been much good at math, Charlie."

"How many, Ally?'

"Just one," she said. "*You.*"

"Got ya, Professor," Charlie crowed. "As *I* was going to St. Ives. The man with seven wives wasn't going to St. Ives. He was going away from St. Ives."

"Well, yes. And if he'd been wise, he would've left his seven wives there," the professor muttered.

"What about you, Charlie?" Ally asked. "Are you the marrying sort?"

"Seven wives," they heard the professor muttering to himself in the back seat. "What was the fellow thinking? Well, Charlie," the professor said in a louder voice, "what *about* you?"

"Whoa. You need to give me a moment to reflect on that one." At last he said, "Okay, I can't give you a definitive answer, but I will admit that I once knew a young woman I thought I might be able to marry. But that was a good long while ago, and it hasn't happened since."

"It couldn't be *that* long ago," Allie said. "You aren't even thirty yet, are you?"

"So Charlie," the professor sang out, "give us all the gory details. I've never heard *this* tale before."

"Sorry to disappoint you, but there's not really a lot to tell. It was when I was still in college. I went with a certain girl for most of a year. During that time we got really close, and sometimes I did imagine us having a future together.

But then something quite weird happened – something I'm *not* going to go into – and we had a major blow-up. She was furious with me and I was furious with her, and we ended up turning our backs on each other and just walking away. The whole thing was pretty painful for me, to be truthful about it. But, in time, one tends to get over things like that."

"One does?" the professor said.

"Oh, Charlie," Ally said, "you didn't even try to sort it all out?"

"Back then I was young and stupid. Now I'm just old and stupid."

"You're neither," Ally said. "Now you're just a little bit older and quite a bit wiser."

They drove along the road that skirts Carbis Bay and then on into St. Ives. Ally cautiously navigated the narrow, bustling streets of this little town renowned for its picturesque harbor, sandy beaches, and world-famous museums, a town that is both a haven for artists and a prime destination for tourists. Ally's flat was tucked away on a back street, a short walk from the Tate Gallery.

"Come on up for coffee," she said, "and after that I'll show you the sights. And of course, Professor, I shall lead you straight to the best places to buy your CDs. There's a couple of ratty old places that do offer loads of used CDs. These days, not so easy to buy them new unless you go online."

"Works for me," the professor said, beaming her a smile.

Charles was surprised by how neat Ally's little flat was. No bohemian squalor for her. It consisted of two floors: on the lower one, a tidy sitting room with sofa and two easy chairs (and no television set, Charles noted, though it did have a small Bose radio-CD player), and an efficiently laid-out kitchen-dining area; on the upper floor, two small bedrooms and a spacious bathroom. French doors led from her bedroom to a small open deck, where, she said, she did most of her painting. To Charles, the flat smelled only faintly like an artist's studio.

"Black for Charles, white for the professor," she said, handing them mugs. "Tea for me."

"*Meur ras*," said the professor, lifting his cup.

"You're most welcome," Ally replied. Then they sat and sipped in companionable silence for another minute or two.

"Ally," Charles said, "have you ever heard of a place called Polminster?"

She thought for a long moment before replying. "Actually, after racking my brain, no. There are a lot of places in Cornwall that begin with Pol-, but I've never heard of a Pol*minster*. Maybe you mean *Porth*minster?"

"No, I'm quite sure your father called it the Polminster Manuscript. Right, Professor?"

"By Tre, Pol, and Pen, ye shall know all Cornishmen," the professor intoned. "Three of the most common elements in Cornish place names, and also surnames. Some of you Yankees, I believe, are rather keen on a show called 'Poldark.' Pol means 'pool,' by the way."

"Polminster . . . ," Ally mused. "Hmm. It rings no bell. One of the main beaches right here in St. Ives is called Porthminster Beach. And there's a hotel with that name, too. But that's definitely Porth-, not Pol-."

"I'm guessing the 'Pol-' is merely camouflage," the professor said. "The important part is 'minster.' "

"Minster?" Charles said. "Isn't a minster a great church or cathedral, you know, like York Minster or Westminster Abbey? Surely there aren't any minsters in Cornwall."

"No, there aren't, other than Truro Cathedral, but the word can also simply mean a 'church,' " the professor said. "In this case, I believe it does."

"So you think Daddy had a specific place in mind when he gave the manuscript that name?"

"That's what I *suspect*," the professor said. "He's been extremely tight-lipped about where this manuscript came from."

"But do you recall him snapping at you a couple of days ago, when you started to say something about Polminster?" Charles said. The professor nodded. "Wouldn't that suggest you were on the right track?"

Just then Charles' cell phone buzzed. He looked completely taken by surprise, and had to fish about hurriedly in his backpack just to find it.

"Yes?" he said, sounding nonplused. "Oh, Jack! Of course . . . No, no, I didn't forget . . . Yes, I really want you to come . . . Well, right now I'm actually in the town of St. Ives. You could come tomorrow? Terrific . . . You what? You have a surprise for me? Jackson, I don't want any surprises. Surprise me no surprises . . . Okay, I'll need to work out the logistics on this end and get back to you. If you can let me know what time the train is supposed to arrive in Penzance, I'll find a way to meet you there . . . Good, then I'll see you at some point tomorrow. Jack, it will be great to see you."

Charles put away the phone and looked at the inquiring faces of the other two.

"That was Jackson, my old college roommate. I'd invited him to come and stay with me for a few days in Oxford. Guess it's going to be Cornwall. Hope that's okay with everyone."

"Of course," Ally said. "The more, the merrier. And it sounds like he has a surprise."

"Apparently so. No idea what *that* could be."

"Is Jack a scholar, too?" Ally asked.

"Jackson? A scholar?" Charles said with a loud laugh. "That's a good one, Ally."

11

The three of them walked into the little town's busy commercial area, and Ally showed the professor what she thought were the most promising places to look for CDs.

"In that one," she said, pointing to a place called Sullen Syd's CD CITY, "you should find just about everything. Check the discs for scratches before you buy them. If they're enclosed in plastic wrap, make Syd open them for you. He can be a little bit slippery, our Sullen Syd. Well, happy hunting, Professor. Meet back at the flat at five?"

"Five it is," he replied.

"Here," said Charles, holding out a twenty-pound note. "Spend it wisely, sir. Dave Brubeck? Fats Domino? Leonard Bernstein's *Candide*?"

"I can't take your money, Charlie."

"You *have* to take my money. A deal's a deal."

The professor relented and accepted the bill. "Buddy Holly's *Greatest Hits*," he said, "if I can find it."

"Hard to do better than that," Charles replied.

"Happy hunting, Professor," Ally said. "See you at five. C'mon, Charlie, time to show you the sights." And the two of them headed off, leaving the professor at the mercy of Sullen Syd.

"Let's walk around the harbor, shall we?" Charles said.

"Absolutely."

They passed small shops catering to the tourists, offering beach towels, postcards, plastic cricket bats, cheap soccer balls, sunglasses, and the like; passed a fish and chips place, several B&B's, and also a few more upscale restaurants and guest houses. Tourists jammed the narrow passages as well as the wider street, Quay Street, that ran in a clockwise direction around the small harbor.

"Let's walk out on the quay," Charles said.

"Smeaton's Pier, it's called," Ally replied.

They walked along the wharf, passing The Pier Coffee Bar and then the small building that housed the Harbour Master. Ally now donned her sunglasses against the bright glare of the afternoon sun.

Charles breathed in the fresh air, strongly flavored with the salty tang of the sea and the smell of fish. Several fishermen's boats were snugged up against the pier.

"The Cornish Mermaid," Charles said, reading aloud the name of one of them. "I do like the painting," he added, grinning at Ally.

"Well, Charlie, if you are keen on Cornish mermaids,

and I hope you are, I can show you a real one," Ally said.

"Umm, not quite sure what you are suggesting," he said, looking at her with tilted head.

"Not *me*, silly. I'm just an ordinary mortal, alas. No, but there's a little country church not far from here that has a wonderful bench-end carving of a mermaid. Maybe I could take you there tomorrow on my lunch break. It's no more than a ten-minute drive. Given your penchant for mermaids, I think you will quite like it."

"You have lots of good ideas, Ally."

"Charlie, you don't know the half of it." She put her arm through his and squeezed it tightly against her.

They walked on out to the end of the pier and stood there for several minutes, drinking in the wonders of the sea, the air, the sunlight, and the light afternoon breezes.

"How far is it to that lighthouse?" Charles asked, pointing off to the northwest across the harbor.

"Lighthouse Island. Just a couple of miles. There's a boat that takes tourists out to it. Do you know about that lighthouse?'

"Know about it? Uh, no. Should I?"

"That's Godrevy Lighthouse, Virginia Woolf's lighthouse."

"It is?"

"It's the one she had in mind when she wrote her novel. Of course the novel is set off the west coast of Scotland – Isle of Skye, I think – but it's this lighthouse that was its inspiration. Her family, the Stephens, often vacationed here when Virginia and her brother were young. Her name, Virginia Stephen, is recorded in the visitors' book. The story goes that her younger brother wasn't allowed to go. She uses that in the novel. Have you read *To the Lighthouse*?"

"Sadly, no."

"'Sadly' may be the right word. It is not a feel-good novel."

They sat on a low stone wall and ate fish and chips from out of the greasy papers in which they'd been wrapped – cod for Charles, plaice for Alwyn – and they shared a can of Double Diamond Pale Ale, passing it back and forth.

"Don't lick you fingers, Charlie," she admonished. She fished a small bottle of hand sanitizer from her handbag.

"When you eat fish and chips with your fingers," he said, "it's part of the deal that you lick your fingers."

"Guess that proves you really aren't a gent," she said. "But you should probably still use this." Nodding, he accepted the hand sanitizer.

"*Meur ras*," he said remembering the phrase the professor had used earlier. As an afterthought he added, "Do real gents eat fish and chips out of greasy wrapping paper? Umm, do real gents even *eat* fish and chips?"

"Rhetorical questions, Charlie?"

They spent much of the evening listening to the professor's new treasures. He was especially delighted with a Roy Orbison CD he'd found. Charles flipped through the highly diverse group of CDs the professor had purchased, which included Charlie Parker and John Coltrane. The professor's choices brought some smiles and an occasional groan.

"Professor, what's *this* doing in there?"

"Oh, dear, I didn't mean for you to see that."

"The Zombies? . . . Professor!"

"Oh, Charlie, just reliving a tiny bit of my own youth, you know. When I was still a wee lad, 'She's Not There' was a big favorite of mine. Almost as good as The Beatles, I always thought. Charlie, I was just a callow youth."

"What's the problem, Charlie?" Ally said. "That's a really good song."

"British Invasion," Charles said scornfully. He didn't really mean it. He was just twitting the professor. "For shame. Sir, I'll need to reconsider my ideas about your musical tastes."

"Professor," Ally said, "he's just teasing. He knows that that's a really good song. Right, Charlie?" Charles didn't say anything. "*Right*, Charlie?"

"Yeah, okay. I'll grant that it's not half bad. Anyway, Professor, we all have our idiosyncrasies."

"Yes, we all do," Ally said, "and especially you, Charlie." Her tone of voice said she wasn't speaking entirely in jest. Then turning to the professor she said, "Are you getting hungry, sir?"

"Not especially. I had just enough extra time to treat myself to a lovely cream tea in one of your quaint little tearooms. Ah, fresh-baked scones and newly gathered strawberries. There's nothing quite as delectable as fresh, juicy Cornish strawberries in early June."

"You, Charlie?"

"Our fish and chips is doing me fine. Perhaps just a very light supper?"

"Cheese, apples, maybe a sandwich?"

"Sounds perfect."

⁜ ⁜ ⁜

"Ally," the professor said as they were finishing their light repast an hour later, "you wouldn't have a computer handy that I could fool with for a bit, would you?"

"Sure thing. Just let me fetch my laptop. When you say 'fool with,' I hope you mean 'look some things up?' "

"Oh yes. Want to see what I can come up with in regard to a little notion I've just had about 'minster.' Best I follow it up before it slips from my mind, as my thoughts have a habit of doing."

She was back in a minute. She set the laptop down on her kitchen table and turned it on. "Let me just log in. Half a sec. Okay, sir," she said after a moment, "here you go."

"Aha," the professor declared five minutes later. "I *thought* I remembered that, and by Lloyd George, I did."

"What have you remembered, sir?" Charles asked.

"There's a little church up in North Cornwall that's called Minster. Actually, its real name is St. Materiana's, but it's commonly known as Minster Church."

"Is that the one on the cliff top near the village of Tintagel?" Ally asked. "If it is, I've been there."

"No, it isn't, but I know the one you mean. That's the other church in Cornwall dedicated to her. There's one in Wales, too, actually. But the one I'm thinking of is eight or ten miles from Tintagel, closer to the coastal village of Boscastle. It's quite remote, and not much frequented by tourists, not like the one at Tintagel. I've been there just the one time, but as I recall, it's quite a picturesque spot."

"How is it likely to be connected to the manuscript?" Charles asked. "Just the fact that the church and the manuscript have the 'minster' element in common doesn't seem to prove anything."

"You're probably right. And yet, my boy, I can't get away from this nagging feeling I have. Ever had one of those, a scholarly intuition that just won't let go of you? I've only had a few of those, but almost every time it's proved, in the end, to be correct. Well, as I've done in the past, probably best to let it simmer away for a few days. Maybe I'm just a clueless old fool, as they say. But if it won't let go of me, then maybe we should run up there and have a look. If nothing else, it will make a pleasant outing for you."

"Sir, you didn't get to hold the Bosworth Chair of Medieval Studies because you are a clueless old fool."

Charles lay on the day-bed in Ally's sitting room reading one of Colin Dexter's Inspector Morse novels. Since he'd arrived in Oxford to do his research, he'd been reading his way through the whole series. It had pleased him to discover that the house where the fictional inspector lived was just a few blocks from his flat in North Oxford.

Following his usual nightly routine, Charles read for forty-five minutes before setting the book down and snapping off the light. At the point where Charles had stopped, Morse was testily informing someone who'd inquired about his first name that he wished only to be called "Morse." It amused Charles that the inspector never revealed his given name – though the author had offered the tantalizing hint that it began with the letter E.

Five minutes after he'd doused the light, Charles heard soft footsteps coming down the stairs. Someone approached the sofa, pulled back the duvet, and slid in next to him.

"Come to try and corrupt me?" he whispered to her.

"I would never do such a thing, Charlie," she murmured. "I've just come to wish you a very pleasant good night."

Then she pressed her warm body firmly against his.

12

Charles slept in; by the time he'd roused himself, Ally had already left for work, and the professor was nowhere to be seen. But he found fresh coffee in the little kitchen awaiting him, and beside the coffee maker, a note: "Back to get you at 11:45 to take you to your rendezvous with a mermaid. I enjoyed saying goodnight. A."

Charles helped himself to an English muffin from the breadbox, popped it in the toaster, then poured himself a mug of coffee. In the fridge he found butter and marmalade and orange juice. It was close to the breakfast he normally ate at home, though there it would have been honey on the muffin, not marmalade.

He read some more of the Morse novel while he sipped his coffee. Then, feeling more fully himself, he went up and showered in Ally's bathroom. Since it was still only ten, he had plenty of time before Ally came to fetch him to get cracking on making a typed copy of his transcription of the Middle English poem that was possibly by Chaucer.

But when Charles reached into his backpack for the folder containing his transcription – *no folder*. What the heck? He emptied out the entire contents, but the folder simply wasn't there. He was certain he'd brought it since he was eager to have a readable, hard-copy version; that was essential before he could do any serious editing and annotating. Until he had that, it wasn't possible to know what they had: a work by Chaucer; a work by one of his fifteenth-century imitators; or something factitious?

"Well, hell's bells!" Charles said out loud. He didn't know what could have happened to it.

At that moment the professor came through the front door, a thick file under one arm. "Morning, lad, finally up?" he said, grinning. "On a normal day, Charlie, you'd have been standing outside the Bodleian, champing at the bit, eager for them to get the place opened up so you could get in and get at it. Not today, though, eh?"

"Professor! Is that my transcription?"

"It is your transcription and also five copies of it. Just made them at the photocopying place. Like you, I was champing at the bit for them to open up. They were only a few minutes late."

"Whew. I wish you'd left a note, though. I'd begun to think we'd been robbed yet again."

"Entirely safe and sound, Charlie. Those folks were efficient, and it was only 5p per page. You got good value from your twenty-pound note after all. So why don't you keep one copy, I'll keep one, and we'll give one to Rhys to put in his safe. The other two I'll mail home for safekeeping. And maybe we should make electronic files of them, too. Give us backup to the physical copies. You can do that with your phone, can't you?"

"Yes, I believe I can," Charles said. He didn't reveal

that he'd already done that with the pages of the original manuscript.

The professor's mention of his phone caused Charles to scoop it up from the little table beside the sofa and check it for messages. He'd missed a pair, both from Jackson. Jackson, they informed Charles, was coming on the mid-afternoon train and would arrive in Penzance about nine-thirty that evening. Charles quickly typed in the return message: "See you then." He didn't type "C U then," not wanting to demean the English language.

Ally came in with a rush. "All set?" she said to Charles. "Oh, Professor, Daddy wants you to call him. Says it's urgent. Apparently the police have some fresh information about your car." She handed him her phone. "Daddy's number is on this." She held out a scrap of paper. "We should be back in an hour." She grabbed Charles' arm and hustled him out to her little car.

They sped along the narrow coastal road that led out of St. Ives in the direction of the village of Zennor. On the way Charles observed the chimney stacks of several abandoned tin mines, mines once so vital to Cornwall's economy and now just picturesque reminders. Then, from maybe a mile away, he saw the tower of the little church of St. Senara rising above the rolling countryside, the sea a quarter of a mile off to their right. Ally pulled up and parked beside the church, which stood precariously close to the little side road.

After they'd climbed out, Charles paused for a moment by a small memorial plaque inserted into the church wall near the entrance porch. The inscription on the plaque was written in both Cornish and English. "John Davey," Charles said, reading the English portion aloud, "last person to possess any considerable knowledge of the Cornish language. Died, 1891."

"Yes," Ally said, "sadly, Cornish is now extinct as a spoken language. Various people are said to be the last living speakers of it, including this poor chap. People like my father would love to see it revived, like they've been doing in Ireland, but there's not much hope of that actually happening here. Well, come on, Charlie, time to meet your mermaid."

She led him straight to the mermaid bench-end in the little south transept of the nondescript church. There she was: longhaired, bare-chested, and fish-tailed, and holding her mirror and comb, a mermaid's usual accoutrements.

"So, what do you think?" Ally asked.

"Looks a lot like a mermaid," he said.

"That's it?"

"Well, no. I like the way the wood grain blends with the lines of the carving. Not the work of a master carver, I'd say, but someone with a genuine aesthetic sensibility. Ally, tell me her story."

"Ah, her story. Sure. The old legend is that there was once a young man who sang here in the choir, his tenor voice the loveliest anyone had ever heard. And one evening as the choir sang, sitting right on this very pew, a beautiful young girl appeared, a young girl no one had ever seen before. For several weeks, every time the young man sang, here she was. And then one evening after the service was finished, she spoke to him and persuaded him to go with her down to Pendour Cove. There they became lovers. And then she lured him out to sea. After that fateful evening, the two of them were never seen again."

"She was a selkie," Charles said. "She could only be in mortal form for a very limited amount of time before she had to return to the sea."

"So Charlie, what would you have done? Would you have gone with her?" Ally tilted her head and folded her arms across her chest.

Charles gave a nervous laugh. "Umm . . . probably a good thing we'll never know the answer to that question."

"I've noticed, sir," she said, "that you do have certain susceptibilities."

"Probably so. Anyway, how about I commission you to make a painting of her for me?"

"If you can't experience the real thing, then you'd like to have the next best thing to it?"

"I really do like your work – honestly, I do. That's *not* mere flattery. I would really like to buy one of your paintings."

"For you, sweet Charlie, I would do almost anything. My work isn't normally representational, but for you I shall make an exception."

"Doesn't need to be fully representational. You are the artist and you should have full artistic license. Do whatever your aesthetic principles tell you."

"Well, okay then," Ally said. And taking his face in her hands, she planted a small kiss on his lips. "That," she said, "is what a mermaid tastes like. Just so you know."

13

Late in the afternoon of the previous day, a hundred and twenty miles to the northeast, off-duty Police Constable Martin Goodrich pulled his old Ford Cortina into the garage bay of the Stevenson & Sons Auto Repair & Retrieval in Yeovil, Somerset. The car was due for routine servicing.

For the first few minutes the young policeman sat in the waiting area and glanced at an old RAC magazine. Becoming bored with that, he got up to take a little stroll to stretch his legs. He exited through the back door of the main shop and stepped over to a second building that housed the body shop. He stood and watched as a fellow was putting the finishing touches on a paint job. PC Goodrich looked at the work admiringly, for the car – an old Morris Minor – sparkled beneath its fresh coat of light green paint.

"Looking good," he said to the fellow, whom he now recognized as being Colin Stevenson, one of the sons of the garage owner and an old school mate of his from a few years back.

Colin looked up. Recognizing the PC, he replied familiarly, "Just about got 'er licked, Marty." He stood for a moment next to the young policeman and gazed with pride upon his handiwork. "Got a bit more tidying up ta do on the interior, then she'll be all set to go."

"What year is it, Colin?" PC Goodrich asked.

"Believe it be a '64. Not quite sure. 'Round about there, anyways."

"Who does it belong to?"

"Oh, it be ours. Brother just bought 'er t'other day."

It was at that point that PC Goodrich remembered the bulletin they'd received that very morning about a stolen Morris Minor. The theft had occurred somewhere down in Cornwall. And the missing car was just about this model and year.

"I like the new paint," the policeman said. "That's one of the classic colors, isn't it. What was the old color?"

"It were black. Much nicer now, eh?"

"Yeah, looks great. And what do you plan to do with it?"

"Oh, well, sell 'er for sure. Fetch a pretty penny. Lotter folks out there eager to have one o' these old uns."

"Colin, no offense intended," PC Goodrich said, "but could I see the paper work on the car? We received a notice about a missing Morris, and the description was very similar to this one. Just ta do my duty, like."

"Well, don't know about that. My brother did all the official stuff. He's gone off somewheres just now, so's we can't be askin' 'im, can we?"

"Well, then pop the bonnet for me, would you? I'd like to take a quick look at the vehicle registration number."

"Matter o' fact, I tried to find it earlier. Pretty worn down, it is. Couldn't make 'er out."

"Well, let's have a look anyway."

But Colin was right. The number was so well worn it wasn't possible to read it.

"Mind if I have a look inside the car?"

"O' course, Marty. Suit yourself."

The interior of the car, which appeared to PC Goodrich's

eye to be entirely original, looked in remarkably good shape for a car so old.

"Cleaned up good, didn't it?" the constable said, more an observation than a question.

"Think it must'a been a one-owner car," Colin said. "Doubt if they used 'er so much, neither, cuz she ain't got a whole lot of miles on 'er."

"That should enhance the value, I'd guess. Looks like you still have a bit of work to do with the dashboard, then?"

"Oh, yeah. Someone'd mucked about with it. So I had to replace the radio. The one I got in there now ain't the original, but I can do some touchin' up with 'er and make 'er look just right."

"Why'd you have to remove the old one? Didn't work?"

Colin looked flustered by the question. Finally he said, "Somebody'd stuck somethin' else in there, you know. Like a tape deck, or some such. That were the only thing about the whole car that weren't quite right. Had to get 'er out of there and put in a proper radio."

"Looks like the original upholstery has held up really well," the PC said, glancing over the top of the driver's seat at the backseat area. "Almost looks like no one's ever sat back there. Must not have had children."

He ran his hands over the front seats, which he could tell by both sight and smell had recently been cleaned. Then, as he ran his hand along the side edge of the front passenger's seat, his fingers brushed against the hard edge of an object. PC Goodrich ran his hand slowly across the edge of the seat once more to locate the spot. When he found it, he inserted his thumb and forefinger into a crevice that ran along the side of the leather seat.

He got a grip on the edge of a hard piece of plastic, then slowly extracted it. He raised it up to his eyes and read: *Slaughter on Tenth Avenue & Other Show Tunes of the 1930s.*

✣✣✣

As the train sped westward from London, Jackson Lockhart gazed admiringly through the window at the rolling Berkshire Downs. He'd left the city forty-five minutes ago and was now heading toward Bristol, where he would change trains for one that would take him south to Penzance. What he looked out at now was horse country, he knew, not from personal experience but from reading the mystery novels of Dick Francis. It was also where *Watership Down* was set, he recalled, a novel he'd loved in the eighth grade. He studied the high hills as they zipped past, wondering if one of them might have been the author's model for the one he'd called Watership Down.

Before Jack had boarded the train at Paddington Station, he'd had a quick lunch with Clare Reilly at the café of the National Film Theatre beside the Thames. What an impressive woman Clare had become. She'd always struck him as being pretty special, back when they were all in college together. But unlike most of the young women in their crowd, she'd never shown him the slightest bit of interest. No, Charlie Bascombe had been the only boy for her. With a smile, he remembered her singing, on one semi-drunken occasion as they walked in a group back to their dorms, "Charlie is my darling, my darling, my darling, Charlie is my darling, the young chevalier."

"Charlie a chevalier?" someone in their group had said scornfully. "That's a laugh."

"It's called irony, Mike, something you wouldn't know anything about."

"Actually," Charles had said, "my high school basketball coach once accused me of having a cavalier attitude."

"*That* I can totally see," Clare replied, punching his shoulder.

Back then, Jack said to himself with a sigh, they were all just young kids. Now they'd all moved on with their lives and found their niches – for better or for worse.

Jack often missed Charlie and the others during the ensuing years. He felt guilty for having been so caught up in his mad pursuit of his own glorious achievements in the world of finance that he hadn't made much effort to keep up with them. He'd certainly achieved a lot for himself in less than a decade; he was now firmly on the fast track to fame and fortune. But at what cost?

Seeing Clare again had brought home to him the immense value of close personal friendships. In the last few years he'd formed no friendships that came anywhere close to those he'd forged in college. He hadn't had the time, or so he claimed, and most of the people he'd come in close contact with weren't people he wanted to forge close friendships with. No, he greatly missed being around people like Clare. And more than anything, he missed good old Charlie Bascombe. Well, tonight he would see Charlie again.

The train rumbled southward, making briefs stops in Exeter and then Plymouth. Now the landscape they passed through made Jackson think of the novels of Thomas Hardy, novels he and Charlie had read for a seminar they'd taken together and had often discussed. Clare had been in that class, too. In fact, she'd been the star. Charlie and the professor had clashed over *Tess of the d'Urbervilles*, the only Hardy novel Charlie thoroughly disliked. It happened to be the professor's favorite. Bad luck for Charlie. But he'd stuck to his guns – that was Charlie – and his final grade had suffered for it. Yes, that was Charlie, always true to himself and his principles, despite the consequences.

About seven, Jack put down the novel he'd been reading and went in search of the buffet car. There he treated himself to a light snack: a packet of bacon-flavored crisps, a pair of sausage rolls, and a bottle of stout. As he ate, he attuned his ears to the conversations around him. He couldn't help marveling at the variety of English accents he heard. Every day in Charlotte he experienced quite a range of American dialects, Charlotte being a pretty cosmopolitan southern city. But what he heard here seemed far more wide-ranging in its diversity. Maybe, he thought, that was because Cornwall, in the summer, was a popular vacation spot for folks from all over England.

It was still only early dusk when the train pulled into the little station in Penzance, just after 9:30. These long summer evenings in the U.K., when the June twilight persisted until ten or even eleven, were really quite something, Jack thought.

And there on the platform stood Charlie Bascombe, looking just like the Charlie of old. He hadn't put on a pound, and he certainly hadn't improved his sense of dress style. And there beside him, obviously with him, stood a most attractive young woman who filled out her attire in all the right places.

"You dog, Charlie," Jack said to himself, "what have you been up to?"

"Jack!" came Charles' cheerful greeting. "We're over here!"

14

They'd reserved a room for Jack at a small guesthouse – The Moon & Six Pence – just around the corner from Ally's flat. The plan was to get Jackson checked in, and then he and Charles would head off for the pub. It would be just the two of them, since at that hour the professor would have gone to bed; and Ally, knowing that the two old friends should be left to themselves on this reunion night, had turned down their offer to join them.

As the young woman walked away, Charles noticed Jack's eyes lingering on her retreating form until she was out of sight. Charles couldn't help laughing. "Some things never change, do they, Jack?" he remarked.

"What's that?" Jackson turned his gaze back toward his old friend.

Charles gave Jack's shoulder a squeeze. "C'mon. Let's go find a pub."

The Golden Lion, one of St. Ives's oldest public houses, was just a short stroll away. As it was a Friday evening, the place was packed with a mixture of regulars and tourists.

Clutching their pints, the pair of young men managed to nab a low, two-person table just as a couple of others vacated it.

"Cheers, amigo," Jack said, looking across at Charles and hoisting his glass.

Charles hoisted his glass, too. "Welcome to Cornwall, Jackson Browne," Charles said, using one of his old nicknames for his friend, a nickname he hadn't used in nearly a decade. Hearing the familiar phrase on Charlie's lips brought a grin to Jack's face.

"Charlie, what did you mean back there when you said 'some things never change'?" Now it was Charles' turn to grin.

"I caught you, Jack. You were checking out Ally as she walked away. You were famous for that in days of yore." Jack's familiar, smiling eyes looked across at Charles above the mug's rim as he sipped his beer. Jack looked older now, his dark hair showing the first very faint traces of gray at the sides. He would soon have a distinguished look, Charles thought. But his deep-set, amber eyes were the same as always.

"Charlie, you can't blame a guy for looking," he replied. "Hell, you must've been looking too. Anyway, what's the deal with Ally? Something going on with you two?"

"No, no, not at all. But she's great, isn't she? No, I only met her a few days ago, over on the Lizard where the professor and I are staying. Her father's an old friend of the professor. On Sunday we'll be heading back over there. Tomorrow, you and I will have the whole day to explore this great little seaside burg. Maybe we can hit the beach for a few hours. Ally works in a local art gallery and Saturday's her busy day, so we won't see her till evening."

"This pub is great," Jack said, looking around and soaking up the ambiance. He ran his eyes over the people packed up against the bar, the guys in the back section shooting pool – or some pool-like game – and the noisy crowd clustered in front of the dartboard. His eye halted for a moment on the figure of a young redhead who was scrawling numbers on a chalkboard next to the dartboard. On most of the walls, Jack saw notices posted for all sorts of local events, including one for the group that would perform here Saturday night.

"I went to a couple of pubs in London," Jack continued, "but none of them were as atmospheric as this one. And it doesn't hurt that this place has a good share of attractive women. Check out the redhead by the dartboard. Wow, what a babe."

"Like I said, some things never change, like you and your redheads. Let's see. Martha Paxton was first. Then Lynsey Sveboda. After her, Rachel Kleinmann, I think." Charles pursed his lips. "Who've I missed?"

"Susan Laningham, Charlie. How can you possibly forget Sweet Sue? Man, I certainly haven't."

"Oh yes, Jackson Lockhart certainly had a thing for redheads. As for the one by the dartboard, would you like to meet her?"

"What? You mean you know her?"

"Not yet. But give me a moment."

"Ha, ha to that. Not unless a certain shy introvert has changed a lot more than I think he has. Anyways, I'm pretty sure she's with that hulking guy. The one with the black beard and hairy arms. The troglodyte tossing the darts."

"Oh, him. He's no problem. I could take him easy. He may look like the real deal, but I'm sure he's just a big wuss."

Jack's loud guffaw caused a lot of others to turn their heads in their direction, including the redhead.

"*You* could take him? Oh yeah, Charlie, sure you could."

"Hey, c'mon, I know jiu jitsu."

"Yeah, sure you do," Jack said, smiling across the table at his old college roommate. "Man, it's so great to see you again, Charlie, sitting here with you and nattering about old times is just what I've been needing. Listen, my brother, this coming week we're gonna have us some really good times – starting right now."

Charles, nodding his agreement, lifted his pint glass and took a deep drink. Then he wiped his lips with the back of his hand.

From the darts area came cheers of victory. "A double seventeen!" cried the redhead. She rushed over and hugged the burly bloke with the black beard. The troglodyte.

"Must've been playing 301," Charles said.

"Oh, wow. Now I remember your exploits in darts. Dorm league champ, several years running. You still play?"

"Not really, but I have played a couple of times in Oxford pubs. They tease me because I throw a dart like a baseball, using my whole arm. The real pros just flick their wrists. Still, I've held my own against 'em."

"I'm sure you have. But hey, here's the big question. What the heck are we doing in *Cornwall*? Whatever happened to *Oxford*? I'm not complaining. Cornwall's been awesome so far. But what happened to Oxford?"

Charles sighed. "Yeah, it would've been a lot simpler to

have you come stay with me in my flat in Oxford. What upset that plan was the professor receiving an urgent request from an old friend of his, Rhys Tremayne, Ally's father. The guy lives on the Lizard, about an hour from here. Somehow, he'd come into possession of a mysterious manuscript and wanted an expert opinion on it as soon as possible. He asked the professor, but the professor insisted that I was the perfect fellow for the job. I was reluctant at first, but, well, you know me. What's a guy to do? A mysterious and previously unknown manuscript that I would have first crack at? I couldn't resist that, Jack.

"So, we hustled down here to have a look. I assumed it would only take a couple of days and then we'd scoot back to Oxford. I figured I'd get back before your visit. Then things got complicated."

"Happens sometimes. So how did things get complicated?"

"The day after we got here I started in on the manuscript. It was fascinating and mysterious, just as advertised. After only a couple of hours I knew it had the potential to be a scholarly blockbuster."

"Whoa. And you also knew it had the potential to put a young, virtually unknown scholar, on the map."

"Well, okay, that thought did cross my mind. But then, on our third night at Mr. Tremayne's home, someone walked off with our car."

"Someone swiped the professor's car?"

"Actually, it was his wife's car."

"Uh-oh."

"It gets better, Jack. Right after we discovered the car was missing, we learned that the manuscript had disappeared as well. Apparently stolen right out of Rhys Tremayne's super-secure safe."

"Jeez. *That* must've pissed him off."

"Well . . . one would have thought so. But his reaction was kind of weird. We'd already notified the police about our car, but Mr. Tremayne told us *not* to tell the police about the manuscript. In fact, he insisted on it."

"Why in the heck wouldn't he want to tell the police?"

"That's the question, isn't it? It seemed to me there was either something fishy about the manuscript, or else something fishy about how Mr. Tremayne came to have it in his possession."

"Wow. Do you think the two thefts could be connected?"

"No obvious reason why they should be. But, Jack, ever since we got to Cornwall, we seem to have entered the wacky world of Alfred Hitchcock."

"No, not quite. Ally isn't nearly as willowy as one of Hitchcock's heroines."

"But she is a blonde. Anyway Jack, I've left out one other little event. When the car was stolen, the professor's personal collection of CDs – possibly more dear to his heart than even a mysterious medieval manuscript – was still in it. If you think Mr. Tremayne was irked at losing the manuscript, you should have seen the professor."

"*The Lady Vanishes*," Jack said, "*The Thirty-Nine Steps*. Sounds like early Hitchcock, definitely pre-*Rear Window*."

"I think it's more like *Rebecca*, Jack."

Jack nodded his agreement.

"Anyway, the only good news out of all of this is that before the theft of the manuscript, I'd made a transcription of the particular poem that intrigued us the most. So having that, it's still possible for me to continue working on preparing the text of it."

"Wow. That's quite a tangle of weird events, my friend. So then, when everything turned to muck, you just said screw it and hightailed it to St. Ives so you could forget your troubles by frolicking with Rhys Tremayne's sexy daughter with whom you'd struck it lucky!"

"*Jack*, that's not it at all."

"Kidding you, Charlie. Go on with your tale."

"Well, okay, we did come here partly to give ourselves some breathing space. But the main reason we came was so we could start reconstructing the professor's CD collection; and also because Ally needed to ship a painting she'd just sold from the gallery where she works. When she extended an invitation for us to come along with her, the professor said yes and then so did I."

"There you go, blaming it on the professor," Jack said. Charlie made a face at him. "Would've been damned hard to turn down such an offer. It's lucky for you Ally's not a redhead. But being as she isn't, I promise not to horn in."

"It's lucky for *Ally* she's not a redhead, knowing your track record with them."

"Alas, 'tis true," Jack said with a sigh. His eyes wandered once more toward the redhead beside the dartboard.

For the next couple of minutes, the two young old friends sat in companionable silence, happily soaking up the genial atmosphere of The Golden Lion pub.

"Jack," Charles finally said, "when you called the other day, you said something about a surprise. What did you mean?"

"Oh, man, between listening to your tales of woe and meditating upon redheads, I let the most important thing slip my mind. Now you've reminded me, Charlie, you'd better brace yourself. Here it comes."

"You can skip the dramatics. Here *what* comes?"

"Charlie . . . you get three guesses to tell me who I just saw in London."

"There are probably eight million people in London and you're giving me three whole guesses?"

"Three whole guesses."

"Umm, Mick Jagger?" Jack shook his head. "Princess Di?" Jack shook his head emphatically and made a scornful noise with his lips. "Charles Dickens? Jack the Ripper? Twiggy?"

"That's more than three, and you haven't even come close. Guess I'll have to tell you."

"Guess you will."

"The person I just saw in London happens to be Clare Reilly, Charlie. *Your* Clare Reilly."

Charles blanched. Then he breathed in a deep breath. "*Clare*? . . . In *London*? . . . Is she on a trip or something?"

"No. She's living and working there. For a branch of her law firm. She says she's likely to be in London for a couple more years."

"Umm . . . Jack . . . does she know I'm living in Oxford?"

"She *didn't* know it, but she does now, once I explained to her what I was going to do this week. Charlie, Clare spoke glowingly of you. When she learned I was coming to visit you, she looked like she felt left out. She didn't say it in so many words, but I could tell she really misses you."

"Clare in London . . . Well, how about that? . . . Clare from County Clare . . . living in London."

"Ha, Ha. I remember you used to call her that. And I remember once when she told you she'd never even set foot in Ireland, that you promised to take her there. Remember that?" Charles sat quietly. He did indeed remember the conversation Jack was alluding to.

"Well, Jack," Charles finally said, followed by a big sigh, "I appreciate you saying it. Somehow, though, I doubt that Clare really misses me."

"If you think that, you would definitely be wrong."

For another lengthy moment, Charles Bascombe just sat there staring down at the pint glass in front of him. Then he lifted it and finished off the final inch.

"Clare from County Clare," he said softly, more to himself than to his friend. "No, Jack, that's one piece of news I certainly didn't expect."

At closing time, the two young men exited the pub, along with assorted stragglers, and began strolling along the now-dark street toward their lodgings. They weren't drunk. At least, not quite, though three pints was more than Charles was used to having at one time.

"I did rather fancy that redhead, you know," Jack mused, as they walked side by side.

"I was all set to introduce you, you know."

"Sure you were. And you were all set to handle her hulking boyfriend, weren't you, Charlie?"

"I was, man, I was. I'm an expert at judo, you know."

"Judo? I thought you were an expert at jiu jitsu?"

"Well, at one of those j-things."

Unbeknownst to Jack and Charles, the very couple they were talking about were no more than a dozen paces behind them. Were they following them?

When the two young men reached the corner where they needed to separate, Jack to his B&B, Charles to Ally's flat, the redhead and her hulking boyfriend stood where they were and watched as each of the young men went on his way. They remained standing there for another five minutes. Then they, too, drifted off into the night.

15

It was nine-forty-five and Jack and Charles, both rather bleary-eyed, were drinking coffee in Ally's sitting room when they heard footsteps quickly approaching the flat's front door. It was the professor.

"Charlie," he panted out excitedly, "guess what? I've just been on the phone with the police. The car's been found, perfectly safe and sound. Maybe even better than before."

Jack, who hadn't yet met the professor, set his cup down and leapt to his feet. He held out his hand. "I'm Jack, sir," he said, grasping the professor's proffered hand. "Charlie and I go way back."

"A pleasure to meet you, Jack. A friend of Charlie is a friend of mine. Charlie and I go back a good ways ourselves. But please, call me Bill," he said, giving the young man a paternal pat on the shoulder. "Charlie – who lives in some earlier age I can't quite place – hasn't been able to bring himself to do that. Thinks it's disrespectful. Plain silly, long as we've known each other."

"Charlie being Charlie, sir."

"Yes, I should say so."

"Professor," Charles said, "what's all this about the car?"

"Safe, sound, and spruced up to boot. Those Stevenson fellows – Robbie and his brother, the guilty parties – went and took out all the scrapes and dents and even slapped on a fresh coat of paint. The lads did an excellent job, apparently. When they were done, they probably had customers standing in line for the lovely thing."

"Same color as before?"

"Not a bit of it. Now she's light green. What they call porcelain green, a classic color for an old Morris. Not sure how my wife will feel about the new color, but if we're lucky, she won't notice."

"Won't notice that an old black wreck is now a princely thing that's been painted a lovely shade of green? Won't notice that Robbie Stevenson has turned Mr. Hyde into Dr. Jekyll?"

"Ha, ha. Good one, Charlie."

"So Professor, where's the car now?"

"In Somerset. Yeovil, the town's called. The local police still need to hold it, but they'll probably let us have it back in a few more days."

"That's great news, sir. And your CDs? Any word on them?"

"Ah, yes indeed. And that's mostly good also. Quite a lot of them turned up at a local resale shop. Robbie must've unloaded 'em there for the odd pound or two. Can't do anything about the few that were already sold, but most of them are still there." He told them how the police had found the plastic CD case, which cinched the deal that the car was theirs.

"Sir, that's terrific news."

"Charlie, young Robbie Stevenson may not be quite the dummy we've taken him for. He told the police the reason they had the car was because I'd *sold* it to him."

"*Sold* it to him? That's rich."

"Claimed he paid us thirty-five hundred quid for it. In cash."

"Well, sir, that *was* your second asking price," Charles said, scratching his chin, "after he balked at your asking for five thousand."

"He couldn't produce any paperwork to verify the sale, of course. But the brazen rascal claimed we'd only had a verbal agreement."

"*That* sounds pretty feeble," Jack said.

"He showed them the scrap of paper on which I'd written my contact information, but they weren't having any of it. So, looks like the poor lad's facing a heap of trouble. But you know, I'm rather inclined not to press charges against him, since we'll be getting the car back, fresh paint and now dent-less, as well as most of the CDs. I'd rather just avoid any additional unpleasantness. You agree?"

"Professor . . . that man steals cars!"

"Well, I suppose he does. But don't you think he's more a child than a man? You saw him, Charlie. Don't you think a bit of compassion might be in order?"

Charles looked at Jack and shrugged his shoulders. "Jack,

you think *I'm* naïve. Get a load of my mentor here."

"It seems to me, sir," Jack said, "that you are taking a very charitable view of the matter. Proves that the milk of human kindness still flows in the veins of some folks in this selfish world of ours." Charles extended his leg and gave Jack a kick in the shin.

"It pleases me, Jack," the professor said, "to see that your heart is warmer than that of your friend."

"Sometimes Charlie gets hamstrung by the inflexibility of his principles."

"He does," the professor agreed, "indeed he does."

The bemused look on Jack's face throughout this conversation suggested he was enjoying poking fun at the other two men.

"By the way, Professor," Jack went on, "where *did* you stash the thirty-five hundred quid the guy paid you for the car?"

"Hardy, har, har," the professor said.

"Yeah, *Bill*," Charles added, "where *did* you stash the lolly?"

The professor offered a self-deprecating smile. "I'm beginning to realize," he said, "that I'm outnumbered here."

In the next moment the three men looked up at the sound of approaching footsteps. In came Ally. She clutched a St. Ives Bakery carrier bag.

"Anyone for lunch?" she asked. "I've brought Cornish pasties." She held up the carrier bag and the smell of warm pasties filled the room.

"Oh, splendid, Alwyn," the professor said. "Been here nearly a week and have yet to partake of a proper pasty."

"Well," Jack said, "I've never partaken of one in my life, but I'm open to the full Cornish experience." He shot Charlie a wink.

"Didn't think we'd see you till tonight," Charles said to Ally.

"I'm not intruding on a boys-only gathering, am I?" she said.

"Certainly not," Jack said, flashing her his brightest smile. "We'd never turn away a winsome lass bearing Cornish pasties."

"Winsome, hmm?" murmured the professor, pondering the word. "Can't disagree with that."

They crowded about Ally's small dining table. She produced plates and placed the pasties on them.

"These are all traditional pasties," she said. "Wanted you to have the real thing, not any trumped up silliness that some benighted folks go for these days." She set a knife and a fork down beside each of them, then started in on her own using just her hands.

Jack cut into his pasty and took a moment to savor the smell. "Umm," he said, "so far so good." He took a bite and gave Ally a thumb's up. "This is great," he declared. "What's in it? Not any of that yucky stuff I'm told they eat in Scotland, I hope."

"No worries, Jack," Charles said. "No animal parts you'd rather not know about."

"Four basic ingredients," Ally said, "beef, onions, potatoes, and turnips – all neatly enclosed in a fresh-baked pastry."

"Turnips?" the professor queried. "Ally, I believe what

you are referring to are called swedes."

"Actually," Charles said, "I believe what she's referring to are called rutabagas."

Ally and Jack exchanged pained looks.

"Jack," Ally asked, "you wouldn't have a couple of extremely pedantic friends, would you?"

"It's a common trait amongst people in their line of work, I'm afraid," he replied.

"Ouch," Charles said. The four of them shared a brief laugh, then returned to devouring their pasties.

"Ally, this pasty really does taste great," Jack said. "You can bring me lunch any time you'd like to."

"Not likely," she said. "Today you get Cornish hospitality, as it's your first full day in Cornwall. But here on out, my dear sir, no more fetching and carrying from me."

"Jack's right," the professor mumbled, mouth still half full. "These are outstanding pasties. It's the swedes that make them special."

"Rutabagas," Charles said.

"Turnips," Jack said.

"Pedants," Ally said.

"But Charlie," the professor remarked, changing the subject, "when Ally turned up I was just getting to the best part about the car."

"The stolen car?" she said.

"It's been found," Charles said.

"Oh, splendid."

"So what's the best part, Professor?" Jack asked.

"Well, I told you about the plastic CD case they found inside the car that was a dead-giveaway, didn't I? Clear proof

126

it was our car. And then later, when the cops were making a thorough search of the car, they turned up one more thing." He paused for dramatic effect.

"Don't stop now," Jack said. "What'd they find?"

"Well, it was just a small index card. A small index card on which some rather obscure figures had been scrawled in pencil."

"Obscure figures? What sort of figures?" Ally asked, her eyebrows arched.

"Abbreviations and numbers."

"Could they read them?" Jack said.

"They could," the professor replied. "And this is what they said: 'fols. 28r-39v.' "

Now Charles' eyebrows shot up.

"Okay, Professor," Ally said, "don't be coy. Clue us in."

"Yeah, I hate coyness," Jack said.

For a moment, neither the professor nor Charles spoke. Perhaps they enjoyed trying the patience of Ally Tremayne and Jackson Lockhart.

"Charlie," the professor finally said, "why don't you explain it to them."

"Sure. Well, it's quite simple, really. The figures penciled on the card were made by me. They refer to the pages in the manuscript of the poem I was working on. They stand for eleven manuscript leaves, or folios – folio 28 recto to folio 39 verso. I was using the card to mark my place as I was transcribing the poem. Whenever I took a break I stuck it in there so I could pick up right where I'd left off. I must've left it in the manuscript when I'd finished the transcription."

"But wait," Ally said. "The card was found inside the

car?" She put the first two fingers of one hand against her chin. "If you left the card in the manuscript, then that must mean that somehow the manuscript got into the car. And that somehow the card had slipped out of it, maybe when someone picked it up again."

"Sounds like it to me," Jack said.

"But what would the manuscript have been doing in the car? How could it have gotten there, when it was locked away inside my father's office safe? Someone must have taken it from the safe and then put it in the car. And then when the car was nicked, the manuscript was also."

"Sounds like it," Jack said.

"It does sound like that," Charles said, "and yet that's not necessarily the case."

"Why not?" Ally asked.

"That's a logical explanation for why the card turned up inside the car, and probably the right one. But it doesn't necessarily explain what happened to the manuscript."

"But Charlie," the professor said, "if the car thieves didn't steal the manuscript, how would the index card have gotten into the car?"

"That's one of the things we need to figure out, isn't it? But, sir, it's just one of the things you and I need to think about." For a long moment he sat quietly, lost in thought.

"To tell you the truth, sir," he said at last, "I'm not sure what we've gotten ourselves into here. Events concerning this manuscript of Ally's father seem to be turning into something other than what either of us anticipated. Maybe we should just wash our hands of the whole business, go and retrieve your car, and head on back to Oxford."

"Charlie Bascombe," the professor said, some sternness in his voice, looking hard and long at his protégé, "I'm sure you don't really mean that."

Charles Bascombe, his lips firmly compressed, nodded his head slowly, then looking the professor in the eyes, said, "No, sir, I guess I don't."

16

In the lounge on the seventeenth floor of the Mersey Building, Clare Reilly stared out through the corner double-paned glass window toward the rotunda of St. Paul's Cathedral, over on the north side of the Thames. Having no windows at all in her little office cubicle, she took her work breaks here whenever she could. Down below her she could see Blackfriar's Bridge and off to her right, no more than a quarter mile, the roof of the Globe Theatre replica. Just beyond it rose the square tower of the Tate Modern. To the left of the Globe the late morning sun glinted on the silver metal railings of Millennium Bridge. Many tiny figures scurried across it on this Saturday morning in early June.

Clare's thoughts took her back to two days earlier and her conversation with Jackson Lockhart. She heaved a sigh. What a shock it had been to run into Jackson at the British Museum. She never would have expected *that*. It had been great to see Jack, but it had also brought a host of semi-buried things back to the surface. Especially, of course, her highly conflicted thoughts and feelings about Charlie Bascombe.

By now, Jack was probably down in Cornwall visiting

with Charlie. She tried picturing the two of them together, picking up right where they'd left off – joking and matching wits and quite likely competing with each other in some kind of athletic contest. She couldn't help smiling, remembering how those two knuckleheads loved competing.

So Charlie was up in Oxford living the scholarly life, she mused. Well, no big surprise there, knowing Charlie and the things he loved. She heaved a small sigh, thinking about how close she and Charlie had once been. And that now their lives were separated by ten years of living. Wasn't that long enough for them to get past all the anguish they'd caused each other? Maybe yes, maybe no.

So Charlie was living in Oxford, she thought again. They'd been just sixty or seventy miles apart for several months and hadn't even known it. Clare hadn't been to Oxford yet, though both Oxford and Cambridge were high on her list of places she wanted to be sure to visit while she was living in England.

She hadn't asked Jack not to tell Charlie she was in London. She knew Jack wasn't capable of keeping mum about that and, in fact, she realized that she wanted Charlie to know it. By now he surely did know, and she wondered what his reaction had been. Would it have pleased him? Would it maybe even prompt him to contact her? Considering where they'd left things a decade ago, that didn't seem too likely. But people do change over time. Maybe the years had softened his anger. They had softened hers. Her initial bitterness toward him, as real as it had been, had long since dissipated. Perhaps it had been the same with him. One could always hope.

Clare took a final fond glimpse toward the dome of St. Paul's. She knew that once her stint in London was over, she would really miss this view. She finished her last swallow of coffee from her mug. It was cold but she didn't mind. What, she wondered, were Jack and Charlie doing at that very moment?

✠✠✠

After tidying up her little kitchen, Ally Tremayne headed back to the art gallery for a busy Saturday afternoon of work. Professor William Wentworth climbed the steps to the guest bedroom to take his afternoon nap.

"So," Jack said to Charles, "to the beach?"

"You are a mind-reader, hermano. Let me grab a couple of Ally's beach towels."

Charles and Jack lazed on the beach for most of the afternoon – soaking up the Cornish sun, reading, dozing, people-watching. Charles had no bathing trunks so he'd improvised by cutting off the legs of an old pair of jeans.

On such a perfect Saturday afternoon in early June, the beach was packed. Jack swam out several hundred yards by himself, then floated for a while on his back. The chilliness of the water belied all those claims about the warming effects of the Gulf Stream, but even so, Jack found it refreshing. Unlike Charles, who wasn't keen on water sports, Jack had always been an excellent swimmer.

When he came back in, Jack joined a rabble of children in an impromptu beach soccer game. He'd been an outstanding player in his youth, and he could still move with quickness and agility. In the various intramural sports he and Charles played together in college, Jack had been better at soccer,

Charles had the edge at basketball and tennis. In touch football and in softball they'd been about equal.

While Jack was doing his own thing, Charles lay back on his beach towel and closed his eyes. Since last night, he'd given a lot of thought to what Jack had told him about Clare – that she was living in England, had spoken warmly of him, and acted like she'd been left out when Jack spoke of visiting Charles. Clare, Jack had said, looked even lovelier now than she had ten years ago. Charles tried to picture her now, but he couldn't quite do it. He had a fixed picture in his mind of her at twenty-one.

What should he do? he wondered. Contact her? Try to see her? But did he really want to reopen old wounds? Clare, apparently, was ready to do that. Charles recalled Ally rebuking him for not having resolved things with Clare long ago. In his heart he knew Ally was right.

Charles sighed. He should come up with a plan, and soon. But with everything else that was going on – the missing manuscript, with its career-making potential; the bizarre events surrounding the professor's car; and the weird, inexplicable behavior of Rhys Tremayne – he tried to persuade himself to let the Clare conundrum ride a bit longer.

Then an obscure word from Chaucer's "The Franklin's Tale" shot suddenly into Charles' mind: *sursanure* – it was a medical term referring to a wound that had healed on the surface but that still festered beneath the surface. Fearing that the term might characterize his feelings toward Clare, Charles sighed again.

Then from the depths of his mind a decision suddenly

emerged. He *would* seek her out. He *would* sit down with her. And the two of them would act like adults and achieve some kind of final resolution. Okay, he'd *done* it. It actually came as a huge relief. But it also scared the bejesus out of him.

Charles Bascombe sighed. He turned over onto his stomach to get some of that blazing Cornish sun on his back.

✢✢✢

"I warned you, Jackson," Ally said. "But oh no, you didn't believe me."

Jackson Lockhart's face, neck, and arms were decidedly pink from several unprotected hours on the beach.

"People think they won't get burned by the U.K. sun," she said. "They don't usually make that mistake twice. Not down here, anyway."

Ally, the professor, and the two young men were sitting at a table in the restaurant portion of the White Hart. When Jack suggested going back to The Golden Lion, Ally balked. "No, no, never on a Saturday night," she said, "not unless you don't mind a relentless assault on your eardrums. Their live performers compensate for their lack of skill with an amplitude of volume."

"This so-called Polminster Manuscript," the professor said, shifting the subject away from Jack's sunburn, "what could've happened to the bloody thing? Who could have taken it, and why? Ally, your father has not been forthcoming with us. Why not? Why won't he tell us how he came by the blooming thing? And why wouldn't he tell the police about the theft of something with such potential value? And, the big question, does the accursed thing contain a lost poem by Chaucer, or not?"

The professor glared at the young woman as if he expected her to know the answers to his questions. Ally raised her hands, palms forward, and scrunched in her shoulders.

"Charlie," Jack said, "at lunch today you said the manuscript might not have been stolen when the car was. Then you just left it at that. Would you mind elaborating?"

"Well, the fact that the note card I used to mark my place was found in the car doesn't *necessarily* mean the manuscript was still in the car when it was snatched. It does indicate that the manuscript must've been in the car at some point. But the card could have slipped out when someone was handling the manuscript, and it's possible that the manuscript was removed before the car was taken."

"The manuscript was placed inside the car for a while but was taken out again before the car got nabbed? Seems pretty unlikely to me," Jack said.

"I suppose," Charles said. "Still, if the manuscript thief needed somewhere temporary to stash it until the coast was clear, the car would have been a good choice. Away from the house and in a place where no one would think to look. That's assuming, of course, that the theft of the car and the theft of the manuscript aren't directly related."

"But Charlie, who might have done that?" Ally asked.

"Sorry, Ally, but the obvious candidate is your father."

"*Daddy?* But *why?*"

"Maybe he wanted to avoid there being any further inspection of the manuscript. I'm sure he knew from my earlier comments that I'd been wanting to know how he came by it. But," Charles went on, "there *is* another person in the house about whom I've been wondering – "

"Maria!" the professor blurted out, guessing what his protégé was about to say.

"Maria? The maid?" Jack said. "You think she could have been an accomplice?"

"Fiddlesticks!" Ally said. "Of course she's devoted to Daddy. And to me also. But after my mother left – she and my mum were especially close – Maria and Daddy's relationship cooled off a good bit. Anyway, I can't see her conspiring with Daddy to do something nefarious."

"Why did their relationship cool off?" Charles asked.

"Oh, it's probably because she blames Daddy for not taking better care of my mum. Mother has her idiosyncrasies – a *ton* of them, actually – and after so many years of her nagging at him, Daddy was getting sick of it. I do love my mum, but I also have a great deal of sympathy for Daddy. He put up with a lot from Mother for a long time. But I think Maria still blames Daddy, still thinks he let Mum down. Maria can be quite judgmental, in her quiet way. I learned at a young age never to get on her bad side. She's always been extremely devoted to Mum."

"Manderley," Charles said.

"Manderley," Ally said, nodding.

"Manderley?" Jack said. "Ah, I get your drift. Hitchcock." Charles nodded.

Ally had tilted her head sideways, seeming to reflect on the suggestion of Maria and Manderley.

"Professor," Charles said, following the lengthy silence, "the other day you said something about a little church up on the North Coast of Cornwall. Minster Church, near Tintagel. Why did that pique your interest? Just the similarity of the name?"

"Ah, the Minster Church. St. Materiana's. Obscure and mysterious little church indeed. Not much visited by tourists, if at all. Probably just a small congregation of locals. But mind you, there's quite an odd coincidence involving that church, one that might provide an important link to Ally's father."

The other three remained silent, waiting for the professor to go on.

"You see, a chap I was once acquainted with at Oxford ended up becoming a clergyman at that church. I wonder if he could still be there." Charles noticed that the professor's fingers, held before his face, had formed a perfect gothic arch.

"If he's still there," the professor continued, "he's surely well on in years by now. I knew him pretty well, but your father knew him much better. The pair of them became quite close friends, one of the few your father had at Oxford besides me. Your father and Neville were rather kindred spirits. A New College man, Neville was, and quite a promising young medievalist. A bit like you, Charlie, if we were to turn back the clock about forty years.

"Poor chap found himself torn between two strong desires – his genuine sense of having a clerical calling and his deep love for early literature and old books. Of course, it was the latter that brought him and your father into close association. Yes, now I reflect on it, he and Charlie share a good many traits. A shy, quiet, unassuming chap; a self-taught paleographer with an unquenchable love for the old manuscripts. Now what was Nev's full name?"

"The name you want wouldn't be Neville Smallwood, would it?" Ally said.

"Ah, spot on, my dear! The very chap!"

"I have a feeling," Charles said, "that Ally has just told us something her father wouldn't want us to know."

"You guys have lost me," Jack said, shaking his head.

"The professor believes in the efficacy of scholarly intuition," Charles said. "My scholarly intuition tells me that Neville Smallwood might provide a vital clue to a lot of the matters we've been struggling with."

"Charlie, mine does as well," the professor said.

"Well, in that case what my scholarly intuition tells me," Jack said, "is that it's time for us to go and track the geezer down."

"Indeed," said Professor Wentworth.

"Indeed," agreed Charles Bascombe.

"What my scholarly intuition tells me," Ally said, "is that you'd better go and track the geezer down."

17

En route to the Lizard on Sunday morning, the four of them stopped off at Marazion to visit St. Michael's Mount. The tide was out, so they trekked across the damp and slippery stones of the causeway to the island's ancient fortress.

Jack and Charles stopped off at the English Heritage office to buy tickets, and the professor showed his member's card. Ally, because she'd visited so often, was content to sit by the little harbor and read her paperback copy of *Mrs. Dalloway* while she waited for them. The professor climbed the steep hill with them, stopping to point out the little stone in the cobbled pathway known as the Giant's Heart, a stone supposedly associated with the old folktale about Jack the Giant Killer.

"Cormoran," the professor said, "that was the giant's name. Something to stash away in your mental lumber room, Charlie."

When they reached the top, the professor told them he would leave them to it.

"What's your plan, if you aren't coming with us?" Charles asked.

"Just going to go down and laze beside the water," he said, stepping over a chain beneath which hung a sign that said "No Admittance Beyond the Rope."

"Umm, sir," Jack said, pointing to the sign, "I don't believe visitors are allowed down there."

"Young man, did you read the sign?"

"Uh, yes sir, I did. That's why —"

"It says 'No Admittance Beyond the Rope.' Do you see any rope?"

"Well, no. But there's a chain."

"Indeed, there's a chain. A chain, Jackson, is not a *rope*. So, I shall see the two of you back in Marazion in a couple of hours." Then he loped off down the path behind the chain, the chain that was not a rope.

The professor found himself a comfortable perch amongst the rocks on the western side of the Mount. He lay back and let his mind roam, lulled by the soughing of the surf. William Wentworth enjoyed being alone. He tended to agree with John Milton's Adam, who once observed that there are times when "solitude is best society."

For an hour and a half, Jack and Charles traipsed along with the other many visitors on their tour of the ancient fortified structure. They listened as their guide spoke about its complex history and the widely varying functions it had fulfilled over time – including castle, fortress, monastery, and baronial manor house. They enjoyed viewing the chapel, the manorial rooms with their antique furnishings, the paintings and suits of armor, and the embattled tower. Charles Bascombe had always felt a deep disdain for "Stately Homes," but he had to admit that this one, probably because of its many medieval aspects, was more to his taste.

High on a wall adorned with many different coats of arms, Charles noticed one that had three Cornish choughs on it. He wondered whose coat of arms it might be. It was similar to the one Rhys Tremayne had called Thomas Beckett's but not identical to it.

"Well, that was really cool," Jack said, when their tour had wound up. "I enjoyed that. And you did, too. Admit it, Charlie."

"Yes, I'll admit it."

Now the two young men were strolling back down one of the main paths from the castle toward the island's small harbor. It was late morning, and the many tourists who'd now shown up in greater numbers moved past them on their way up to the castle.

Suddenly Charles felt a tug at his shirtsleeve. "Don't look now," Jack said in a low voice, "but on that path over there is someone I think we've seen before."

"Hmm? What?" Slowly coming alert, Charles glanced in the direction Jack had indicated by the movement of his head. On a smaller path running parallel to theirs, maybe twenty yards distant, a slender, redheaded woman was moving purposefully through a clump of trees toward the castle. She was the same attractive young woman they'd noticed by the dartboard two nights before in the St. Ives pub. She was striding right along, and because they were moving downward and she upward, she soon passed from sight.

"That was her, right?" said Jack.

"Yeah, I'm pretty sure it was," Charles said. "Whoever her is."

"Interesting coincidence – if it *is* a coincidence. You don't suppose she's here because we are, do you?"

"No, she probably works here. She was on an employees-only pathway. And as far as I could tell, she didn't pay us any notice."

"No hulking boyfriend this time, at least. But if we see her again, Charlie, this time you'll really have to introduce me," Jack said, grinning.

"Oh, okay. Caveman boyfriend or no, I shall introduce you."

"You're a real pal," Jack replied, and they both laughed.

As they went through the archway near the ticket office, they spotted Ally sitting in the shade on a stone ledge overlooking the little harbor. She'd seen them, too, and waved. They went to join her.

"Any sign of the professor?" Jack asked, as Ally stuffed her book inside her handbag and rose to her feet.

"Yes. He's abandoned us. Seems there's a quaint little tearoom in Marazion he's especially fond of. We'll probably find him there just finishing the dregs of his Earl Grey and wiping away the crumpet crumbs. But it's a good thing you didn't dally, because the tide's coming in. We'd best hurry, or we'll have to take one of the launches."

On the causeway, water was lapping at the stones. "We can make it," she said, "but we'd better step out. Once the tide starts rolling in, it doesn't mess about. Fifteen minutes from now, this whole area will be submerged. We get caught in the middle, we'll have to swim for it."

They marched briskly across the treacherous stones, making the crossing in a couple of minutes. By the time they neared the sandy beach at Marazion, water was squish-squashing beneath their feet.

"Ugh. I do hate wet feet," Ally said.

She bent down to remove her damp shoes, and while she was doing that, she noticed Jack glancing back across the causeway.

"Looking for something?" Ally asked.

"Not some*thing*, some*one*. But, she's not there hurrying after us. We're definitely the last ones to get across."

"Some*one*? And who might that be?"

"Just a girl we noticed back there," Charles said. "Someone we're pretty sure we saw the other night in St. Ives. A redhead, actually. Just to let you know, Jack has a terrible weakness for redheads. He's been lusting after this one ever since we saw her and her hulking companion."

"You don't mean the redhead in a green pullover who went up the path toward the castle a few minutes before we met up?"

"Sounds like the one," Charles said.

"That was Dargan. Dargan Owens. I know her quite well."

"Dargan?" Jack said. "Kind of an odd name."

"Comes from *dearg*, an old Gaelic word for red," Allie said. "Dargan and I were in boarding school together, though we moved in rather different circles. Her mother and mine were best friends. After her mother died, Mum actually paid Dargan's tuition. More recently my mother's given Dargan a part-time job at the guest house she owns in Porthleven. Dargan helps out there quite a bit, though her main job is here with the National Trust.

"But Jack, you'd be well advised to quell your lusts and steer clear of that one. No doubt she's quite luscious, but Dargan has spelled trouble for every guy who's ever had anything to do with her. What's more, that hulking companion of hers is one of the local baddies. Make any moves on Dargan, and you'll find yourself on the wrong side of Thick Mick. You don't want to do that."

" 'Thick'?" Jack asked. "Meaning muscular?"

" 'Thick' meaning 'stupid.' Fella couldn't find his arse using two hands and a mirror, as they say."

"They *say* that?" Jack said, surprised by the crude expression.

"But yes," Ally went on, "Mick's physique is rather

impressive also."

"Well, we've got no worries there," Jack said. "Charlie can handle him. Charlie knows tae-kwon-do."

"Jiu jitsu," Charles said.

"Ha, ha," laughed Ally. "Oh yes, I really believe *that*. Good one, Jack."

When Charles gave Ally a you-mean-you're-doubting-me look, she grabbed him, pulled him to her, and planted a kiss on his cheek. "Our sweet Charlie is a man of many parts," she said. "Ha, ha, ha. Tae-kwon-do. Charlie, maybe you'd show me some of your moves if I asked politely?"

As they drove through the entranceway to the house on the Lizard, Charles glanced at the pair of choughs atop the flanking columns. They made him think of the coat of arms he'd seen back at the castle. He'd have to ask Rhys Tremayne about it.

"Remember," the professor said, "don't say anything about the old fellow we plan to track down in North Cornwall. Mum's the word, right?"

"Right," the other three chorused.

"We mustn't let Ally's father get wind of it."

"Right," the other three chorused again.

"We're just going up there to see some of the marvelous sites, right?"

"Sir," Jack said, "we get it."

"Just so we're clear," the professor said.

"We're clear, sir," Ally said, rolling her eyes.

They pulled to a stop beside a dark green Ford Charles hadn't seen before. As they climbed from Ally's roadster,

Maria came down the front steps lugging a large carryall. Behind her came another woman who most definitely wasn't Ailish Tremanye. She was a gaunt, prune-faced woman whose graying hair was pulled back tight against her head. Her triangular-shaped face and slightly slanted eyes gave her a somewhat reptilian look. To Charles she appeared to be at least sixty, but if she were Ally's mother, she was more likely in her mid-fifties. As Charles had guessed, she was indeed Ally's mother, Rhys Tremayne's first wife, a woman whom the professor once described as being "a bit of a lizard."

"Mother!" Ally leapt from the car and hugged the woman, who beamed a smile at her daughter.

"Well, if it isn't the professor," the woman said, with a lack of enthusiasm. "I didn't expect to see *you*."

"Lowenna," he replied, "it's lovely to see you again," his tone belying the sincerity of his words. There was obviously no love lost between these two.

"Mother, these are my American friends," Ally said, "Charlie and Jack." The woman merely glanced in their direction and offered the two young men a curt nod. She wasn't exactly a warm and welcoming person, Charles thought. But then, lizards usually aren't.

"I'm sorry I can't stay longer, Ally. I didn't expect anyone to be here, and I'm running far behind schedule. I just needed to collect a few things. Now I really must be rushing off."

"No time for a cup of tea?" Ally sounded disappointed.

"No dear, not even time for that. I shall try and see you in St. Ives sometime soon."

"I hope you will, Mother. Come any time that's convenient for you. You are always welcome."

Maria opened the rear door of the dark green car and placed the heavy carryall on the seat. She then held the driver's door open for Ally's mother. Lowenna Tremayne gave Maria a small hug, then stepped into the car and closed the door firmly. A moment later she was driving back down the gravel drive. She didn't wave goodbye.

Ally stood and watched until the car was out of sight. So did Maria. Then, for the briefest moment, Maria and Charles exchanged glances. Did Maria notice the questioning look in the young man's eyes? Did Charles notice a trace of guilt in Maria's?

Maria moved quickly away from the others and up the steps to the house. She passed through the door but left it open for them, assuming they'd be coming right behind her. Maria's sudden disappearance, Charles thought, even though she hadn't slammed the door in their faces, had been borderline rude. She seemed a bit nervous about something. Or maybe a bit guilty?

Charles thought about the momentary glance he and Maria had exchanged. Was there any special significance to it? Then he thought about the carryall Maria had placed on the back seat. It had been quite large. Large enough to contain more than just Lowenna Tremayne's personal belongings. Large enough to hold a medieval manuscript.

✠✠✠

Later that afternoon Rhys Tremayne returned, after spending the weekend in Truro with his wife. That evening he took all of them out to dine at a posh restaurant in one of the scenic coves along the Lizard's south coast.

Despite the coolness of the evening, they sat outside on a spacious deck that offered a spectacular view of the rocky shoreline. A lighthouse blinked off in the distance to the right, and behind it a dark bank of clouds rose malignly. It promised a stormy night to come.

"Wonderful seafood here," Rhys said as they studied their menus. "A splendid chowder, the most delicious mussels you'll ever eat, and quite an amazing array of fish choices." Charles was still in the mood for Cornish pasties but didn't wish to offend his host by ordering one, though pasties were on the menu. "Order away," Rhys said. "Tonight you are all my guests."

"Well, sir, if you don't mind, please allow me to buy the wine," Jack said, as he studied the wine list. "Let's try several different whites, okay?"

"Quite okay," Rhys said. "Might I recommend the Château du Jaunay Muscadet?"

"You got it," Jack said.

"Sir," Charles said, "that wouldn't be the Eddystone Light we can see out there, would it?" He pointed off to the southwest.

"No, but not a bad guess. You can't see the Eddystone from here, though if we were down around Lizard Point, we could. No, what you're looking at is called Wolf Rock. Been the bane of many a ship, despite the lighthouse. Quite a treacherous area out there. The Isles of Scilly lie just a few miles behind it."

Picking up on the reference to the Eddystone Light, Ally softly intoned: "Oh, me father was the keeper of the Eddystone Light, and he slept with a mermaid one fine night." Then she glanced at Charles and winked.

"I never did any such thing," Rhys said, feigning shock. "Being the offspring of a mermaid is *not* how you came by your capriciousness, Alwyn."

"How did she come by it?" Jack asked.

"Well, she certainly didn't get it from *me*," he replied.

"That's for sure," the professor said, and they all laughed.

When their meals arrived, they tucked in eagerly to lemon sole, seaweed-cured mackerel, and *moules marinieres*. And for a time they eschewed conversation until Jack finally said, "The Moon & Sixpence. That's what the B&B I stayed in was called. What's that all about?"

"Title of a novel, I think," Rhys Tremayne said.

"Somerset Maugham," Ally said.

"Okay, but what's it mean? Something deep and mysterious?"

"I'll confess that I don't actually know," the professor said. "You, Charlie?" But Charles hiked his shoulders and held out his empty palms.

"Dear me," Ally said, "our learned scholars are at a loss? Well, I'll give it a try. I believe it's some kind of commentary on people's contrasting values. If I'm remembering right, it stems from some little tale or anecdote about two dissimilar men. One of them is so captivated by the sight of the silvery moon that all he can do is gaze at it. As a result, he doesn't notice that there's a sixpence lying in the roadway at his feet. The other man immediately spots the little silvery disk of the sixpence, but he's so fixated on it that he misses out on the beauty of the moon."

"One's a hopeless romantic and one's a crass pragmatist?"

Charles said.

"A philistine," the professor said.

"That's the general idea," Ally said.

"Sounds like me and Charlie," Jack said. "One guy caught up in his pursuit of filthy lucre, one guy caught up in his dream of discovering a lost poem by Chaucer."

"Well, wait a minute . . . ," Charles said.

"Speaking of lost works of Chaucer," Rhys said, "while you're away on your jaunt to North Cornwall, I'll have Charles' transcription of the poem typed up. Then when the lad gets back, he can get right to the editing without delay."

"Thanks. That would be very helpful," Charles said. "I'm eager to have at it. But sir, while we're speaking of ancient things, I have a question for you. At the castle today I noticed a coat of arms with three choughs on it. It looked pretty similar to the one hanging in your library. If you're familiar with the one I saw at the castle, what can you tell us about it?"

"I do know the one you mean, but alas, there's disagreement about whose coat of arms it is. You are quite right, though, about it being similar to mine. Mine, as you know, has the arms of Thomas Beckett."

"Mr. Tremayne, all these Cornish choughs. What's the deal with them, anyway?" Jack asked. "You folks seem enamored of them."

"Yes, as well we should be. The chough is our national bird."

"National?"

"Well, calling Cornwall a nation is rather hyperbolic. But that's how I prefer to think of it. Technically, Cornwall is a Duchy. Wales and Scotland *are* countries. Cornwall, alas, isn't."

"But choughs. How did they come to have that honor? They don't seem like an obvious choice for a royal bird."

"Ah, well, then let me explain. You see, Cornwall is both the birthplace and death place of King Arthur. And even though our greatest king fell in the final battle against his rebellious son Mordred – that's what *we* believe, though some chroniclers claim that Arthur *didn't* die – we believe it was Arthur's spirit, not his body, that survived. Arthur's spirit, we believe, has lived on down through the ages in the chough."

Ally picked up the tale. "When Arthur, along with countless others, was killed in the terrible battle, the battle-field was bestrewn with corpses. The choughs, who are carrion birds, descended upon the bodies and picked their bones clean.

"The feet of the choughs waded in the blood of Arthur and his men. And on that fateful day of destiny, both the bills and the feet of the Cornish choughs were stained red by the blood. To this day, Arthur's blood may still be seen on their feet and bills. While many British legends contend that Arthur didn't actually die but was carried off to Avalon to have his wounds attended to, that isn't what we believe. We don't believe that Arthur is alive. We believe that when the choughs drank his blood, they imbibed King Arthur's spirit. They preserved it and still carry it. When the choughs disappeared from Cornwall for many years, they took Arthur with him. But now that the choughs have returned to Cornwall, King Arthur's spirit has come back as well."

"That's pretty cool," Jack said. "I like it. Way better than believing that an actual person will return. So, King Arthur *has* returned; in spirit, anyway."

Rhys Tremayne beamed a broad smile at Jack. Charles and the professor exchanged glances. Jackson Lockhart had just scored one for the team.

"And tomorrow, Rhys," the professor said, "if your offer of Ailish's car still holds, I'll be taking these lads to the very place where Arthur was conceived and born, and also to where he fell in battle."

"Tintagel and Slaughter Bridge," Ally said. "Two of my favorites. Wish I could go with you."

"Of course the offer of the car is still good. And of course these lads must go there. I'll make you a list of some other places as well. So what do you reckon, William, be away for a couple of days? Back on Tuesday evening?"

"Possibly, though perhaps a day or so more. Unless these chaps get bored."

"I still have more than a week before I need to catch my plane at Heathrow, so no hurry as far as I'm concerned," Jack said. "Like Arthur and the choughs, I'm beginning to get Cornwall in my blood."

"Do take your time. Those places are worth it. But, I'm most eager to get on with the editing of the poem. *Chaucer's* poem. It *has* to be his, I feel certain of it. Don't you, Charles?"

"It does reflect many characteristics of Chaucer's work," Charles agreed. "If it isn't by him, someone has been extremely clever."

"Surely no one could be *that* clever," said their host.

✠✠✠

They returned to the house, and Ally, needing to depart for St. Ives, said her farewells to the professor, Jack, and Charles.

"I hope to see you again before we leave for Oxford," Charles said to her.

"Well, you had better do more than hope," she replied. "How about if I come back for dinner on Wednesday evening? You'll surely have returned by then. Maybe you'll be able to extract your nose from that musty old poem and find a little time for me. Maybe we could take another walk down to Loe Pool."

"If you're coming back," Jack said, "maybe you could bring us some pasties?"

She looked sternly at Jack for a moment, her brow creased. "Well," she said, "maybe just one last time." She hugged Jack for a moment, then hugged Charles a bit longer. And then she was gone.

The two older men said their good nights to Jack and Charles and disappeared to their bedrooms. The two younger men remained in the sitting room in front of the fireplace.

"You know, Charlie," Jack said, "I think that young woman is fonder of you than you realize. She hasn't fooled me, though."

"It's her nature to be warm and friendly."

"Yes, I'm sure it is. But in your case, Charlie, I think it's more than that."

They sat quietly for a bit before Jack went on. "So, amigo, what are your thoughts in regard to Clare?"

"Ah. Good question. This will probably surprise you, Jack, but I've decided I'm going to try and see her, either in London or Oxford. There's no denying Clare and I have unfinished business. It's time to attend to it."

"Amazing. Ten years later Charlie Bascombe finally comes to the realization that he still has unfinished business with the woman."

"Be fair, Jack. Way back then, she really hurt me a lot."

"And vice versa."

"Yeah, and vice versa. I know I was unfair to her."

"Well, sounds like you're making progress."

"I've never been the swiftest guy on the planet in some respects."

"You think?"

"Ally chided me for not having resolved things with Clare. And she was right."

"Took a nudge from Ally to get you thinking straight?"

"Helped, anyway."

"Good for Ally."

"You know, Jack, she's quite a talented artist. I've agreed to buy one of her paintings, and I've commissioned her to do another."

"Really? Of what?"

"A mermaid."

"Well, good. Just so it's not a painting of a chough. I've about had my fill of those bloody things."

After a further hour of mostly meaningless chatter, the two young men climbed the stairs to their bedrooms on the third floor of the tall house. Charles changed into his pajamas, and when he heard the shower running in the bathroom, he went and retrieved his laptop from where he'd placed it atop the wardrobe. He fired it up and opened the file containing the manuscript pages he'd photographed with his cell phone.

He hadn't looked at them since Thursday night, three days ago. His desire to get back to them hadn't been far from his mind the whole time.

He pulled up folio 28r, the first surviving page of the text. He felt sure that only one leaf was missing and that this was the second one of the poem. He enlarged the verses on the screen and examined them closely. To his experienced eye the individual letters of this tidy book hand looked entirely authentic. Nor could he find any faults with the language; every word of the Middle English was one he knew could be found in the Chaucer concordance. All the French borrowings, all the southeastern dialectal forms, all the typically Chaucerian syntactic patterns, even the sometimes slightly strained rhymes of the octosyllabic couplets – they all were typically Chaucerian. Perhaps the verse was a bit stilted, he thought, but if this was one of the poet's early efforts, that wouldn't be amiss. The poetry wasn't quite vintage Chaucer; but you couldn't expect vintage Chaucer from a novice poet.

Engrossed as he'd become in studying what was on the screen before him, Charles didn't hear Jack's barefooted entrance. He didn't realize that his friend now stood behind him, peering over his shoulder.

"Holy cow, Charlie! Is that a page from the missing manuscript? You've got the whole damned thing photographed? Charlie, you sly old dog."

"Jack! Oh, man, you startled me. Listen, Jack, I'd prefer that no one know about this. Not Ally, not the professor, and most especially, not Rhys Tremayne. This was supposed to be my secret and mine alone. Now that you know, you have to promise me you won't let anyone else know."

"No worries, dude. I won't let the cat out of the bag. Your secret's safe with me. Cross my heart and stick a needle in my eye."

"If you tell anyone, it won't just be a needle I'll stick in your eye. It'll be my dagger that I thrust into your sunburnt throat."

"Your *dagger*? Oh, man, Charlie, you have a *dagger*?"

18

Despite never having been behind the wheel of a right-hand drive car, Jackson Lockhart insisted upon driving Ailish Tremayne's maroon Jaguar saloon. No surprise to Charles, Jackson drove the only way he knew how, with panache. Charles sat in front with him, keeping a close eye on the GPS, though the route to the north offered no particular challenges. Professor William Wentworth, comfortably ensconced in the back seat, kept up a running commentary about sites and place names.

"Well, sir," Jack said at one point, "that information about the village of Indian Queens is really interesting." He glanced at Charles and rolled his eyes.

They'd set off from the Lizard right after breakfast on a sullen-skied Monday morning on what was alleged to be a two- or three-day tour of ancient Cornish sites. Rhys Tremayne had supplied them with a list of not-to-be-missed places, and they intended to visit *some* of them, though their primary goal was an old church near Boscastle on Cornwall's northwest coast and the aged clergyman – Neville Smallwood – they hoped to find there; and maybe, through him, to extract some essential information about the so-called Polminster Manuscript.

"That was a splendid castle we saw yesterday," Jack said, as they sped up the A30. "Anything like that in our future?"

"No, nothing so impressive as St. Michael's Mount," the professor replied. "At Tintagel there's just some rather tattered castle remains, though the place is most interesting in itself. What's most special about Tintagel is the setting and the atmosphere, not the castle. That stretch of coast is one of the most spectacular in Cornwall. You lads should spend a few hours walking a portion of it. You'll find it delightfully scenic."

"Works for me," Jack said.

"And for me, too," Charles agreed. "But let's have a good look at Tintagel first. Tintagel Castle, where King Arthur was conceived and born. Where Merlin wangled his quid pro quo with Uther Pendragon – Uther getting a night of sex with the Duke's wife in exchange for fulfilling Merlin's own desires."

"Which were what?" Jack asked.

"The child. The little boy produced by that illicit union. Merlin planned to whisk him away, off into obscurity so he could be raised in safety."

"Yes, now I remember," Jack said. "I always wondered which of those dudes was the randier, lecherous Uther or wily Merlin. Always seemed to me the old guy must've been a frigging voyeur, getting his jollies by peeping through the curtain all night. What a guy, pimping out the wife of one of the king's most loyal liegemen! Nice going, Merlin."

"Oh, lad, no need to be so judgmental," the professor muttered. "Perhaps Merlin's actions do look a bit dubious, but you must remember he did all of that for the larger good. And as for Uther Pendragon, the poor fellow couldn't help himself, overwhelmed by his passions as he was. After all, the fellow was in love. Happens to the best of us, you know."

"He was in *love*?" Jack said. "Well, I guess that's *one* word for it."

"Happens to the best of us, Professor?" Charles said. "Might you be speaking from experience?"

For a long moment the professor didn't reply. "You may find it hard to believe," he said at last, "but I was young once myself."

"No," Jack replied, "I don't find that hard to believe at all."

For the next several minutes they drove on in silence. Charles, with the professor's collection of newly acquired CDs on his lap, began flipping through them. He found one to his liking and slid it into the player. *The Lovin' Spoonful' Greatest Hits*. Soon the three of them were belting out "What a Day for a Daydream." When that CD finished playing, Charles put in one by The Monkees, and then the three of them began belting out "I'm a Believer." For some reason, in the midst of that song, Charles' thoughts were on the face of Clare. Of Clare Reilly. Clare Reilly from County Clare. A woman who right at this moment, he knew, was not so very far away.

The Monkees, the professor thought, with a modicum of scorn. They'd had some catchy tunes, no doubt, but for him they represented the ultimate example of what he called "pop crap." He'd watched them once on TV, and once had been enough. That was in the fall of 1968, the year he'd arrived in Berkeley, California.

Yes, he thought, he really had been young once. He'd just turned eighteen that fall, a callow young Brit. The culture shock of suddenly finding himself in Berkeley – after spending his first two years of university study in Oxford's stuffy, tradition-laden environment – had been totally mind-blowing, to use the terminology of the time. But after his rather terrifying first few weeks, he quickly became enamored of the vitality and engagement of Berkeley's students and professors.

At UC Berkeley, young William Wentworth had quickly made friends. He'd also had his first love affair. He'd gone to concerts at the famous Fillmore West venue in San Francisco – seen the Dead, Jefferson Airplane, Big Brother and the Holding Company. Having been raised on Elvis, Roy Orbison, and Buddy Holly, he never fully warmed up to acid rock, though he'd found the raw, primitive stylings of Janis Joplin unnervingly seductive. He'd also never fully overcome his fear of being stuck amidst a raucous crowd – his ochlophobia – but he tried his best to be a "go with the flow" kind of chap. And despite all that was going on at the Cal campus and in the Bay Area – the anti-war rallies, the Black Power upheaval, the early manifestations of the Women's Movement – he still managed, somehow, to have a thrilling academic year. Ironically, it was the Berkeley profs more than the Oxford ones, who'd turned him on to medieval studies.

Yes, at Berkeley he'd had his first experience of being overwhelmed by love. Her name was Stephanie. She'd been shockingly uninhibited, and being two years older than he was, she was already a seasoned veteran of the Sexual Revolution. She'd taught him a lot. But then after a few exhilarating months, they drifted apart. That was probably a good thing for young William, at least as far as his academic studies were concerned. But what a ride it had been.

"Professor?" Charles' voice reached him through the fog of his memories. "Lost in a brown study?"

"Hmm? Oh, Charlie. Lost in a brown study? Yes, yes, I suppose I was."

"Not thinking about lost loves, were you?"

"Oh, well, umm, yes, maybe just a bit."

✢✢✢

At nine-thirty on Monday morning, Alwyn Tremayne unlocked the front door of the Once & Future Art Gallery in St. Ives. She flicked on the lights, then moved through the main display area toward a little office at the back of the building. She turned on the lights there, too, logged onto the computer, then readied the coffee maker for her boss, the gallery owner, who would likely appear around eleven. The woman wasn't an early riser.

The Once & Future was among the finest of St. Ives's numerous galleries, exhibiting works by artists of local, national, and international acclaim. The owner had generously allowed Ally to display three of her own paintings in prominent positions in the Future section, and it pleased her whenever patrons paused in front of them. The gallery had yet to sell any of her works, most likely because everything in the O&F was vastly overpriced. The online prices she had posted on her own website were far more modest, but any sales she made there would be pure profit since no substantial cut would have to go to the gallery.

Ally smiled to herself when she thought about how Charlie had offered to buy one of her paintings. And how he said he'd commission her to make a painting of the mermaid they'd seen at Zennor Church. Was he being facetious about that? Well, it didn't matter because she was going to make that painting. In her mind she already had a clear conception of what she might do. Maybe tonight she would make a start on it.

She thought about Charlie, Jack, and the professor, now making their way to Tintagel and to the Minster Church. She wondered if they would turn up anything significant. She had met her father's friend Neville Smallwood a couple of times. Her own father was certainly an eccentric, she mused. But as for Neville Smallwood, that fellow really took the biscuit.

✢✢✢

"Church up here just a bit we should stop and see," the professor said from the backseat.

"Would that be Altarnun?" Charles asked, looking at Rhys Tremayne's list. The name of the church had four hand-drawn stars after it. Must be a winner, Charles thought.

The little village of Altarnun was only a mile or so off the main road, and a few moments later Jack snugged the Jag into a parking spot close to a graceful little humpbacked bridge. Beyond it was an arched gateway, and on the upsloping hill beyond that rose the elegant structure of the church of St. Nonna, "The Cathedral of the Moors."

"Charming place," Jack said, taking in the sight.

"Where Doc Martin got himself hitched," the professor said.

"Come again?"

"Doc Martin? The TV show? You don't know it? I thought all Americans were mad about it."

"I guess they must not carry it on ESPN," Jack said.

"Cretin," the professor muttered.

The two young men soon had their cameras out and were shooting shots of the Cathedral of the Moors, inside and out. The baptismal font and the carved bench ends of the pews were spectacular and made Charles think of the mermaid carving he'd seen with Ally at Zennor Church. But these were carved in a far more sophisticated style than the rather rough-hewn mermaid at Zennor.

"Nice place to get hitched," Jack said, as they walked back to the car. "I was thinking of Vegas, but now I'm having second thoughts."

"Cretin," the professor muttered beneath his breath.

When they entered the small village of Tintagel, the professor said, "Anyone interested in having a picnic lunch? We could go down and sit on Barras Nose while we're eating. From there you lads will have a splendid view of the castle and the headland. Pull off just around this next corner, Jack. There's a pasty shop that can't be beat. That sound okay?"

"Sounds great," Jack said.

"To me, too," Charles said.

"They really load them with swedes at this shop," the professor said, "exquisite swedes."

Charles and Jack exchanged a quick glance but didn't say a word. They weren't going to take the bait.

"Truly exquisite swedes," the professor said again.

"Yes," Jack finally replied, "I heard you the first time."

Fifteen minutes later they sat on a large, square-ish rock at the tip of Barras Nose, a point of land that extended out just above the heaving Atlantic. The sight of Tintagel headland and castle, across the little cove to the south, was magnificent. So, too, was the stunning blue sky above them.

"*Cielo azul,*" Jack said, looking at the cloudless sky.

"*Azura caelum,*" the professor said.

" . . . comin' my way, nothing but blue skies, from now on," Charles' voice rang out, startling the seagulls, who'd been attracted by the smell of pasties.

"Well, lads," the professor said when they'd finished eating, "let's go and take a peek at Merlin's Cave and Tintagel Castle, shall we? Then you lads can set off on your cliff walk. And while you're doing that, I just might go and try to suss out the Minster Church. Or better yet, maybe I'll just check into the hotel and take a nice long nap."

✦✦✦

The professor did treat himself to a nap in his room at the small hotel in Boscastle. Then, feeling more refreshed, he wandered out into the village in search of sustenance.

He wandered into The Cobweb Inn, just up the road. It was teeming with visitors, mostly families with rambunctious children, but he didn't mind. He found an empty two-person table off in a corner and settled in. After perusing the menu, he ordered a beef potpie with chips and a pint of ale from a local brewery, and while he awaited his food, he began reading a paperback copy of Thomas Hardy's *A Pair of Blue Eyes*. He knew that the semi-autobiographical novel, based in part on the author's love affair with Emma Gifford, who became his first wife, was set in this very area, near Boscastle.

Absorbed in his reading, the professor didn't notice a man and woman who took a table across the crowded room from him. The young woman wasn't someone he would have recognized, even if he had noticed her, though she was quite attractive and had dark red hair. Her companion was a swarthy bearded fellow, stocky of physique, with a jutting, not quite Neanderthal, brow. The young woman, noticing the professor, leaned toward her companion and whispered to him. Then the not terribly bright-looking fellow gazed across the room at William Wentworth with his small, squinting eyes. She whispered something more, and he slowly nodded his head.

Nearly an hour later the professor, having read through the first fifty pages of the novel, finished the last bits of crust from his meat pie, and drained the final inch of ale from his second pint, stepped over to the bar to settle his bill. On the way to the door, he edged past the table where the redhead sat with her burly companion. The professor couldn't help noticing the attractive young woman. What a lovely glow to her peach-like skin, he thought. And a lovely pair of blue eyes too, he thought, smiling to himself.

He exited the pub and strolled leisurely back toward the hotel. It was now nearly six o'clock. Probably about time for his young friends to come straggling in from their arduous cliffwalk.

The stocky fellow and the attractive redhead also exited The Cobweb Inn, not far behind the professor. They watched him cross the street and navigate the still crowded sidewalk as he moved on down toward the corner. Their eyes remained on him until he'd entered the front door of The Riverside Hotel.

The young woman said something to her companion, and he nodded. Then the two of them moved off in the direction of the car park.

✣ ✣ ✣

After Charles and Jack settled into the room they were sharing in The Riverside Hotel, Charles slipped down to the small lobby and logged on to the public computer there for the use of their guests. He typed out a very short email message, its wording having been carefully worked out in his head. Then he retrieved the little piece of paper from a pocket on which he'd written Clare's email address. He typed it in.

He read over his message a couple of times, and finding it okay, he hit send.

19

A couple of miles from Boscastle, Jack swung the car left off the main road and onto a narrow lane barely wide enough for a single vehicle. Ivy-covered stone walls lined both sides, and the tall trees that overhung the lane formed a virtual tunnel.

"Really hope we don't meet another car," Jack said. He looked rather nervous.

"Oh, no worries," the professor said. "Folks in these parts are highly skilled at backing up."

The lane descended into the gloom, but as they crept along they began to despair of ever finding a church in so desolate a spot. Finally on their left they noticed a small opening through the wall, though still no church in sight. The car crawled onward for another hundred yards, and when they rounded a small bend, there below them on the left, barely visible, lurked a tall gray edifice, shadowed by trees.

"Gotta be it," Jack declared. "No good place to park, but I'll stop up here by this gate and squeeze up close. Why don't you two climb out first."

"Well, sir," Charles said to the professor, "shall we go and have a look?"

"It's why we're here," he replied.

"I'll stay with the car," Jack said, "just in case I need to move it. Don't want anyone bashing into Mrs. Tremayne's fine ride. You two can go and reconnoiter to your hearts' content."

"Guess we'll have to walk back up to where we saw the opening to those steps," Charles said.

"Argh," said the professor, nodding his unenthusiastic agreement.

When they finally passed through the small opening, there before them was a long and steep set of steps leading down to the building they'd seen from the lane. To their left, an unkempt graveyard extended downward on the hillside toward the church; to their right, tall trees bent over the steps and filtered out much of the sunlight. Amidst the lichen-covered headstones of the graveyard, blackberry brambles and huge green ferns grew with abandon. At the bottom of the steps loomed a gray and blotchy-looking stone structure. To Charles, it looked unusually tall and narrow for a church. "Not exactly a cheery place," he muttered to himself, "even on a bright Tuesday morning. Wouldn't want to see it on a dark and stormy night." Oddly – or so it seemed to Charles – it had a green door. He hadn't seen any other churches in Cornwall with green doors. A very Celtic color, anyway.

He moved down the steps, his legs still a bit sore from the previous day's hiking. The professor descended behind him at a slower pace. From somewhere amidst the graveyard Charles heard the sibilant cooing of a wood pigeon – *coo-COO-coo-coo, coo-COO-coo-coo*. It was a plaintive, melancholy sound.

Charles found the entrance porch, built as an extension on the right side of the building. He paused for a moment in that cool, dark space before trying the door latch. There'd been no signs of anyone being about the grounds outside the building, and only silence emanated from within. To Charles it seemed a lonely, desolate place. He decided he would wait for the professor so they could enter together.

When Charles twisted the iron ring and pushed the door open, the loud noise shattered the enveloping silence. If anyone was about, they would surely have heard *that*.

Charles stepped inside and was immediately struck by the coolness of the air and by the distinctive smell of the place – the smell of oldness, dampness, and solemnity, Charles thought – if one could smell solemnity. Definitely solemnity, not sanctity. To Charles, sanctity seemed in short supply in this rather forbidding place.

Charles moved across to the center aisle, then turned and looked toward the choir and the altar. He was struck by the plainness of everything. No elaborately carved rood screen, no beautiful stained glass windows behind the altar, no elevated organ loft, no ornate lecturn, no carved bench ends or striking baptismal font like what they'd seen at Altarnun. Only the bright reds and blues of the knitted covers of the kneelers placed on the pews offered a slight bit of color.

Charles ran his eyes over the various memorials to the dead on the sidewalls, then glanced upward at the massive timbers of the vaulted roof. He was disappointed by the absence of roof bosses. All in all, he thought, the Minster Church was a pretty nondescript – one might even say drab – edifice, stuck off in a remote and rather daunting spot. No wonder no one was around on a weekday morning.

But, in fact, someone *was* around. Through a door to one side of the choir – perhaps from the sacristy? – stepped a small young woman wearing a faded, oversized denim shirt and carrying a pail of what must have contained cleaning items. The look on her face said she was as startled to see Charles as he was to see her.

She set the pail down and then moved slowly and rather anxiously down the center aisle towards him. "You've come to see the church?" she inquired in a soft, timorous voice.

"Hello," Charles called out to her. "Yes, the professor and I have come to see the church." He pointed back toward the professor, who stood in a dark back corner examining a memorial plaque.

"Lovely," she replied, her hands fluttering nervously in front of her like a pair of white birds. "There's a guest book on the small table, if you'd be so kind as to sign it. Also on the table are some brochures about St. Materiana's. You're welcome to take one."

When Charles signed the guest book, he noticed that the last visitor to the church had signed it in late April, six weeks earlier. Not exactly a popular place, was it? He picked up one of the small printed brochures and studied the elegant handwritten title on the front of it. Someone was a master calligrapher. He flipped the pages quickly and was struck by how impressive a production the little booklet was. Quite a contrast to the church it described.

"The vicar was terribly proud of it," she said. "He had the most beautiful handwriting."

Professor Wentworth came and stood beside Charles. He smiled at the shy young woman. "Thank you, miss," he said, accepting the brochure she handed him. "You wouldn't happen to know if the vicar is available today, would you? Neville Smallwood? He's an old acquaintance of mine. He *is* still the vicar, isn't he?"

Once more the young woman's hands were all aflutter. "Oh, crumbs," she said after some hesitation, "I'm so terribly sorry to tell you this, but the vicar is gone."

"Gone? Off on a trip?"

"Oh no, sir." She seemed quite upset and quickly wiped a tear from her eye with her small white hand. "His funeral was yesterday, sir. His grave lies just at the bottom of the cemetery. I could show you, if you wish."

"Anna!" came a loud voice from the front of the church. "Where've you gone off to now, missy?" A tall, stout woman suddenly appeared through the sacristy door, then turned and stared down the aisle toward the three of them. "Didn't know we had guests today." She strode towards them, her face struggling to produce an unaccustomed smile.

"Good morning. I'm Mrs. Brashler, church sexton," she said. "Ah, found the brochures, I see. Lovely. And signed the guest book, too. Professor Wentworth?" she said, looking at their names. "I believe I've heard that name."

"Neville and I were friends at Oxford," he said. "Anna just told us the sad news. My sincere condolences." He bowed his head slightly as he said that.

"And mine," Charles added.

"Died Sunday as he was preaching," she said. "Just how he would have wanted it, I 'spect. Preachin' on one of his favorites, the Book of Jude. He'd just quoted the verses, 'Now unto him who is able to keep you from falling, and to present you faultless before the presence of his glory . . . .' Then he slumped right down and succumbed before our very eyes. Terrible sad it was. But beautiful, too, in a way."

"I'd like to go and visit his grave," the professor said. "Pay him my respects."

"O' course, sir. Anna will show you. Then, missy, it's back to your chores for you," she said a bit sternly to the young woman.

"Umm, one more thing, Mrs. Brashler," the professor said. "This may be asking a lot, but do you think it might be possible for us to visit the vicar's study? He and I share academic interests, you see, and we'd been working on a project together that he very much wanted me to come and have a look at." He threw a sidelong glance at Charles as if to say, that fabrication isn't so *very* far from the truth, is it?

A cold glare emanated from the woman's eyes. Her entire torso seemed to fill up with air. "Sir, I *think not*. No one's ever allowed into his study, not even me. The vicar was a very private man, and he has things in there of considerable value. I s'pose his executor will have to be allowed in. But until that time, it shall remain securely *locked*."

"Oh, well, fair enough," the professor said amiably. "I quite understand. Once the executor's done that, perhaps I can contact him directly."

"She can be a bit of a dragon," Anna murmured softly to Charles. He grinned at the young woman, who grinned back. Then both of them wiped their grins away before the woman had a chance to notice.

"Sir," Anna said to the professor, "would you like me to show you the grave now?"

"Yes, missy," the woman said, "you do that. Then leave these gentlemen alone and get yourself back to your chores." She swung about and marched back down the aisle toward the door to the sacristy. Back to her dragon's lair, Charles assumed.

After they'd spent a few minutes at the graveside, the professor said to Anna, "Oh, just one last thing. The vicarage. I didn't see it anywhere. Is it near here?"

The young woman pointed through the trees to the right of the unkempt graveyard. "It's off through there," she said. "There's a graveled path just up beyond the east end of the church that leads to it. Only takes a minute or two. Maybe 200 yards from here."

"Neville lived alone, I believe?"

"Oh yes, he quite loved his solitude."

"So there's no one else who stays in the vicarage?"

"No, no one else. I come in the morning and tidy his kitchen and sitting room every Monday and Thursday, but he's such a neat man there's rarely much to do. Other than me, hardly anyone else ever sets foot inside the vicarage."

"Well, thank you so very much, Anna. We've probably kept you long enough, dear girl. Wouldn't want to create any difficulties for you with you-know-who."

"Here be dragons," Charles said to Anna with a grin.

"No, not dragons," she replied. "There's just the one."

"Find the geezer?" Jack asked, as they climbed back into the car.

"After a fashion," the professor answered, leaving it at that. "So Charlie," he went on, "how do you feel about breaking the law?"

"Normally, I tend to be against it."

"Ever been arrested for housebreaking?"

"No, not up till now," Charles replied.

"Housebreaking?" Jack said, a question in his voice.

"Breaking and entering," Charles said.

"Ah," Jack replied, nodding. "So they rebuffed you, eh? Going to have to go a more devious route."

"When were you thinking of doing that, Professor?"

"It will have to be tonight, wouldn't you think? In the wee, wee hours."

"We're coming back here in the *wee, wee hours*?"

"Like two thieves in the night."

"Only two?" Jack said. "C'mon, guys, can't I play too? What am I, chopped liver?"

"Of course you can play," the professor said. "We'll need you to be our lookout and to drive the getaway car."

"We're coming back here in the wee, wee hours?" Charlie said again. "Sir, this place is creepy at ten in the morning."

"Not to worry," the professor said. "You'll have *me* with you."

"And besides," Jack said, "should the need arise, you can always use your judo."

❖❖❖

A green Ford Fiesta, driven by a prune-faced woman named Lowenna Tremayne, crawled slowly around the hairpin turn in the road above the village of Boscastle. She was being suitably cautious on the slick and narrow roadway. The car moved on down across the humpbacked stone bridge and entered the village, passing gift shops on the left and the entrance to to The Riverside Hotel on the right. She drove on for another hundred yards through the village and then turned right into the entrance to the public car park. She purchased a sticker from the pay-and-display machine and placed it on the dashboard before locking her car.

The woman crossed the street and entered the Primrose Cottage Café. She looked about for a moment. When she spotted the couple already seated at a table near the front window, she went over and joined them. They were far younger than she was, maybe in their early twenties, though in the man's case his age wasn't quite so easy to ascertain. He was a broad-chested fellow with thick, unruly black hair and an imposing black beard. When the woman looked at him she saw a man who exuded rather brutish masculinity, though he wasn't what she would have called good-looking. The young woman, however, definitely *was* good-looking. She looked slender and fit, and her peaches and cream complexion perfectly complemented her glossy red hair.

The woman sat down and ordered her morning tea, and after the waitress brought it, a lengthy discussion ensued, the two women doing almost all the talking.

✠✠✠

Jackson Lockhart took up his post up behind the church near where the gravel path to the vicarage began. He'd hidden the car in a dark spot off the lane several yards behind a farm gate. It was eleven-thirty at night.

The professor told him he couldn't predict how long they'd be – maybe just a few minutes, maybe quite a bit longer – so Jack had come armed with a heavy sweater and a flask of coffee. Aside from the sweater, the coffee, and his own two fists, though, weapons had he none.

It was eerie hanging out in the darkness by himself. Occasionally he heard the sounds of nocturnal creatures scurrying in the bushes, maybe rabbits or badgers or some such. He really didn't know. And it didn't help matters that a dratted owl somewhere off in the woods kept sounding his *who-WHOO, who-who-WHOO* at irregular intervals.

After nearly two hours of waiting, Jackson had begun to get worried. They surely should have been back by now, he thought. What could be keeping them? He wondered if he should abandon his post and go in search of them. Well, he'd give them fifteen more minutes. If they weren't back by then, he would.

※ ※ ※

"We're just going to bust our way in?" Charles asked, as he and the professor, aided by the professor's flashlight, stumbled and bumbled up the narrow path in search of the vicarage.

"I'm hoping that won't be required," the professor replied. Then Charles heard a jingling sound. The professor's right hand was inside his jacket pocket.

"You nabbed some keys?"

"Let's give them a try before we resort to crowbars, shall we?" he said. "Nabbed them? Oh well, they were just hanging right there on a peg in the sacristy, just above a little label that said 'Vicarage.' I'm guessing these are what Anna uses when she comes to do her tidying."

"So you just nabbed them. Just helped yourself when no one was looking."

"Really, Charlie, 'borrowed' would be a much more suitable word."

The totally dark structure now appeared before then. No dogs barked, no security light suddenly flashed on, no loud voice of a dragon-lady shouting "hold it right there."

"Charlie, aim the light on the door and I'll try the different keys in the lock," the professor said. There were only three keys on the ring, and the largest of them, the first one he tried, slipped easily into the lock. He turned it and they heard the clicking sound of the bolt releasing.

The professor pushed the door open. Silence and darkness. The two of them stepped inside and Charles closed the door behind them. They were in. No crowbars required. Good thing, since they didn't have one.

The professor shined his light about the old-fashioned sitting room – overstuffed chairs, floor lamps, shelves with bric-a-brac and framed photos above a pair of low bookcases. Near the front door was an umbrella stand and a longcase clock. A staircase ascended to where the bedrooms most likely were. The doorway to the right of the staircase, Charles guessed, probably led to a small dining room and the kitchen.

At the far end of the sitting room was another door. The professor headed toward it. "I suspect what we're in search of will be in there, if it's anywhere. Coming?"

"Lead on, McDuff," Charles said.

"Misquoted as usual," the professor muttered. He turned the door handle, but it didn't open. The room was locked.

The professor fished out the key ring and tried each of the keys.

"No luck?" Charles asked.

"Argh," the professor muttered, shaking his head. "You don't suppose there's a secret password, do you?"

"Lacunae?" Charles suggested. "Palimpsest? Hapax legomenon? Or maybe just 'Speak friend and enter'?"

"Some help you are, Bilbo Baggins," the professor muttered grumpily. "Well, what do we do now, lad? Knock it off its hinges like Chaucer's Miller?"

"Hang on," Charles said. "Let's not go bashing it just yet. Here, let me have the flashlight." He ran the light around the room, looking for a potted plan or any place where an extra key might have been stashed. Hte saw no obvious candidates.

"Time to track down a crowbar?" said the professor.

"No! Not yet!"

"I'm just eager to get into the blooming place, Charlie. We're so close, my lad, we can't allow ourselves to be thwarted now."

Charles stretched up on tiptoes and ran his hand across the top of the doorframe. When his finger encountered a small object, he pushed it down to the end of the frame and it fell off. It made a little tinkling sound when it hit the wooden floor.

"Charlie, what would I do without you? You, Bilbo Baggins, have the makings of a proper burglar," the professor said.

The key fit the lock perfectly. And a moment later they stepped through the door and into Neville Smallwood's private study – a place where no one except the vicar himself was ever allowed to go.

✢✢✢

The fifteen minutes Jack had given himself were nearly up when he saw car lights moving slowly down the narrow lane toward the church. Then he heard the sounds of the vehicle's tires. He hoped he'd pulled the Jag far enough up the farm track as to be out of sight, but he wasn't sure.

The car stopped in front of the gate where Jack had parked that morning. Its lights went out. Jack heard a door open and close, then the sound of footsteps. It sounded like it was just one person.

The footsteps moved back up the lane toward the opening to the stair steps that led down to the church. Whoever the person was, they weren't using a flashlight. Must know their way about, Jack thought. He wondered if it might be that fearsome dragon-lady Charlie had told him about. Not likely to be the timorous little Anna.

What should he do? Jack wondered. Go and warn Charlie and the professor? Or stay at his post and hope that whoever it was had merely come to perform some innocent task at the church?

As Jack considered his options, the owl in the woods started in again with his dad-blasted *who-wooing* routine.

20

"I'm going to risk turning on some lights, Charlie. We need to see what we're doing."

"The windows have heavy drapes, sir. I think that should be all right."

The room had an overhead ceiling light, in addition to a pair of desk lamps and a tall standing floor light. They turned all of them on. The sudden illumination caused Charles to shield his eyes.

They stood in the middle of the long room, slowly taking everything in. There was a lot to take in. Charles' gaze halted for a moment on a framed wall poster. It depicted a great many things, but at the center of it was a boney, witch-like woman with sword and breastplate, wearing a pan for a helmet. She was striding boldly toward the gaping mouth of Hell, a wild-eyed look on her face. There were many lesser female figures in the poster also, all wreaking various kinds of havoc. Physical disasters were depicted all across the work. It was certainly a hellish-looking vision, Charles thought.

"Mad Meg," the professor said, standing next to Charles and looking at it too. "Attributed to Bruegel. Looks almost like Hieronymus Bosch, doesn't it? Probably influenced by him."

"What sort of a man would want *that* hanging on his wall?"

"A very odd one."

"You ain't just a-kiddin'," Charles said. "What do you suppose it means, Professor?"

"No real agreement on that. Is she greed personified? Or the crazed leader of a frenzied band of women undaunted by Hell itself? Lots of theories, Charlie. No critical consensus. Is it anti-feminist or pro-feminist? Is it a satire? And if so, of what?"

"Whew. It's quite fascinating. It isn't something I would want on *my* wall, though."

"Oh, Charlie, what have we here?"

All along the external wall beneath the drape-enshrouded windows, ran a pair of long library tables shoved together. They were covered with various bits and pieces of medieval manuscripts. All along the back portion of the table near the wall were pots filled with inks in several colors and many different kinds of writing implements.

"Looks like someone raided a medieval scriptorium," Charles said. "Look at all this stuff."

"And Charlie, you need to take a look at this." The professor pointed to two manuscript pages that lay side by side.

"Wow. They look virtually identical," Charles said. "But wait a minute. The one on the left is far older. It's the original. The one on the right . . . ."

". . . is a modern copy," the professor said. "A copy so good that were it to be aged a bit, no one would be able to tell them apart."

"He was a forger? Professor, you've always spoken of him as being a man of impeccable morals. Does that make any sense?"

"Well, I wonder, I wonder." The professor held his chin in his hand. He spent the next five minutes silently examining all the items laid out on the table.

"Charlie," he said at last, "I don't think he was a forger in the sense you mean. I think he was just doing what medieval scribes actually did – make copies of the manuscripts that came to them."

Charles nodded his agreement. "He was taking each of these bits of manuscript and then laboriously mastering each scribal hand he encountered," Charles said, wonder in his voice. "He was reliving the Middle Ages."

They continued studying all that lay before them.

"Man," Charles said, shaking his head in disbelief, "he was *good*."

"Well, if he'd been doing this for the last fifty years, he'd had a lot of practice."

They both wandered about the study for the next ten minutes, amazed by all they found there. Portions of genuine manuscripts hundreds of years old. Evidence to suggest that Neville Smallwood had taught himself how to prepare large sheets of vellum and parchment and had a small supply on hand ready for use. A variety of inks and dyes, several quills of different styles, and some other more specialized writing implements. There was a sharpening knife, a pumice stone for smoothing parchment, as well as binding materials and calf-skin covers. There was even a small oven for ageing the newly copied pages.

"I wonder where he got the original manuscripts?" Charles said aloud.

"At first glance, at least, they don't appear to be items of great value," the professor said, "nor things that most collectors would be clamoring for. There are dealers who handle things such as these, and not necessarily unscrupulous ones, either. Moral treatises, like the one you described as being in the Polminster Manuscript, aren't rare at all. Nor are early medical texts."

Charles moved down to the far end of the long room where a small alcove had been curtained-off from the rest of the room.

"Let's see what we have here," he said softly to himself. Charles reached up to the top right end of the curtain and then pushed it open. It was dark in the alcove, but Charles saw a string hanging down from a naked light bulb. He pulled on it and a small ceiling light came on.

"Oh, man." Charles gazed at the three shelves that filled

the alcove. "Sir, you'd better come and have a look."

The professor had been caught up in examining a deep red ink in one of the small pots on the library table. "How in blazes did he *do* it?" he mused. "Scholars have yet to learn the secret of the origins of that particular ink. My word, are you telling me that old Nev figured it out on his own?"

"Sir," Charles said again more insistently, "I *really* think you'd better come and see this."

✢✢✢

Now the noise Jack heard wasn't just the scurryings of nocturnal critters. It was the sound of footsteps on the path leading to the vicarage. Oh crap, he thought, the person who went into the church must've come out again on this side. Now whoever it is is heading toward the vicarage. I'd better do that, too.

Jack had no trouble hearing the footfalls of the person on the path ahead of him. Must be wearing heavy boots, he thought. Jack, who was wearing his favorite pair of Adidas sneakers and was naturally light on his feet, moved almost noiselessly. Better stay close, he thought. But maybe not *too* close.

It was dark on the forest path and the person ahead of him didn't carry a flashlight. But Jack's vision had long since adjusted to the darkness; he could just make out the bulky figure of the person moving in front of him. Whoever it was, they certainly weren't small. Now Jack could see the shape of the lightless building in the trees just ahead. The person he was following was nearly there. But he (or she?) didn't approach the front door. Instead, they moved off into the darkness of the trees to the right of the building.

Jack stepped off the path and took up a position behind the trunk of a huge beech tree. It was damned chilly standing there in the dark woods, now that he wasn't moving. He was glad he'd worn his heavy sweater. He worked the fingers of both hands, loosening them up and warming them. Then he took turns running one hand over the back of the other and rubbing the palms of his hands together. His hands were the only weapons he'd brought with him – should it come to that.

⁜⁜⁜

The shelves in the alcove held half a dozen bound manuscripts. Alone on the top shelf lay a thick volume that was already familiar to Charles, for he'd virtually lived with it for several days last week. He felt a very strong emotional connection to it.

"These are the finished products," the professor said. "Obviously, these were his pride and joy. That one on top, Charlie, is that one *ours*? Is that the Polminster Manuscript?" He pointed to the thick volume on the top shelf.

Charles carefully lifted it down. He opened it to folio 28r, the first page of the Chaucerian poem. And there it was, just as he'd seen it in Rhys Tremayne's study.

Charles nodded. He felt powerful emotions as he held it – affection, relief, astonishment. There were many unanswered questions swirling in his mind, but for now he was just grateful they'd been able to recover it.

"So what do we do now, Professor, just take it?"

"Indeed. We take it. Then we return it to its rightful owner, Rhys Tremayne."

"If he *is* its rightful owner," Charles said.

"Well, at this point it's not likely to have a lot of value to Neville Smallwood, what?"

"No, probably not."

"Think we should take the other manuscripts while we're at it?"

Charles made a moue at his mentor. "Sir, I hope you're just kidding."

"Oh dear me, yes. Merely a joke, Charlie, and not a very good one, either. Though I would dearly love to see what they contain. Wouldn't you?"

"Sir, by a real stroke of fortune we've found what we came for. Let's not press our luck, okay?"

"Right you are, Charlie, right you are. Put the curtain back the way you found it, won't you lad? We need to make certain that everything looks just the way it did when we got here. Then let's get the hell out of Tombstone, eh?"

"Dodge, sir. I believe it's Dodge people get the hell out of."

✢✢✢

In the bedroom closet of her flat, Ally Tremayne always kept a few canvases stretched and gessoed so that when inspiration struck, she'd be all set to go. Now she selected one of the largest of them and placed it on the easel. She reached for the pencil sketch she'd made during her lunch break and studied it for a long moment. It depicted the interior of Zennor Church during a service.

Toward the right-hand side of the sketch a young man stood before the other members of the church choir. He was singing. The figures in the choir were fairly indistinct, whereas the young man was drawn in more detail. He, however, wasn't the chief focus of the drawing.

Depicted on the left-hand side of the drawing was a young woman. She sat alone on the last pew. The sketch was laid out so that it focused on her, her figure a good bit larger than anything else in the drawing. Her face and hair were especially emphasized. Her body was swathed in a long hooded cloak, the hood thrown back to reveal her cascading hair. The cloak had a pair of large side pockets. Poking out of the top of one of them was a portion of a comb. At the top of the other pocket was another object which, on close inspection, could be seen to be the top half of a hand mirror.

The long cloak, Ally thought, should probably be painted using a dark green pigment, so that the woman's whitish face and honey-blond hair would be set off by it. At the very bottom of the cloak, though just barely showing, would be the most crucial item. The greenish-gray tip end of a bifurcated fish tail.

In Ally's sketch, the facial features of the young man who was singing hadn't been drawn in at all; for the young woman sitting on the back pew, the drawing provided a few more details. But the sketch was too small to be able to do real justice to either of them. Given the much larger size of the painting, however, doing that would be quite possible. In fact, the artist had every intention of turning those two faces into miniature portraits. She smiled at the thought of it.

✣✣✣

Charles placed the study key back atop the doorframe where he'd found it. Then he and the professor took final glances about the sitting room to be sure they hadn't left any tell-tale signs. As far as Charles could see, they hadn't. Then Charles stepped for a moment into the kitchen. When he returned he was holding a plastic carrier bag that said "Sainsbury's" on it. Inside the bag, wrapped for safekeeping in a borrowed tea towel – they surely wouldn't notice the loss of a single tea towel, Charles assumed – was the Polminster Manuscript.

They exited the vicarage front door, which locked automatically behind them when Charles pulled it shut. The professor flicked on his flashlight. Its feeble beam did little to illuminate the dark pathway, but the two men, elated by the success of their mission, weren't bothered by that. Now they would hurry back to the car where the stalwart Jack awaited. It was time to leave Dodge in their rearview mirror.

✠ ✠ ✠

After watching his two friends come out of the vicarage and begin to make their way down the path, Jack remained stationary behind the beech tree. He planned to do nothing unless the person hidden in the shadows around the side of the building made a move.

It wasn't until Charles and the professor had gone a ways down the dark path that the watcher finally emerged and set off behind them. Jack had figured that when Charlie and the professor came out of the vicarage, some kind of confrontation, maybe even a physical one, would occur. But that hadn't happened. The person had simply waited until they were a safe distance ahead before setting off in pursuit of them. Jack hung back another half a minute before doing the same.

It was eerily silent as he moved through the darkness. Jack could barely hear the muffled footfalls of the person ahead. This time the guy (or gal) must've been making more of an effort. Even the dratted owl was keeping mum. Every now and then Jack caught a brief flash of the professor's light, maybe fifty yards up ahead.

Then, to Jack's surprise, the watcher in the woods suddenly swung off the main path. He was following a different path that led toward the church. Probably heading for his vehicle, Jack thought. Wants to get out of here before Charlie and the professor become aware of his car.

Jack was relieved that no confrontation had occurred, but he was also rather confused by these events. What was this all about? Apparently the watcher in the woods had simply been monitoring Charlie and the professor's activities. Why would he do that? Pretty weird, Jack thought.

"Jack?" came Charles' loud shout. "Where *is* ya, dude?"

"Here ah is," Jack shouted back. He hurried up the path toward them.

"Answering the call of nature?" the professor said. "Had a bit too much coffee?"

"No, not really. But I have some interesting things I need to tell you about."

"As do we," Charles said. He held up the Sainsbury's carrier bag. "It's the manuscript, Jack. We actually *found* the blessed thing. So if you ain't chopped liver, my friend, we ain't either."

"Hear that?" said the professor. "Sounds like a car engine." He glanced off in the direction from which the sound had come.

"Oh, yes," Jack said. "It's a car engine all right. Sir, we haven't been entirely alone tonight."

"Really? Someone else has been in the woods? Who was

that?" the professor asked.

"I really don't know. But on the way back to the hotel I'll tell you what I do know."

"My word," said the professor. "Sounds a bit ominous. Well, why don't we go, then. Been quite an eventful evening, hasn't it. Have to say, though, that I'm rather pleased with the outcome."

"Umm, sir," said Charles, "aren't we forgetting something?"

"Hmm?"

"The keys to the vicarage. We've got to put them back. If those keys go missing, it will be a dead giveaway."

"Oh my, so it would. Well, Charlie, would you mind doing the honors? My tired old legs are pretty well shot."

"You want *me* to go down inside that creepy old church? Alone? Thanks a lot, Professor."

"Well, returning the keys *was* your idea."

"No sweat," Jack said, "I'll come with you. The two of us together should be a match for any dragons, or even a dragon-lady, shouldn't we?"

"I wouldn't be too sure about that," said the professor.

21

After sleeping late on Wednesday morning, Charles, Jack, and Professor William Wentworth packed up and prepared for the drive back to the Lizard. They were on the road by eleven and spent a good portion of the ride listening to *Porgy and Bess.*

"Sullen Syd didn't have a lot of serious music to choose from, but at least I found one real gem," the professor said, "one I didn't even have in my old collection."

Conversation was minimal as they listened to the Gershwin classic. But when it got to "I've Got Plenty O' Nuttin'," Charles and the professor couldn't stop themselves from joining in. If Jack had known the words, he would have, too. So he tapped out the rhythm on the steering wheel and waggled his head back and forth to the lively tune.

"Old Ira," Jack said when the song was over, "he was a heck of a good lyricist."

"Indeed he was," the professor said, "though he didn't write the words to that one. In fact, he only wrote a couple of these lyrics."

"Really?" Jack said.

"Most of 'em were penned by a fella named Heyward. The fella who wrote the novel Gershwin's work is adapted from."

"Ira did write one or two of the best ones, though," Charles said. "I'd bet money 'It Ain't Necessarily So' was one of his."

"Well, you ain't necessarily right," the professor said,

"though from time to time you've been known to be."

"I'll take that as a compliment, Professor."

"Listen guys," Jack said, a note of foreboding in his voice, "there's something that's been nagging at my brain the last hour or so. I don't want to rain on your parade or anything, but I'd be interested in knowing what you plan to tell Mr. Tremayne when we get back to Manderley. Do you intend to just hand him the manuscript and say, 'Here you go, sir. We just happened to stumble upon your missing manuscript while we were looking at sites in North Cornwall. Maybe you'd like to have it back?' "

For a moment both Charles and the professor were silent. "Oh, my," the professor finally said. "I hadn't given that any thought. Charlie, what *are* we going to tell Rhys? How will we explain ourselves?"

"Well . . . umm . . . I suppose we could cook up some yarn about visiting the Minster Church and . . . er . . . finding it by chance in Neville's study, following his unexpected death."

"Yes, well, let me think about that," the professor said.

"What if he doesn't *want* it back?" Jack said. "What if his intention all along was for the thing to vanish?"

"Hmm, yes," said the professor, "more food for thought."

"You know what I would do?" said Jack.

"What would you do?" asked Charles.

"I wouldn't tell him about it at all. For now, just keep it quiet. Act as if all we did on our trip was exactly what we were supposed to do, visit a bunch of ancient sites. You can regale him with a lot of guff, Charlie, about all the cool stuff we saw. That will surely please him. We'll just keep mum about the manuscript until we see how the land lies."

"Interesting suggestion," said the professor.

"It's a brilliant suggestion," Charles said. "I knew there was a reason I asked Jack to come down to Cornwall. It wasn't just so he could check out redheads."

"Speaking of redheads," said the professor, "let me tell about the one I saw in Boscastle."

✣✣✣

"Anna," came the harsh voice of the dragon-lady, "would you mind letting Mrs. Tremayne into the vicarage this morning? She left something with the vicar she would like to retrieve."

The Mrs. Tremayne she was referring to was the prune-faced Mrs. Tremayne, not the current one, whom she'd never met.

"Yes, ma'am," Anna replied. "I'll just get the keys." She stepped into the sacristy and stared at the row of pegs from which all the various keys dangled. But the peg for the vicarage keys was empty. That was strange.

Oh, there it was, on the next peg over, on top of the keys for the tool shed. Very peculiar, she thought. She wondered who could have done that. She was certain it hadn't been her. That was something she'd never done before. In fact, it was rare for anyone but her to use the vicarage keys. Well, maybe the dragon-lady had needed to use them for some reason and put them back incorrectly. Of course that woman would never admit to making a mistake. She was the only person Anna knew who *never* made mistakes. Anna decided it might be better not to say anything about the keys.

Anna couldn't help wondering what Mrs. Tremayne could want from the vicarage. She knew, of course, that the woman and the vicar had had a long-standing friendship.

189

But she was quite sure their relationship had been limited to nothing more than just sharing the occasional cup of tea. What could the woman have left in the vicarage that she needed to retrieve?

✦✦✦

Despite his brain being more than just a little bit zombified from their late-night activities, Jack pushed the Jaguar quickly down the A30 through the light traffic. The professor was dozing in the back seat, and Charles sat up front beside Jack, poring over the manuscript he held cradled in his lap. He was going through it slowly, page by page.

As they tooled along, Jack once more noticed the Indian Queens exit as they zipped past it. He smiled, remembering the professor's long-winded exegesis on the village's peculiar name. Anyway, the sign told him they were now on the final leg of the drive, no more than forty-five minutes from their goal.

Jack had noticed the exit sign to Indian Queens but not the dark green Ford that had been cruising along about a hundred yards behind them, ever since they passed Launceston. Why would he? Ford Fiestas, in the U.K., were about a dime a dozen.

"Oh no!" Charles suddenly blurted out. Then he slammed the heel of his right hand hard against his forehead. He blew out a noisy breath. Jack glanced over and saw the agitation and exasperation written on Charles' face.

"Charlie?" came a drowsy voice from the back seat. Charles' sudden expostulation had awakened the professor. "Everything all right?"

"*Son of a b* . . . ," Charles started to say before catching himself. "Holy Moses, Professor, Holy Moses. No sir, every-thing is not all right. It appears that we've screwed up royally."

"Screwed up? How so, lad?"

"Dammit, Charlie," Jack said, "what have you gone and done now?"

"This execrable thing," he said, holding up the manuscript in disgust. "Crap, I really hate to say it, but it *isn't* what we thought it was."

"The manuscript?" the professor said. "Not what we thought it was? Charlie, I'm not following you."

"Sir, this execrable thing I hold in my hands *isn't* the Polminster Manuscript. Or at any rate, it isn't *our* Polminster Manuscript."

"Charlie, I'm still not following you."

"Sir, this *isn't it*. Must be a copy, I guess – a really *good* copy, but still a copy. Sir, what we have here isn't the same manuscript Mr. Tremayne showed us last week. It isn't the one I sweated over for large parts of three days in Rhys Tremayne's library. Believe me, sir, it isn't. And I should know."

"*Now* you tell us," Jack said grumpily. "Took you this long to figure that out?"

"Charlie, what makes you think that?" said the professor.

"Because whoever assembled *this* one made a mistake, that's why. They made a very simple yet very telling blunder."

"Charlie, I looked that manuscript over quite thoroughly myself. I saw no blunders."

"What'd they do?" Jack asked.

"They put it together wrong. When they bound it – and now I think about it, it looks like it's a newer binding – they botched it. They misarranged the individual sections. They aren't in the same order as the one I worked with."

"Surely not," the professor said.

"They did, sir, I swear it. They messed up. They reversed two of the sections. It's a very small mistake but definitely a mistake. And that one little mistake makes all the difference. The Chaucerian poem starts in the right place, fol. 28r, no problem there. But the order of the two sections that come before it have been reversed. In this manuscript the lapidary section comes before the moral treatise section. In our manuscript, it was the other way around."

Charles' companions said nothing for several seconds. Finally the professor said, "You're dead certain?"

"Absolutely."

"Well," said the professor – now it was his turn to breathe a loud sigh – "that rather sucks, doesn't it."

"What should we do," Jack asked, "head on back? Take another crack at it?" But he got no response from the others. Each of them seemed to have fallen into a deep funk.

"Well," the professor finally said, "here's the crucial thing. We now have a manuscript copy of the poem we wanted. And given Neville's assiduousness, it's presumably a perfectly accurate copy. So we can use that one to compare with the transcription you made. If I don't miss my guess, they will turn out to be identical. There's *that*, anyway."

Charles, lost in thought, still hadn't responded. Finally he said, "Sir, I have a funny feeling about all of this." He paused again for a lengthy moment before saying, "I have a notion, sir, that we have been snookered."

"What?" said the professor.

"Duped," Jack said, "conned, hoodwinked, bamboozled."

"It did seem to me that this whole rescue-the-manuscript thing had been pretty damn easy," Charles said. "Too easy? Have we gone and done exactly what somebody wanted us to do?"

"Who is this 'somebody,' Charlie, and why would they want us to find a copy of the manuscript and bring it back?" the professor asked.

"Beats the hell out of me," Charles replied.

"Curiouser and curiouser," Jack said. "You know, I've been having a terrific time down here in Cornwall. Man, this Cornwall place is really outta sight. Makes one feel kinda like he's stumbled straight into some old Hitchcock film."

"Ha, ha," the professor grumbled. "I am not amused."

22

Ally turned off the main road and onto the gravel drive toward home. She'd been able to leave the gallery early today and was really looking forward to seeing Charlie, Jack, and the professor again. Especially Charlie. It seemed odd to her how fond she'd become of him in such a short time. It had only been a week ago they'd first met, that noon in the kitchen when he'd initially mistaken her for her stepmother. Right from the start she'd felt some strange attraction to him, something she really couldn't account for.

With a smile, she thought about the painting she'd been working on the past two evenings. It wasn't at all like anything she'd ever painted before. She'd never had much interest in making representational art, but somehow it was coming together surprisingly well. Maybe she'd been inspired by the subject matter. Or maybe she'd turned some corner she hadn't expected to turn. Rather like her unexpected feelings for Charlie.

Tonight would be hard, she thought. For one thing, her stepmother would be there. She and Ailish got along just fine, really, but they both preferred to keep the other at arm's length. Given how much each of them cared for Ally's father, that was probably a good thing. Otherwise they might find each other engaged in a competition for his affection. She didn't want to become her stepmother's rival.

Tonight would also be hard because it might turn out to be the last time she would ever see Charlie. In the next day or two, he and the professor would be going back to Oxford and resuming their lives there. Maybe Charlie, in the days and weeks to come, would have a few additional dealings with her father that involved tidying up the manuscript project. But a return trip to Cornwall probably wouldn't be needed.

Well, maybe this evening she and Charlie would have a chance to spend some time alone. She hoped so. Maybe they could take that cliff walk she'd suggested when she last saw him. She hoped he hadn't forgotten.

✢✢✢

In the privacy of his bedroom, Charles closed the door firmly. He took the manuscript they'd brought back from the Minster Church out of the Sainsbury's bag and placed it carefully on the low table next to the window. He opened it to the beginning of the poem they hoped was by Chaucer.

Then he photographed folios 28r to 39v. He wondered if he should photograph the entire manuscript but decided that would be pointless. The order of the individual sections of the manuscript couldn't be ascertained definitively just from the photos – since photos could be shuffled about much more easily than the bound sections of the manuscript.

He paused for a moment to stare out the window at the sloping, terraced garden beneath him. He loved this view and would miss it once he was back in Oxford. The gray-blue sea in the not-too-far distance looked choppy today, the waves topped by whitecaps. Charles raised the window, leaned out, and inhaled a deep breath. The sea-scented breeze brushed coolly against his face. He took another deep breath. Bracing. Windows in the U.K., he'd come to realize when he first arrived in Oxford, rarely had screens on them. Seemed kind of odd to someone from the U.S. It wasn't as if there weren't any insects in the U.K. Seemed to Charles there were more midges in the U.K. than anywhere he'd ever been.

Charles retrieved his laptop from atop the wardrobe and placed it on the table next to the manuscript. Time to get at it. He logged on and then pulled up the file containing the photos he'd taken the week before of the poem in the Polminster Manuscript. Then, with the Minster Church manuscript opened to fol. 28r, where the Chaucerian poem began, he found the corresponding page on his laptop.

Looking at them side by side, Charles was struck by how remarkably similar they were. Which one was really the original, he wondered, and which one the copy? Or was either of them actually the original? He felt quite sure that one of them was. And, he suspected, it was the one in the photographs, the one he'd transcribed last week. But he couldn't be one hundred percent certain.

For the next several minutes he examined the corresponding pages minutely. He could see that there were some differences between them, though they were very slight differences. The hands in which they'd been written were virtually identical. The work of the copyist had been impeccable. The number of verses on the pages was, of course, the same, and the amount of space between each verse and the amount of space between each couplet were also the same. But in the vicarage text, the individual letters were just slightly larger, with the result that the verses filled the manuscript page just a little bit more. What especially struck him was that he found no discrepancies in the written words of the two texts – *none*. The two manuscripts mirrored each other perfectly. Every variant spelling, every manuscript abbreviation, even one place where the scribe had written in a small correction – all those things were there without exception. It was almost like looking at a photocopy.

That fact in itself, Charles believed, proved that one of them was copied from the other, copied with the clear intention of making them exactly the same. And so, they virtually were.

Charles felt certain that if a medieval scribe had been the copyist, there would have been many small variations. In Charles' experience, when one medieval scribe copied the work of another, there were *always* discrepancies. Aside from the fact that each of the scribal hands would have been peculiar to the individual scribe, the occasional spelling variation always occurred. And any scribe, coming upon the small, corrected error in the manuscript he was copying, would have corrected that mistake to begin with, not copied the mistake and *then* written in the correction. Even if it was the same scribe copying his own work, he wouldn't have intentionally duplicated his mistake. Nor would the handwriting, even of the same scribe, have been so letter-perfect. Everyone's writing varied slightly from one exemplar to another. Here, there were almost no variations at all.

Through the open window Charles heard the sound of car wheels on the graveled drive. The growl of the engine was familiar to Charles, too. It was Ally's little roadster. He got up quickly and leaned out of the window. He turned and looked toward the small portion of the drive that was visible from his room. But he'd missed her; she'd already gone past. Charles glanced over at his travel alarm on the small table beside his bed. Four-fifteen. He knew that the plan was to have a late meal, certainly not before eight, so maybe he and Ally would have time to take the cliff walk she'd mentioned last Sunday. The thought pleased him.

While they were still fresh in his mind, Charles jotted down a few quick notes about his manuscript observations. Then he shut down his laptop and returned it to the top of the wardrobe. He shoved it to the far back. He put the vicarage manuscript back inside the Sainsbury's carrying bag and lay it flat on the wardrobe, just behind the decorative scrollwork along the top. Neither the laptop nor the manuscript was now visible. They were his secrets.

Charles could hear Ally's footsteps as she rushed up the central staircase to the second floor. He heard the sound of her bedroom door closing. She'd be changing out of her work clothes and into her walking clothes, he hoped. And he also hoped she was as eager to take their cliff walk as he was.

All afternoon the song "Bess, You is My Woman Now" had been stuck in his head. Earlier, Charles had wished the thing would just leave him alone. Now he found himself humming it with pleasure.

When Charles reached the sitting room, he found it empty. Through the partially open door of Ailish Tremayne's study came the sound of music. Bach's Brandenburg Concerto No. 2, one of his favorites.

He tiptoed over and peeked through the cracked door. Ailish Tremayne sat in one high-backed wingchair, Jackson Lockhart in another. Charles ducked back out of sight, not wanting them to know he was there. Jack has found his redhead, Charles thought, a smile on his face. Far be it from him to intrude. Besides, he had other desires on his mind.

Ally came bounding down the central staircase. She was dressed in blue jeans and an oversized, red-checked flannel shirt. In her hand she clutched a dark blue windbreaker. She paused for a moment on the bottom step, looking at Charles, who had donned a gray Waverly College sweatshirt and an ancient pair of gray corduroy trousers, obviously his cliff-walking garb, not his dinner garb. Ally, too, could hear the music coming from her stepmother's study. She raised a finger to her lips, which formed a "shhh."

She tiptoed down the last step and moved right up against Charles. She embraced him fully and enthusiastically. Only after several seconds did she release him. Then she took a step back and stood there studying his face. She liked what she saw. Charles, for his part, liked what he saw, too.

Ally, still on tiptoes, moved toward a little alcove just inside the front door. She snatched an old jacket of her father's from the coatrack there. "For you," she mouthed silently. Then the two of them, still not having exchanged a spoken word, slipped out the door and headed toward the path that led down to the sea.

✣✣✣

Clouds were banking up out in the west. Once more rain was probably in the offing, but not until sometime later that night. A stiff breeze buffeted the waves beneath them, and a gaggle of seagulls swirled about the cliffs, the air filled with their loud squawkings.

"Noisy buggers," Ally said.

"Very few introverts among them," Charles said.

"Maybe they could teach you a thing or two," she said.

"That being a loud-mouthed bird is extremely irritating?"

"No one will ever accuse you of being a loudmouth, Charlie. There's little danger of that."

After reaching the cliff path they walked about a mile along it before seating themselves on a bench that overlooked a scenic little cove. They'd met no other walkers on this blustery, sun-occluded late afternoon. Charles was glad he had the warm jacket Ally had snatched for him.

"Well, so what about your trip?" Ally said. She snuggled up against his side, her thigh up against his, her arm threaded through his. "Did you find Neville Smallwood? Was he as eccentric as I told you he was?"

"Well, we did find him, at least after a fashion. And yes,

he was every bit as eccentric as you'd said."

"You found him after a fashion?"

"We found him lying in his freshly dug grave. In the cemetery beside the Minster Church. Turned out the poor chap had kicked the bucket just two days earlier."

"Oh, goodness. I wonder if Daddy knows? That man was someone he really liked and admired. But Charlie, if he was dead, how could you find him eccentric?"

"I'll tell you how. In the dead of night, we broke into the vicarage and into his study. That room told me all I needed to know in order to believe that he was one of the most eccentric human beings I'd never met."

Ally arched her eyebrows. "You broke in? Wow!"

"There was a dragon-lady person there who told us that, under no circumstances, could we be allowed into his study. So, since she didn't invite us in, we invited ourselves in."

"Golly. You and Jack?"

"No, me and the professor. His idea, actually. And a darn good thing, too."

"And you found what, Charlie?"

Charles stared out to sea without speaking. After about a minute he felt Ally's elbow nudging him in the ribs, but she didn't say anything.

"Ally," Charles finally said, "listen. I've just made up my mind to do what I'd told myself earlier I shouldn't do. I'm going to tell you everything."

"*Everything*? Sounds like you have a lot to tell."

"Umm-hum, a lot to tell. But don't expect me to be able to explain it all because I can't." Charles remained quiet yet again, his eye following the swooping, swirling movement of a single seagull. "I found a quiet one, Ally, see him?" he said, pointing. "That guy there. Flying all alone. Must be an introvert."

He sighed, then started in again on his tale.

"Of course we didn't get a chance to speak to the man since he died before we got there, but the things we found in his study told us an awful lot. That poor fellow had got himself stuck in the Middle Ages."

"Not like you."

"No, not like me. I am not *stuck* in the Middle Ages. Fascinated by them for sure, but not stuck in them. Neville Smallwood was stuck in them. The guy was actually recreating them with parchment and vellum. He was making his own manuscripts just as if he were a medieval scribe. And he was an absolute perfectionist. He was so good that it was virtually impossible to tell the copy from the original."

"So he was forging manuscripts?"

"That was my first thought, too, but that wasn't it. He was simply remaking them for his own pleasure. It was like it was a hobby that had turned into an obsession."

Ally leaned her face toward Charles and gave his cheek a little kiss. "I like listening to you," she said. "When you finally get going, you can become quite passionate. Perhaps my introverted seagull has hidden dimensions."

"If you like listening to me," he said, "then how about not distracting me." He felt her elbow give him another little jab in the ribs.

Over the next half hour Charles told Ally all about what he and the professor had found in Neville Smallwood's study. And he told her what he'd discovered later on about the manuscript they'd brought away with them; how they'd originally believed it to be the Polminster Manuscript but then discovered it wasn't; that it was an astonishingly good copy but definitely a copy. He told her that he'd now been able to verify that fact by comparing it to the photos of the real manuscript he had on his laptop.

"Photos? You'd kept photos of the original?"

"Thought it might be a wise idea."

"Yes, well, I should say so."

"But Ally, here's where things get sticky. What I've come to suspect is that we've been fooled. Manipulated."

"Manipulated?"

"I'm afraid we may have done exactly what someone wanted us to do."

"Seriously?"

"Yes. It appears that for some reason, someone wanted us to find the copy in Neville's study and bring it back with us. Wanted us to think we'd found the original."

"But why, Charlie? And who would want to do that?"

"Yes, those *are* the questions – why and who. And maybe we should add where, too. Where is the original manuscript? What's become of it? Was it really stolen along with the professor's car, or not? But that's another matter. For now, what we really need to figure out is what to do with the one we have. Do we just hand it over to your father? And if we do, how do we explain how we came to have it? Do we tell him we think it's not the original manuscript? Or just let him think that it is?"

For another long moment they both sat in silence, staring out at the sea as it thrashed up choppy, gray waves.

"Brrr," Ally said, snuggling more firmly against his side. He put his right arm around her and held her more tightly against him.

"Here, why don't you put on my heavier coat?" Charles said.

"No, no, I'm fine. But I do like having your arm around me." He turned his body toward her and put both arms around her, pulling her against his chest.

"Umm, that's even nicer," she said.

"I think," Charles went on, "that for some reason, what someone really wants us to do is give this version of the manuscript to your father."

"Do you think they may want to embarrass him or even humiliate him? Get him to try to pass it off as an original and then have its fraudulent nature discovered?"

"That possibility has crossed my mind. But the one thing that continues to really puzzle me is why your father didn't want us to inform the police about the theft of the original manuscript. At first, right after he discovered the theft, he seemed truly upset. But only a few moments later, not so much. He almost seemed relieved. The professor and I aren't sure he even wants the original manuscript to be found. The whole time we've been here, he's refused to tell us anything about the provenance of the manuscript. Not our business, he's insisted. Well, that seems kind of fishy to me."

"Charlie, I can't believe Daddy would have done anything illegal to get it," Ally said.

"You would know that better than I. I've been wondering, though, whether he might be trying to protect someone."

"Someone like Neville Smallwood?"

"Yes, quite likely."

"Poor Neville," Ally said. "Daddy's going to take his death very hard. He was his closest personal friend. Other than the professor, Neville was about the only friend he had."

"Ally, what your father seems to care about most is just one thing. He really, really wants the professor and me to prove beyond any doubt that the poem in the manuscript is Chaucer's *Book of the Lion.*"

"Chaucer's famous lost poem. But without the original manuscript, could you really do that?"

"That would definitely be an obstacle. But if other Chaucer experts, after studying my transcription of the poem, concluded that the text we have is almost certainly by Chaucer, that would still make quite a big splash in the scholarly world, even without having the physical manuscript to back it up. And your father would have the scholarly authority of Professor William Wentworth, one of the most eminent Oxford scholars, in support of him. In fact, the mysterious disappearance of the manuscript would probably add some additional spice to its celebrity."

"And Daddy would also have your word to back him up, right?"

"Yes, for what mine is worth – though at this point in my career that wouldn't count for a whole lot."

"But you could produce your photos of the original, couldn't you?"

"I could. Though it would be hard to verify their authenticity without the physical manuscript."

"How soon were you and the professor planning to go back to Oxford?" she asked, changing the subject. "Not tomorrow, I hope."

"I'm sure we'll be here another day or two. There's still a good bit to get sorted out before we go. And then we'll also have to figure out a way to pick up the professor's car in Somerset."

"Listen, if you stayed here until Saturday or Sunday, I could drive you up there to do that. I get to have this Saturday free, for a change."

Charles grinned. "I'll tell the professor," he said. "He might like that idea."

"Maybe you'd like it too?"

Charles gave her an additional squeeze but didn't reply. For the next several minutes they just held each other.

⁜ ⁜ ⁜

Earlier that day around mid-morning, Anna had gone with Mrs. Tremayne to the vicarage so the woman could retrieve the item she'd lent the vicar. As they walked along the gravel path, Anna couldn't help noticing the large bag the woman carried over one shoulder. It looked heavy.

Anna unlocked the vicarage and let the woman in. And then at her request she opened the study for her. Anna peeked in curiously, since she herself had never been allowed to go in, but before she'd been able to see much, the woman shut the door swiftly behind her, practically slamming it in Anna's face. Really quite rude. But Anna knew she'd better oblige the woman in every way she could. No sense getting her mistress, the dragon-lady, any more riled up than need be.

Anna occupied herself in the vicarage kitchen for a few minutes while the woman looked for whatever it was she wanted to find in the study. It seemed to Anna that the woman was taking longer in there than she would have expected, just to retrieve an item she'd lent him; but maybe she was having a hard time tracking it down.

As Anna puttered about, she noticed that one of the kitchen tea towels wasn't where it normally was. The vicar must have put it somewhere else, she thought. A bit surprising, since he was a man of strict habits and settled routines. Well, the missing towel would probably turn up, and if it didn't, it was no big loss. Maybe the vicar had spilled something on it and thrown it away.

Anna went back into the sitting room. She stepped over to the study door, stooped down and peeked through the old-fashioned keyhole. It didn't offer much of a view, but she could see the back of Mrs. Tremayne, who seemed to be doing something in a little curtained alcove. Then the woman swung around and looked straight toward the door.

Anna jerked herself upright, hoping the woman hadn't seen her eye through the keyhole. She called out to Mrs. Tremayne, "Can I give you any assistance, ma'am?"

"Oh no," her voice came back through the door. "I've just found what I was looking for." Only a few seconds later she came back into the sitting room.

"So everything is okay?" Anna said, who'd managed to retreat a few steps back toward the middle of the room.

"Oh, yes. Just took a little longer than I expected."

To Anna's eye, when Mrs. Tremayne stepped out of the study, her shoulder bag appeared less bulky than before. Had the woman really come to take something? Or to *leave* something?

Fifteen minutes later, Mrs. Tremayne said her farewells to Anna and the dragon-lady. She climbed into her car and drove away.

As Anna was returning the vicarage keys to the proper peg, the dragon-lady said, "Well, what was she was so eager to find in there?"

"I really don't know, ma'am. She said she'd found it, though it seemed to me her bag was lighter when she went away than when she'd come."

"Well, she must've found what she'd been looking for. She didn't seem displeased when she departed."

As for Anna, she was just glad that for once she hadn't displeased her own quick-to-criticize mistress.

✢✢✢

"So Charlie," Ally finally said, after a long silence, "what do you plan to do with the manuscript you brought back from the Minster Church?"

"Good question, Ally. I'm not quite sure. Do you have any suggestions?"

"Well, I might have. How about this? What if I were to stumble upon the missing manuscript, kind of just by accident?"

"The actual Polminster Manuscript? How could you do that?"

"No, silly, not *that* one. The one I would find is the one you brought back with you. What we would do, though, is pass it off as being the other one."

"You'd stumble upon it?"

"Yes, somewhere in the house. Then I would joyfully present it to my father as if it the original manuscript hadn't been stolen at all. The whole thing that just been some sort of innocent accident."

"Wow. Okay, keep going," Charles said, "this sounds kind of promising."

"I could discover it, for example, under a stack of clean towels in my linen closet – something along those lines. Find it where someone had inadvertently put it."

"Or maybe where a thief had stashed it, assuming it was a place no one would think to look."

"Okay, that too."

Charles nodded. "And then what?"

"How about this? Tonight, right after dinner when we're all gathered in the sitting room for coffee and sweets, I go upstairs for a moment to use my bathroom and then come running down all excited because I've found the manuscript. I rush over to Daddy and give it to him. And, while all that is occurring, you, sir, are making a careful study of Daddy's reactions. Is he beside himself with joy to have it back? Or is he something else?"

"Goodness, Ally, quite a scenario. So the point of the little charade would be to tell us whether or not your father was involved in the disappearance of the original manuscript. If he's genuinely ecstatic at the manuscript's unexpected recovery, he's innocent. If he shows any degree of displeasure, he was probably complicit in the manuscript's disappearance."

"That would be the idea, Charlie."

"Goodness, sounds like something straight from the pages of some old crime novel, Miss Marple."

"Charlie, I do hope you're not implying that I am some

grouchy old bag."

"You aren't some old bag, that's for sure. Grouchy? Well, as for that – "

Ally gave him a little poke and he gave her one right back. Then they found themselves laughing gleefully. For a moment, even the seagulls seemed to join in.

"Well . . . let's do it. Let's give this devious little plan a shot. But let me add just one thing to it. When you bring in the manuscript, be sure to do at a moment when Maria is in the room. It's just possible that her reaction will be as important as your father's."

"Maria? You suspect her?"

"Unless some outside thief really did break into the house and take the manuscript – which I don't believe for a second – then there are only four people who might have snatched it: you, your father, your stepmother, and Maria. You didn't do it, and I'm pretty confident your stepmother didn't. She had neither opportunity nor motive, as they say on TV."

"Okay, Charlie Chan, but still, maybe some outsider really did take it. Don't forget that someone took your car that very same night."

"Yeah, but stealing the car wouldn't have been all that hard to do, sitting out there on the driveway in the darkness, unlocked and unguarded. But breaking into your father's locked study, and then into a safe which few people even knew about – and hardly any knew the combination to – that would have taken some real know-how. Almost certainly an inside job."

"Charlie," she said, "do you really think you should be excluding me from the list?"

"Well . . . I *think* so. Unless there's a side to your character you haven't yet shown me."

"You think you've got me totally figured out, do you?"

"*Totally* figured out? I'm not sure that's within the realm of possibility."

"You can say that again."

"I'm not sure that's – "

Before he could finish, he felt a sharp elbow impacting his ribs.

When they got back to the house an hour later, before going to her own room to dress for dinner, Ally made a short detour to Charles' room. When she left, she was carrying a reusable plastic bag. Sainsbury's it said on it.

23

Clare Reilly leaned against the heavy iron railing above the brown-gray water of the Thames on the south bank of the river. She looked across at Savoy Palace, then shifted her gaze to the left toward Westminster Bridge, the Big Ben bell tower, and the Houses of Parliament. Beyond that, she saw the towers of Westminster Abbey. On this side of the river, well-dressed people moved behind her toward the Southbank Centre.

Clare had stopped for an after-work drink at the Three Tuns with several of her colleagues, but after an hour she excused herself to wander off alone. She planned a leisurely journey home to her little bed-sit just off the Bayswater Road. Even though her flat was extremely modest, she could still just barely afford it; but the location allowed her to walk and jog in Hyde Park. That was compensation enough.

Clare knew that by leaving the pub by herself she'd disappointed Peter Blanchard, the young attorney who'd been trying to court her. She'd gone out to dinner with him once and they'd also taken in a play, but Clare didn't wish to offer the fellow further encouragement. Peter was a good guy for sure, but she didn't want to develop a relationship with him. Never get involved with a co-worker, she believed. Besides, she could be transferred back to the U.S. – or maybe someplace else in Europe – at any time. Best not to develop emotional entanglements.

As she soaked up the London evening, her thoughts turned to Charlie Bascombe. It was two evenings earlier that she'd found the email message from Charlie on her laptop. Realizing what it was, she'd felt a twinge of nervous excitement in her stomach.

She'd read through the message once, then a second time. It was typical Charlie. Brief, somewhat guarded, emotionally neutral. Still, she couldn't help smiling at it. It was the first communication she'd had from him in ten years. Oh, Charlie, she sighed.

Charlie's message said Jack had told him that Clare was now living and working in London. He wondered, his message said, if Clare might be willing to get together with him. He hoped she would be, and that maybe she could come to Oxford some day soon for lunch. Or, if she preferred, maybe he could come to London. He said his schedule was flexible. He said it would be great to see her, that it had been much too long. That was it. Not a single hint about what had happened between them Yes, it was typical Charlie.

Clare had sat there for another minute staring at the computer screen and smiling. Oh, Charlie, she said to herself again, yes, it has definitely been much too long.

That was two nights ago, and Clare hadn't replied yet. Now, as she walked along the south side of the river, she knew she'd better do that this evening when she got home. She'd made him wait just about the right amount of time. She didn't want to seem *too* eager. But it wasn't fair to leave him hanging for too long, either.

Clare climbed the steps to the Hungerford Footbridge and started across. Then she stopped at the mid-point to look downriver. This was one of her favorite viewpoints in London. She could see the dome of St. Paul's, and then a little ways to the left, the slender, wedding-cake spire of St. Bride's Church, still visible amidst all the tall structures that threatened to engulf it – both of them designed, she knew, by the indefatigable Christopher Wren. The river traffic beneath her this evening was light, but when the loud music from a party boat intruded upon her thoughts, she decided it was time to move on.

Clare crossed the bridge and entered the Embankment Underground Station. She would hop on the Bakerloo Line and take the tube to Marble Arch. Tonight she would sit down and give Charlie a reply.

On most evenings during her ride on the tube Clare amused herself by studying all the colorful characters inside her coach. The Underground was great for people-watching. Tonight, though, her thoughts were more taken up by something else – what she should say to Charlie Bascombe.

✛✛✛

Tonight the dining room was illuminated by candles. Charles Bascombe and Professor William Wentworth stood gazing at a very old-looking tapestry, rife with the forms of animals and a mounted hunter, amidst lush vegetation. "Reminds me of some of the tapestries I've seen in The Cloisters Museum in New York," Charles said.

"Do you recognize the subject matter?" the professor asked.

Charles looked at it closely for a long moment. "I'm pretty sure it's not Mad Meg," he said. The professor emitted a soft snort at the remark. "No," Charles went on, "I think it's probably the Saint Eustace legend. The crucifix between the stag's antlers kind of gives it away, doesn't it?"

"Well done, Charlie. No flies on you, eh lad?" Flies? For a moment Charles thought about the lack of screens on the windows in Britain.

Rhys Tremayne was seated down at one end of the long, gleaming table, his wife at the other. The professor was placed on Rhys's left, Charles on his right. Ally, beside the professor, sat across from Jack. The arrangement might have encouraged the three men at one end to spend the whole meal talking shop, but Ailish Tremayne announced at the outset that shoptalk was strictly forbidden. "You can do all of that later over coffee, but for right now, let's have no talk of manuscripts and dusty old poets. Let's hear about Ally's recent paintings. Let's have Jackson's impressions of our beloved Duchy of Cornwall."

Ally happily told them about the new painting she'd just begun, though she kept them focused mostly on her experiments in style and technique. On the matter of what it depicted she seemed a bit reticent.

"Come on, Ally, what's it *of?*" Jack insisted.

"It depicts a very traditional Cornish legend," she said. "Beyond that, I ain't sayin' another word." She held a finger and thumb at one corner of her mouth and made a zipping motion.

"You make it seem rather mysterious," Ailish said.

"Ally likes to be mysterious," Jack said. "Not like my pal Charlie. Good old Charlie's a completely open book. Nothing mysterious about Charlie Bascombe."

Charles shrugged. "What you see is what you get."

"Oh no," Ailish declared. "Brief as my acquaintance with Charles has been, I feel quite certain that his 'Innocent Abroad' image is just the one he's chosen to project."

"Ha, ha, ha," laughed the professor. "She's got you pegged, Charlie," he said.

"She has indeed," Ally agreed. "Charlie's not just some dry as dust academic who thinks about nothing but lost poems by Geoffrey Chaucer or Bach cantatas and fugues. That shy introvert demeanor is merely a pose. I'm quite certain that Charlie Bascombe, in fact, is a bit of a dark horse."

Charles placed the fingers of his two hands against his chest and dipped his head as if to say, "Who, me?"

"Well, all right, I'll grant he has a *few* eccentricities," Jack said. "For one thing, you probably never would've guessed that he's a whiz at darts. Old Charlie can give those blokes in the pub a good run for their money. That's something, I suppose."

"A skill not to be scoffed at," Rhys Tremayne said. "Once upon a time Neville and I – a pair of dull and boring bookworms – were two of the very best in Oxford, you know." A note of sadness had crept into his words, for it was only yesterday, the day before the travelers returned, that he'd learned of his friend's death.

"I remember how you and Neville would creep out of your rooms at night and trudge off to The Bear, where you'd show those pampered Christ Church lads a thing or two," the professor said. "You were the absolute best at hitting the triple ring."

"No, Nev was better. But we made a formidable team."

Ailish Tremayne smiled with pleasure as she listened to the two old friends reminisce about their bygone days in Oxford.

Her husband's happiness meant a great deal to Ailish Tremayne. He was an odd and eccentric man, and many of her friends had wondered at her when she'd chosen to accept his proposal of marriage. She hadn't regretted her decision. They gave each other respect and affection and sufficient personal space, things each of them greatly needed. He had never failed to support her in her career, and he wasn't threatened in the least by her success. The man dearly loved his old books, but he loved his wife every bit as much. Theirs was a relationship that worked quite well.

⁜⁜⁜

In Porthleven, just a few miles from Helston, a green Ford Fiesta sat parked out behind a small guesthouse amongst the several other cars in the guesthouse's crowded car park. The popular B&B was now fully booked for the next three months, and as a result the proprietress had needed to add extra staff for the high season. Charming the guests most mornings and evenings was a slim redhead who served as the hostess. Her thick-bodied male companion helped out with preparing morning breakfast for the guests, and he also helped out by performing routine maintenance for the property. Another young woman, a part-time employee, helped in serving the guests their breakfasts.

This evening, most of the guests were still out at the pubs or maybe sitting down by the harbor watching the boats come in and the dark storm clouds approaching. Porthleven was quite a scenic little village, and some of the guidebooks to Cornwall referred to it as the most storm-battered village in all of England. It still had a small working fleet of fishing boats, and while it had become a popular tourist destination, the village preserved a feeling of authenticity.

In the private sitting room in the guesthouse, a prune-faced woman was conversing with her two assistants, the slender redhead and her burly friend. Their talk this night didn't primarily concern goings-on at the guesthouse. Rather, it concerned events that had occurred during the past couple of days up near the north coast of Cornwall; and it also involved speculations about what might now be occurring at a large manor house not many miles away.

Mrs. Lowenna Tremayne, the prune-faced woman, seemed quite pleased with what she and Dargan and Mick had accomplished. Events had transpired exactly as she'd hoped they might. Now they would just have to wait and see if the seeds they'd sown would produce the results for which she wished.

✦✦✦

They'd relocated from the dining room to the sitting room, and now Charles Bascombe and William Wentworth, seated across from each other on two of the facing sofas in Rhys Tremayne's large sitting room, were poring over typed-up versions of the transcription of the Chaucerian poem Rhys Tremayne had had prepared during their short absence.

Ally, sitting next to Charles, glanced at the pages also, though with inexpert eyes.

Jack sat beside the professor, his eyes flicking back and forth between the two very attractive women in the room.

Ailish and Rhys Tremayne sat close together on the sofa facing the fireplace, Rhys fidgeting and Ailish studying the expressions that flitted across Charles Bascombe's face. If Charles' words didn't often give much away, his facial expressions often did.

"Nice job," Charles said, looking up and nodding his head. "Sir, this looks really good. Thanks a lot for having this done while we were off on our sightseeing trek. This will be very helpful," he said, tapping the sheaf of pages. "Once I've double checked it against my transcription, I'll get right to work on the editing. Sir, this makes me really excited."

"And perhaps it will make you famous, Charlie," Ally said.

"Hardly," Charles said with a laugh. "But it might help to solve a mystery that has eluded Chaucer scholars for the last six hundred years." He returned the document to its folder and set it on the low table at the end of the sofa.

"And maybe it will get you tenure," Jack added.

"One can always hope," Charles said.

"I don't wish to rush you," Rhys said, "but now, I hope,

217

you will give it your full attention."

"No question, sir. This can't wait. The other things I've been doing in Oxford, compared to this, they *can* wait."

"Splendid. Well, who would like coffee?"

"I would," said Ally, "just as soon as I've made a quick trip to the loo. Excuse me for a moment, would you?" She arose from the sofa and hurried from the room.

"How much longer will you be staying?" Ailish asked. "At least a few more days, I hope."

"Oh, that reminds me," Charles said. "Professor, if you don't mind staying on here until Saturday, Ally says she could drive us to Yeovil to pick up your car."

"Oh, Charlie, that would be excellent. I'd been wondering how we would do that. Yes, that would be excellent indeed."

"Could I catch a train from there to London?" Jack asked.

"Most definitely," Rhys said.

"Then you'd better plan to use my old Jaguar again," Ailish said. "With four of you, plus all your luggage, you couldn't possibly do it in Ally's car."

"Yay," Jack said. "I *love* driving that buggy of yours, Mrs. Tremayne. Makes me feel just like the little old lady from Pasadena. Right, Professor?"

"'There's nobody meaner than the little old lady from Pasadener,'" the professor said, slightly misquoting the line.

"'Go, granny, go,'" added Charles. Rhys and Ailish exchanged baffled expressions.

"From one of those old Beach Boys songs," the professor explained. "A bit before your time, Ailish."

Then they heard rapid footfalls sounding on the main staircase, the footfalls of someone who seemed in quite a hurry. Ally whooshed into the room, cradling in her arms a hefty object. With alacrity she moved toward her father, then carefully deposited the object in his lap.

"Daddy! Could this be *it*? Could this be what you thought someone had *stolen*?"

Just a moment earlier, Maria had entered the room with a tray of after-dinner sweets. Seeing what Ally was doing, Maria froze where she stood. Did Charles detect a slight trembling of her hands? Maria quickly set the tray down on an end table and stood there perfectly still, perfectly alert, her eyes on Rhys Tremayne's face.

By then Rhys Tremayne was staring at the large tome his daughter had placed in his lap. A variety of emotions began flashing across his countenance: surprise, shock, wonderment, undisguised delight, perhaps even a tear.

"Alwyn," he said, "oh, my dearest Alwyn."

Then cautiously, gingerly, he began to run his fingers over the thick leather cover of the tome. Finally he opened the volume at random and gazed upon a manuscript page. "Hmm. Something about the spleen, I think," he mumbled to himself. Charles knew he must have opened it to a page in the section on medicine.

A moment later, now with a specific goal in mind, Rhys Temayne slowly turned the leaves of the manuscript until he reached folio 28r, the page on which the poem he cared so much about began. And there it was, Chaucer's famous lost work – or so he hoped.

"Charles, William," he said, "we've *got* it." His last words were spoken so softly that he could barely be heard.

He stared at Ally, who'd sat down next to Charles. "But

219

Alwyn, where . . . ," he began. "How . . . ?"

"Daddy, it was in my linen closet, of all places. Buried under a stack of towels. Don't ask me how it got there. I reached in to pull out a towel from low in the stack and then my fingers touched something a lot firmer than a towel. Daddy, I didn't put it there. Is it really your missing manuscript?"

Ailish said, "It really has to be. Oh, Ally, well done. You've just made your father a very, very happy man."

Apparently she had. Charles couldn't detect any sign of displeasure in Rhys Tremayne's reactions. He seemed truly astonished, there wasn't any doubt about that; he didn't appear at all miffed. The joy shining from his face couldn't be anything but genuine.

Maria's face, to Charles' eye, showed equal bafflement. But *not* equal delight. The poor woman looked totally confused. She had clasped her hands together and was now twisting them nervously.

"Yes, my dear," Rhys Tremayne said at last to his daughter, "this is absolutely it. But *mirabile dictu*, how could it have found its way into your linen closet? I'm absolutely dumbfounded."

"You do look rather gob-smacked, Rhys," the professor said. "As am I." And perhaps he was, since Charles and Ally hadn't told anyone else in the room about their little ruse – though the smirk on Jack's face said it had taken him about half a second to guess what was going on.

For a long moment everyone sat in silence while their host continued to study the object he held in his hands.

"Now *this* is rather odd," he said at last. "Certainly don't know what to make of it."

"What's odd, Rhys?" the professor asked.

"This leather cover and binding. Look at it."

"What about it?" Ailish asked.

"Why, it's nearly pristine. No small cracks or other indications of wear and tear on the spine, no small discolorations on front or back, no frayed bottom edges. Charles, the bottom edge of the back cover? Do you remember how rough it felt to the touch? As if the leather had become abraded from being pulled many times from a shelf?"

"Actually, sir, I can't say I noticed that."

"Goodness me, goodness me. William? Do you think someone could have gone to the trouble of having the thing rebound before stashing it among Ally's towels? Now why on earth would anyone do that?"

"Dear," said Ailish, "that hardly seems likely."

"No, no, you're quite right. Hardly likely. Still, I'm one hundred percent certain that this is *not* the same cover, though much like it. Same thickness of leather, same basic color, made from virtually identical material. And yet, this one is in much finer condition. It's *newer*. Hasn't yet acquired the patina of age. Quite nice, actually. But not the same." The man heaved his shoulders and expelled a deep breath.

"Well," he went on, "at least the contents seem unaltered. All in all, one has to conclude that this really is the Polminster Manuscript. Yes, one must. And yet . . . and yet. William . . . I have to say that I am really baffled."

24

After the professor and the Tremaynes had gone off to bed, Ally, Jack, and Charles piled into Ally's roadster and headed toward Helston. Ally sat behind the wheel, Charles beside her, Jack in back. Taking up Ally's suggestion that the three of them should get away from the house for a bit, they were now en route to "The George" – The Saint George & the Dragon Public House – a popular local pub Ally said would still be open for a couple more hours.

"So," Jack asked, "whose bright idea was it to have the Polminster Manuscript miraculously turn up in Ally's linen closet?" He gave a half-laugh. The surprise plan of attack had amused him.

"Kind of a team effort," Charles replied, "though Ally's more than mine."

"Professor wasn't in on it?"

"Nope. Wanted to keep everyone in the dark," Charles said.

"You definitely succeeded," Jack said, "you dark horse."

"Wanted to see how people would react, especially Ally's father. We hoped his reaction to the manuscript's sudden reappearance would tell us whether he'd been complicit in the manuscript's disappearance. Judging by how delighted he was, that seems to put him in the clear. So Ally was right about her father, and I was wrong."

"But keeping an eye on Maria," Ally said, "that was Charlie's bright idea."

"*Maria*? You suspected *her*?"

"Charlie did," Ally said. "And if I was right about my

father, it looks like he was right about Maria. You probably didn't notice, Jack, but she was doing everything she could to control her emotions. Made quite a brave effort, too, but all the signs were still there. The manuscript turning up in my linen closet must've given her quite a jolt."

"Manderley," Jack said, "Mrs. Danvers."

"Maria showed remarkable aplomb," Charles went on, "carried it off really well. Just not quite well enough. And ten minutes later she slips off to make a private phone call. Why would she do that? Highly suspicious."

"But if she's the one who nabbed the real manuscript," Jack said, "wouldn't she still have it stashed away somewhere in the house?"

"Not if she'd already passed it on," Charles said, "which is what I'm guessing she did. If she'd already disposed of it, having it suddenly turn up again like that must've nearly blown her mind." Ally gave a little giggle.

"Well," Jack said, "let's hope *this* one doesn't get stolen tonight."

"Daddy will be guarding it like a griffon guards his gold," Ally said. "Probably sleep next to it. I can see him in his locked study, lying on his futon right beneath his safe. He's probably already changed the combination, too."

"Griffons guard their gold?" Jack said. "Something I didn't know."

Ally pulled around behind The George and parked in the pub's rear car park. Then the three of them made their way around the side of the building to the front entrance.

"Poor *wyrm*," Charles said, as they passed beneath a colorfully painted pub sign depicting an armored knight seated on a prancing stallion. The knight was impaling the scaly, dark green, open-mouthed creature that slithered beneath the horse's front hooves.

"Worm?" Jack said.

"*W . . . y . . . r . . . m.* The Anglo-Saxon word for dragon or serpent."

"Kind of a big worm. And man, what a set of chompers!" Jack said, in reference to the dragon's long, razor-like teeth. He whipped out his cell phone and clicked a picture of the sign.

The George was surprisingly busy for a Wednesday night. The front section of the pub, once the saloon bar intended for the gents or middle-class patrons, was jam-packed, so they got their drinks at the bar and pushed on through into the back section. This scruffier part of the pub had once been the public bar, where the working class could come in their grubby work clothes and buy their pints a few pence more cheaply. The George, like most British pubs, no longer maintained this Victorian distinction. Now this section, with its bare wooden floors and inexpensive furnishings, had become the games room. It, too, was quite packed, mostly with a younger crowd, but Ally spotted a small table off in a corner a good distance from the dartboard, and they snagged it.

The room reverberated with a cacophony of youthful voices, the *clacking* of pool balls, the *thunking* of darts, and Rod Stewart's gravelly voice telling Maggie May he really should be back in school. A good-sized group had clustered about the dartboard where a fierce battle was in progress.

Charles crammed himself into the small, tight space in

the corner behind the table, giving Jack and Ally a bit more elbow room. Ally looked at her two companions, smiled, and held up her glass of scrumpy. "Cheers," she said, extending her arm toward them. Jack raised his double of Jameson, Charles his half pint of Penryn Pale Ale, and the three of them clinked glasses. "Cheers," the two men replied.

"I'm guessing this is not your father's local," Jack said.

"Uh, no," Ally replied, "not hardly. Nor is any other pub in the whole of Cornwall his favorite local."

"Does he still play darts?" Charles asked. "From what the professor said, it sounded like he was once quite a player."

"Oh yes, I should say he was. You probably haven't been in our billiards room. We don't use it much anymore, but there's an amazing dartboard cupboard in there, probably a hundred and fifty years old. My grandfather was once county champion, and he taught Daddy all the intricacies of the game. When I was a girl, Daddy and I played a good bit. Daddy passed on some of the tricks of the trade to me, too, which I put to good use while at school. Dargan Owens and I could hold our own against the best boy players. We got a big charge out of destroying their fragile egos."

"Charlie has a dartboard in his office at the college," Jack said, "right?" Charles nodded. "Still play much, Charlie?"

"No, not so much the last couple of years."

"At college, Charlie was dorm league champ three years running," Jack said. "He's too modest to ever mention that."

"Modesty is Charlie's middle name," Ally said.

"That's not what he claims," Jack said.

"What does he claim?"

"He claims his middle name is equanimity." Ally tilted

her head. She seemed to be considering that possibility.

"As for Charlie's so-called modesty, ha, ha, if you only knew the truth about *that*," Jack said.

Two of them laughed while the other looked as if his equanimity might be hanging in the balance. Charles balled one hand into a fist, then gave Jack a good-natured punch in the shoulder.

"Ow," Jack said. "I *felt* that. Still, Mike Tyson you ain't."

The darts game had come to an end and so had The Police's "Every Breath You Take," and many of the onlookers began drifting away. Ally, seated to Charles' right, had her back to the darts area, but Jack, to Charles' left, now had a clear sight of the participants. And the guy who'd obviously won – a thick-torsoed, black-bearded fellow who was basking in the adulation of his friends – looked familiar to Jack. Where had he seen him before? Ah, yes, it was at that pub in St. Ives on Jack's first night in Cornwall. Then stepping into Jack's line of sight was the young woman who'd been keeping score on the chalkboard. The slender, attractive redhead was very definitely someone Jack had observed before. Someone he'd *keenly* observed before.

"Don't look now," Jack said to his companions, motioning with his head in the direction of the dartboard, but there's a couple of people over there with whom Charlie and I have already crossed paths."

"Oh, boy," Charles said, now also seeing the couple. "Must be our lucky night."

"Or not," replied Ally, who'd swung about and stared across the room at Dargan and Thick Mick. "If we're lucky, they won't notice us. The truth is, I've never been one of their favorite people."

"Why not?" Jack asked.

"Far too toffee-nosed, in their view."

"You? Toffee-nosed?" Jack said. "Not true at all."

"You, sir, are a gentleman," she replied. Ally reached out and patted the back of his hand, then raised her glass of scrumpy. Jack raised his Jameson, and they clinked glasses once more.

Mick's deep voice suddenly resounded through the room. "All right, then, who's up next? Who's got winners, eh?" he shouted. But Mick got no response. No one seemed eager to be the brash fellow's next victim.

"C'mon folks, who's next?" Mick bellowed once more.

Thick Mick began walking from table to table, trying to cajole or bully one of his friends into taking him on.

"Alf, you ain't played a single game t'night. Yor one helluva player, mate. So how's about it, eh?"

"Hafta pass tonight, Mick. Me arm's a bit sore, like."

"Not no single taker, huh?" Mick shouted. "Well, okay then, ya wankers, here's what I'm gonna do." He pulled out a bill and smacked it down hard on a tabletop. "Twenty quid. Twenty quid to the blighter who beats me. Ya don't hafta put up nuthin'. It ain't a bet, it's an offer. You win, the twenty's yours, free 'n clear. You don't got nuthin' ta lose, but ya shor got somethin' ta win. Twenty quid!"

Mick just stood there for a moment, extending his arms out from his sides, his empty palms forward. Still no takers. "Well, shit," he muttered, disgusted.

As he continued scanning the room, Mick's eyes finally lit upon the threesome seated at the small table in the far corner. Mick paused for a moment to stare at them, a slightly puzzled look on his face. Then recognition slowly dawned.

"Well, would ya look at who's here. Dargan," he shouted across the room to her, "look who's here. It's Ally! Ally Tremayne!"

Dargan Owens turned and looked. As she crossed the room a big smile appeared on her face. She stopped and stood next to the table, her head cocked to one side, one hand on her chin, the other on her hip.

"Well, hiya," she finally said to Ally.

"Hiya, Dargan," Ally replied.

"Hiya, Dargan," Jack added, staring at the redheaded vision, a big silly smile pasted on his face. Dargan ignored him.

"Ally," Mick said, "I remember you used ta toss a right fair dart. Yeah? So how's about a game?"

"Nah, nah, we'll just be finishing our drinks, Mick, and then we'll heading out. Thanks all the same, though."

"What about you?" he said to Jack. "You look like a bloke who could toss a pretty fair dart."

"Never once played," said Jack. "With me, I'm afraid, it wouldn't be much fun. I'd have no chance of giving you a contest."

"Huh," Mick grunted, still staring at Jack. Then he turned his attention to Charles. "How 'bout you?" Mick said, pointing his thick forefinger at Charles. "You got any more balls than this here bloke got?"

Charles wasn't quite sure what he should say, so for the moment he said nothing.

"*Speak up*, laddy, can't quite hear ya. Cat got your tongue or summat?" Mick spat out in disgust.

"As Ally's already told you," Charles finally said, "we were just about to leave. So maybe we could have a game some other time, okay?"

"Some other time? Well, fuck it!" Mick bellowed out. "Ya can't even stay for one little fuckin' game o' darts? Just one little game o' darts and a free twenty quid ta the winner, and all you can do is whine about how you 'really have to go.' What kinda poncy friends ya got here, Ally? A couple o' fuckin' pansies, yeah? That's kinda how it seems ta me."

Charles' chest rose as he sucked in a very deep breath. Then he slowly expelled it. With slow deliberation, Charles began to raise himself up from his chair. He stood there for a long moment, then came around the table and took a step toward Mick. Now the two men were staring each other in the face, though Charles, two or three inches taller, had to dip his head slightly to look Mick straight in the eyes.

"So you wish to have one little fuckin' game of darts, do you?" Charles said. "That's what all this bellowing is about? Well, okay then, why don't we have your little fuckin' game of darts."

Charles reached into his back pocket and pulled out his billfold, opened it, and took out a twenty-pound note. He held it in his hand for a moment, then slapped it down hard on the table.

"Okay, bubba," Charles said, "you can have your little game o' darts. But first you have to accept my two conditions."

Mick stood there looking nonplussed, his arms folded across his stout chest. "Conditions, huh," he grunted. "The pansy's got conditions!" he shouted out to the room, bringing a few titters and gaffaws. "Well, let's hear 'em."

"Forty pounds goes to the winner," Charles said, "my twenty plus yours. If we're going to play this little game of darts, there won't be anything free about it. We put up an equal stake. That's the first condition."

"Like a bet, yeah? Well, that's how ya want it, that's how yor gonna get it. And what else?"

"It won't be just you against me. It'll be a team game. You and Dargan against me and Ally."

Mick opened his eyes a bit wider. He gave his beard a good scratch. He jutted out his bottom lip. At last he began to nod slowly. "Fair 'nough," he said, "fair 'nough. Teams it'll be. That be all right with you, Dargan?"

"Oh, yes indeed," Dargan said. She was grinning ear to ear. "I have to say I like that idea very much. It'll be just like old times, eh?" she said, shooting Ally a wink.

"I'll hold the twenties," Jack said. He scooped up the pair of bills and jammed them in his pants pocket.

Mick and Dargan swung about and headed back in the direction of the dartboard. Several of their friends followed in their wake, wanting to get ringside seats. The Doors' "Riders on the Storm" began playing on the jukebox.

"Charlie," Ally said softly, "I don't think you quite realize what you just got us into. Dargan's a highly skilled player, and as for me, yes, I was once pretty good. But I haven't tossed a dart in a good long while."

"Makes no difference, Ally. So we get creamed. What the hell? If we lose my twenty, no big deal. The only thing I really care about is we don't let Mr. Big Stuff think he can push us around the same way he can bully his so-called pals.

And besides, Ally, it's nothing more than a little fuckin' game of darts, right?"

" 'That which we are, we are,' " Jack declaimed, " 'made weak by time and fate but strong in will, to strive, to seek, to find, and not to yield.' "

"Thanks for that, Alfred Lord," Ally said, looking at Jack askance. "You always did have a way with words. But, since Charlie says it's just a game, I'll try my best to keep that in mind."

"Charlie says it's just a game? Ally, with Charlie, nothing is *ever* just a game. In this darts game, someone's going to be playing for blood. And that someone, Ally, won't just be Thick Mick."

✤✤✤

A couple of hours earlier Lowenna Tremayne had placed the receiver back down and smiled an unaccustomed smile. Maria's news delighted her. Her complicated ruse appeared to be well on its way to working. Poor Maria. The woman seemed in quite a panic, not understanding at all how the manuscript could have suddenly turned up again. Probably best not to explain anything further to her, Lowenna thought.

She'd thanked Maria for letting her know and told her not to worry, that everything was quite all right.

"But missus, how'd it get there?" Maria had said.

"Did he seem pleased?" she'd asked, ignoring Maria's question.

"Oh yes, indeed. Most pleased, the master were."

"That's the important thing, Maria. So you just go about your business as usual. If anything else strange should occur, please let me know. Otherwise, why don't we just let sleeping dogs lie."

Lowenna Tremayne also couldn't help wondering how it was that the manuscript happened to be "found" in Ally's linen closet. That was quite perplexing. Ally's doing, probably. She'd never been able to read what went on in her daughter's mind very well. The two of them were as different as chalk and cheese.

Well, the important thing was that they now had the manuscript she wanted them to have, and that they believed they'd recovered the original version. Yes, that was just what she'd hoped for.

Lowenna Tremayne went so far as to indulge in a small chuckle.

✤✤✤

Clare Reilly had been walking for the better part of an hour – left down the Bayswater Road toward Marble Arch and Speakers' Corner, where she listened for a bit to one lunatic railing about the evils of Brexit (not that she herself was in favor of Brexit) and then a second railing against the evils of genetically modified crops (a point of view with which she had some sympathy).

Then Clare started back in the direction of her flat, strolling along a broad graveled path that angled through Hyde Park. Close to the Serpentine she found an empty bench and sat down. She'd brought along a paperback copy of *Middlemarch*, thinking she might read while there was still some evening light. She opened her book to where she'd bookmarked it, but then began staring off into space. She found herself thinking about the email message she'd sent to Charlie before starting her walk.

Then she found herself recalling that fateful night a decade ago, when she'd made a very stupid decision, a decision that had cost her her relationship with Charlie. Why had she decided to leave the party with Professor René Bouchard – God's Gift to the Undergraduettes, as Charlie liked to call him – the English department's most notorious seducer of co-eds. As handsome and charming as the asshole was, she had despised him as much or more than Charlie had. And yet . . . and yet. Well, that was in another country; and besides, the wench is dead . . . or something like that.

Clare sighed. What would it be like to see Charlie again? she wondered. How would they greet each other? What would they say to each other? Maybe all was forgiven, and Charlie would be delighted to see her. Clare's subconscious desire to see Charlie had definitely emerged into the light of her conscious thoughts. Yes, she really did want to see Charlie again, despite how much his judging her had hurt her.

She'd spent several long minutes mulling over the email message before she sent it to him. She'd wanted it to sound warm and friendly, yet not *too* eager. In the end, she felt she'd got it about right. She'd also given a good bit of thought about what to suggest as to their meeting place. Ideally, Oxford, she'd decided.

She'd considered asking him to come to London for one of the Proms Concerts, which she knew would be starting soon at the Albert Hall. The Proms would be just Charlie's cup of tea. But then she'd realized that going to a late-night concert together might create some real awkwardness, for it would inevitably raise the question of whether Charlie should stay overnight. That sounded to her like a no-win situation. Making him return to Oxford on a late-night train would seem rather cold; yet inviting him to spend the night in her flat the very first time they'd seen each other in a decade could be awkward and might also be filled with certain risks.

No, she finally decided, it would be safer for her to go to Oxford, probably on a Saturday or Sunday, and meet Charlie just for lunch. So she told him she'd really like to come and see him in Oxford, that her weekends for the next month were wide open. She could come on any day that suited him.

The possibility of seeing Charlie again, after ten years without any contact at all, was a bit scary, for sure. Still, Clare had to admit to herself that the prospect of doing that made her very excited.

25

"So, what's the game?" Charles asked. "Around the World? Cricket? Legs?" The four of them were standing in the dartboard area, the onlookers having formed a wide circle about them. The jukebox had gone silent and no one seemed to mind.

"Har," Mick said in response to Charles. "Only one game, boyo, and it ain't none o' them."

"301?" Ally said. "Takes a good bit of math, Mick. You okay with that?"

"Not me, her," he said, jerking his thumb in the direction of one of Dargan's friends. The woman was already at the chalkboard, erasing the scores from the previous game.

Jack felt someone nudge him in the ribs. "Like ta make a little side bet, mate?" said the beery fellow standing next to him. "Mebbe a tenner?"

"Uh, no, no, I think I'll pass."

"C'mon now. What kinda friend're you? Ya wanna bet on yor pals, doncha?"

"Oh, well, okay then," Jack said. He didn't want the guy to think he wasn't loyal to his friends. "Sure, I'll go a tenner."

" 'Course ya will," the fellow said. "A mate's always gotta bet on his mates. Stick by 'em, like."

Mick was toeing the touchline, tossing a few darts at the board. *Thunk, thunk, thunk.* The last one landed square in the bull's eye.

"Mind if we take a few warmups too?" Ally asked. She'd been looking over the assortment of available darts, checking them out one by one for heft and feel.

"Don't mind a bit. Two sets o' three for each of yas, eh?"

Ally, having selected her darts, stepped up to the line. She stared at the board for a moment, then made her first toss; it landed right on the number 19, just a little outside the double ring. Her warmup throw brought jeers of derision from some of the onlookers. "Least she didn't miss the whole fuckin' board!" someone shouted scornfully.

"Your twenty quid's lookin' bloody safe, Mick," someone chortled.

"As if there was any doubt," someone else added.

The rest of Ally's tosses looked at least a bit more promising. None of them threatened the bull's eye, but they weren't as close to being complete misses as her first dart.

Charles' warm-up tosses were more impressive. He was

targeting the bull's eye, and though none of his tosses hit it, they formed a neat little circle around it. But what drew derisive jeers for Charles wasn't the result of his throws, it was his style of throwing. With his left foot forward, Charles rocked back just a little on his right leg and then brought his entire body forward behind his right arm. He looked a lot like a pitcher throwing a baseball.

"Used ta chuck 'em for the Yankees," some wag said, causing a small ripple of mirth.

Amidst a good bit of additional heckling, Charles and Ally finished their warm-ups, then stepped aside.

"Let's throw ta see who goes first, eh?" said Mick.

"Go ahead," Charles said to Dargan.

Dargan stepped up to the line, leaned forward, and with a small flick of her wrist threw her dart at the center of the board. It grazed the outer single bull, drawing *oohs* from the onlookers.

Ally threw next, her dart landing in the 16, midway between the narrow triple and the outer bull. A decent throw, but not as good as Dargan's.

Then it was Mick. Leaning forward, concentrating hard, he stood poised for a moment, then flicked the fingers of his right hand. It was an excellent toss, landing just outside the bull's eye but inside the single bull. "Yay, Mick!" shouted several of his chums.

Charles stepped up and went through his baseball pitcher's routine, then rocked and fired. His dart landed with a goodly *thunk*. It was in the 20 section, just an inch above the single bull. It was an excellent throw, though not as good as either Dargan's or Mick's.

To begin the game of 301, a player has to score a double by landing the dart in the slender outer-most ring on the dartboard. Until that happens, throws produce no points that can be subtracted from 301, the total with which each player or team begins. Likewise, the game has to end by hitting a double, and that throw has to bring the player's total precisely to zero. It sometimes takes a few turns for a team to get started, and the end game is especially tricky, involving both strategy and math. Throws that would make the player's total less than zero don't count.

Since they were playing a team game, the players would alternate their sets of throws. Dargan would go first, Ally next, then Mick, and finally Charles.

Dargan Owens stood poised before the dartboard, her long red hair braided into a single thick braid that reached half way down her back. Jack Lockhart, along with probably every other man in the room, couldn't help admiring the young woman's slender, athletic form. Dargan held one of her bare, lightly freckled arms cocked just above and in front of her shoulder; with the other she was gripping her left thigh. Jack couldn't help admiring her tight leather pants and her black T-shirt.

Dargan's first throw landed just above the double 19, her next two just below it. "So, so close, Dargan," someone yelled encouragingly. Good throws, but counting for nothing.

Ally's very first throw landed squarely in the double 16, opening the scoring for their team and bringing vulgar imprecations from some of Mick's loyal fans. "Beginner's luck," someone shouted. "I got a tenner says ya can't do it again."

Ally's next two throws, a 7 and a single 16, dropped their total to 246. The friend of Dargan's who'd taken over chalkboard duties scrawled the appropriate numbers on the board.

Mick wasted no time putting his team back into the lead, hitting a double twenty on his first throw, a single twenty on his second, just missing a triple twenty – bringing groans and "oh no's" from his pals – but then only a 1 on his third, which just skimmed the wire between the 20 segment and the 1 segment. Dargan's friend recorded their team score of 240.

Charles also concentrated on throwing twenties, and he hit two of them. Then, like Mick, his third dart scored just a 1. His 41 points brought their total down to 205.

"This ain't gonna be no walkover," Jack's betting partner said. "Looks like yor pal and Ally gonna give 'em a fight. Shor didn't expect it."

"You ready for a refill," Jack said, pointing to the guy's empty glass.

The guy nodded and handed the glass to Jack. "Pint o' Penryn, eh?"

"You got it," Jack said and headed off for the bar.

Dargan's next set of throws dropped their score to 161, and Ally's dropped theirs to 181. Mick hit a triple 20, followed by a 1 and a 5. They were now below 100. Charles hit another 20, a 1, and then a triple 20, lowering their total to 100 on the nose. Charles' triple brought a cheer from several of the onlookers, and it was now becoming apparent that quite a few people there wouldn't mind seeing Thick Mick taken down a peg or two by these interlopers.

Jack got back with the drinks and handed the guy his pint of Penryn Pale Ale. "Ta, mate," the guy said, before quickly slurping down about a third of it. He wiped the foam off his mouth with the back of his hand and gave a small belch.

Now some of the people from the saloon bar section, realizing that an epic darts match was underway in the games room, crowded into the room, too. The place was really jam-packed, and the noise of the onlookers increased steadily. Closing time was approaching, but the publican wasn't about to turn off the lucrative flow of booze. If only every Wednesday night could be so good.

The players were nearing the tricky part, the end game. Since the winners could only go out with a double, they had to be very careful not to box themselves in. Once they got below 40, it was important to keep an even numbered score so that a double could end it. An odd number score required a more complex strategy.

Dargan lowered their total to 58. If Mick, on his turn, could hit an 18 and then a double twenty, they'd have it.

Ally's trio of tosses dropped their score to seventy. They were now in striking distance, though it would be difficult for Charles to close it out from there. Difficult, but not impossible. A triple 20, followed by a double 5, would do it.

Mick stepped to the line and concentrated on his target. He leaned forward and barely flicked his wrist. The dart landed in the 18, just above the triple. That brought their score to 40. A double 20 would end it. Mick's second dart sailed straight at the double twenty. It appeared that he had it. But the dart stuck in the board just a whisker above it. A huge *oooh* came from the onlookers' throats – some of them registering their disappointment, some their relief.

Mick's third and final throw *thunked* into the board just a little above his second one. Their score still stood at 40.

Jack's drinking buddy, who'd already downed his full pint, was in desperate need of another. "Yours be Jameson?" he asked Jack. Jack nodded. When Jack reached for his wallet, the guy waved him off. "My shout," he said and scurried off, wanting to get back before the match ended.

Charles, holding two of his darts in his left hand, fingered the dart in his right. He rolled it back and forth between his thumb and first two fingers, trying to relax. As he'd once done long ago when he'd shot free throws in basketball, he sucked in a deep breath, held it for a moment, then slowly expelled it. Charles' entire concentration was focused on the triple 20. He raised his arm and went into his pitcher's motion.

This time Charles hurled his dart with a little extra velocity. His aim looked perfect, and the small pointed missile zoomed straight and true at the very narrow target. The dart smacked up hard against the metal wire of the spider. It bounced back, then fell point-first, sticking in the wooden floor. Charles' throw, so nearly perfect, counted for nothing.

"Bollocks!" someone exclaimed.

Now Jack's buddy arrived back with their drinks. When he handed the glass of whisky to Jack, Jack said, "Ta, mate."

"What happened on that last throw? What'd he get, eh?" The guy was trying to peer above the heads of the people clustered in front of him, hoping to see the chalkboard, but he was too short.

Jack held up a hand, forming an "O" with thumb and finger. "His toss hit the wire and bounced off."

"Crikey," said his pal, using an expression Jack thought had gone out with the Victorian Age. The guy took a deep pull on his pint and Jack took a goodly sip of his Jameson. It suddenly dawned on Jack that he was well on his way to being drunk.

Charles, swallowing his disappointment, gathered himself and prepared for his remaining throws. His second one landed in the 20 midway between the double and the triple rings. That dropped their total to 50. No way he could double out from there, but knowing that Ally favored throwing at the 19, Charles went for the 12 segment, hoping to bring their score to 38. His throw went just where he'd hoped it would, landing in the 12 a little above the triple ring. Had Charles' dart hit the triple, that would have been okay too, since it would have dropped their score to 14. From there a double 7 could close things out.

Now it was back to Dargan. A double 20 would end it. If she failed to do it, then a double 19 from Ally would put paid to the game.

The room grew quiet as Dargan stepped up to the toe line.

Dargan Owens stood absolutely still. She stared at the dartboard with intense concentration. A hush fell over the games room. It was obvious to just about everyone there what she would try to do – land a dart in the double 20. If she and Mick could subtract forty points, they would have a score of zero.

Dargan leaned her weight forward on her right leg, her

right arm now poised out in front of her. She cocked her wrist a tiny bit, pulled her forearm back just slightly, then let fly. The well-aimed dart flew with precision toward the top of the 20 segment of the dartboard. It landed with a soft *thunk*. The dart hit the area exactly between the 2 and the 0 of the number twenty. It was maybe an inch above the double 20. *No score*. The soughing of exhaling breaths filled the room.

Dargan's second throw also looked like a winner. At the last microsecond, it dropped just below the double 20, scoring a single 20. That brought the team score down to twenty.

Dargan still had one chance left. She needed a double 10. If she could get it, it would bring their score to zero – and game over.

Dargan's third toss zipped across the short space toward the board. It landed just barely inside the double area.

"Shit!" shouted Mick. Several of their supporters gave voice to similar sentiments. Dargan's dart had hit a double but not a double 10. It had landed in the double 15, just a hair's breadth beneath the double 10. Because it would put their score below zero, it counted for nothing.

Mick rocked side to side on his feet, his fury palpable. Dargan grimaced and crossed her arms across her chest stoically. She didn't look at Mick. Charles found himself bouncing up and down on the balls of his feet. I think we're going to win this thing, he told himself. I can feel it, I can feel it. We're actually going to win this thing.

Ally took her time moving to the toe line. As she griped her three darts in her left hand, she slowly worked the fingers of her right. She gave her wrist a few revolutions, loosening it up. The eyes of the nervous onlookers watched her every small move.

"Looks like my tenner's gonna be toast, eh mate?" Jack's new pal muttered to him. To Jack's ears, his words sounded more sanguine than glum. "Ally's gonna do it. She's really gonna do it."

"Hope to hell you're right," Jack replied. He downed the last little sip of Jameson from his glass. "My nerves can't take much more of this bloody game of darts."

"Oh, she's gonna do it, oh, I know she's gonna do it. C'mon, Ally, put us outta our misery. C'mon, girl, you can do it."

Jack's pal wasn't alone in his shifting allegiances, for now quite a few others were openly pulling for Ally. Now that the underdogs had a real chance to win, the Brits' deeply ingrained sense of fair play had emerged.

Ally toed the line and assumed her stance. She glanced over at Charles. He was grinning at her. She watched as Charles lowered his right arm down by his side, his hand formed into a fist. She couldn't help smiling as he gave his arm a forward jerk. He was signaling for her to "stick it to 'em."

Seconds later, she did. Ally's throw landed right in the middle of the double 19. And – that was *it*. Her throw scored 38 points – exactly what was needed to bring their total to zero.

"Game, set, match!" Jack shouted. "This game is history!" He and his pal slapped hands. Nearly everyone else was cheering.

Charles grabbed up the jubilant Ally in his arms and swung her about. Then a smiling Dargan, in a true act of British sportsmanship, came over to them and she and Ally exchanged high fives.

"Well, hell, Mick, ya can't win 'em all, mate," someone said to Mick in a feeble attempt at consolation. Mick responded by making a vulgar gesture. There would be no acts of true British sportsmanship from Mick.

Jack, slightly inebriated, clumsily shouldered his way in amongst the group congregated about the winners and managed to hug Ally and then Charles. Jack's more-than-slightly-inebriated sidekick followed in his wake. But his hope of hugging Ally proved vain, for as he groped for her, she sidestepped his attempted embrace and the bloke fell hard against a table, glasses clattering to the floor. "Well, bugger," he muttered, slowly righting himself.

After things began to settle down, Ally motioned to Charles and Jack. "We probably should get out of here while the getting is good. Yes?"

"Yes," Charles said. "Let me make a quick trip to the loo and then let's go."

"Kinda gross back there," warned Jack. He'd learned from his own trips to the loo just how rank the Gents in a British pub could be. This one was right up there.

So Charles shot off to make a quick trip to the loo. Not many seconds behind him, so did Thick Mick.

⁂

It was nearly eleven p.m., and Rhys Tremayne lay in bed beside his wife listening to the sound of her soft breathing. Many nights he did that, since he usually had more trouble getting to sleep than she did. But he found the hour or two before he eventually dropped off to be quite pleasurable. He didn't mind sleeping alone on those nights when her work required her to stay in Truro, but he always found her presence beside him a great comfort.

But tonight, Rhys's brain just wouldn't stop rabbiting. The sudden reappearance of the Polminster Manuscript earlier in the evening had made a stew of his thoughts. The whole thing was befuddling. He felt certain that this manuscript Ally had discovered in her linen closet really was the lost manuscript – how could it *not* be? – and yet how in the world did it get there? He could think of no rational explanation for that. Could he have absent-mindedly left it in the laundry room, and then Maria inadvertently scooped it up amidst a pile of clean towels and taken it to Ally's room? *No.* He'd been getting a little more forgetful in recent years, but not about this. He knew for a certainty he'd locked it in his safe and that whoever took it had somehow gotten in there and filched it. That in itself was quite a mystery – who could have done that and how? – but this latest turn of events was even more mystifying.

And then there was the matter of the manuscript's cover. Charles said he didn't notice anything odd about it, and Charles had worked intimately with the manuscript for several days. If anyone should know, *he* should. And yet Rhys was dead certain it *was* different. He was a man who knew his old books, dammit. Hadn't he spent the last four decades doing little else than working with them?

The covering of the manuscript *had* to have been replaced. But why? And by whom? The only person he could think of who might have done that was his dear friend Neville Smallwood. And now poor Neville was dead. And even if Neville had somehow managed to do it before he died, why would he do that? It wasn't as if the old cover needed replacing. Of course it exhibited the wear and tear one would expect of a book that had been bound at some unknown time during the eighteenth or nineteenth century. But that only added to its sense of antiquity, and in Rhys's mind, to its beauty. The present cover was quite lovely, for sure, but it was almost *too* perfect.

Of course, the crucial thing was the poem. *That* seemed unchanged, thank goodness. Now it would be up to Charles to make the case for the poem being Chaucer's lost work, The *Book of the Lion*. William had been right in thinking Charles was the man for the job. He really did know his stuff. And he had just that little streak of independent-mindedness that Rhys much liked to see. If anyone could stick it to the British academic establishment, it would be this bright, not-easily-daunted young American from Waverly College in Virginia, this youthful scholar who had the imprimatur of William Wentworth, the Bosworth Professor of Medieval Studies at Oxford.

Thinking about how he hoped Charles would establish, once and for all, that the poem was Chaucer's lost work helped calm Rhys Tremayne's perturbations. His thoughts a bit more settled, he too finally fell asleep.

✦✦✦

The Gents, located in what was virtually an alleyway behind the Public House, was dark and extremely smelly. Charles wanted to get in and out just as quickly as his reason for being there would allow.

Zipping up his trousers, he stepped back out into the passageway. Happy to be out of the stinking jakes, he sucked in a deep breath of the slightly less fetid air. And that's when he discovered that his path back to the main part of the pub was blocked by a bulky figure. It took him a moment to realize that the bulky figure standing there in the dark was Thick Mick.

"Ya got more balls'n I give ya credit for," Mick said.

Charles wasn't sure how to reply to that remark, so he just shrugged.

"Shit," said Mick, "you 'n Ally shor was lucky in there. Good idea ya had, makin' it be a team game. But this time, sport, it'll just be you 'n me."

"No, I'm sorry," Charles said, "but we can't stay for another darts game tonight. We were supposed to be out of here a while ago, so we've got to hit the road."

"Darts? Fuck ya talkin' about, mate. You and me, we ain't about to play no fuckin' game o' darts. Darts is over and done with."

"Look," Charles said, "we got lucky in there. You've played enough games to know that that sometimes happens. We play you ten times, you win nine of 'em. Just our luck that this happened to be the tenth game." It wasn't that Charles was slow on the uptake. He knew exactly what Mick was moving toward. But he had to try and head it off if he possibly could.

Charles had made a good effort, but it didn't work.

"Ya know what?" came Mick's menacing growl. "Yor nuthin' but a stinkin' sack o' Yankee shit. Ya think you can come prancing in here and show us up? Well, fuck it, let's see what ya think o' this."

With lowered head, Mick suddenly charged. His intentions were plain – launch his entire body at Charles, ram his head straight into Charles' chest, and smash the guy as hard as he could back into the slimy bricks of the dark passageway.

Charles had little time to react and almost no room in which to maneuver. But with the reflexes of a middle infielder dodging a hard-charging base runner, he twisted his torso sideways and leaned away. He just managed to avoid a direct collision.

Mick's shoulder scraped across Charles' chest and then Mick's head rammed straight into the brick wall with explosive force.

At the moment of impact, Charles heard a loud crunching sound and felt the vibrations made by Mick's head smashing against the hard structure. Mick crumpled to the grimy floor, his lips emitting a soft little gurgling sound.

Mick's eviscerated scalp began to bleed copiously. For a moment Charles was frozen where he stood. Then, gathering his wits, he shouted, "*Help!*"

The sound, and the reverberations, created by Mick's collision with the wall had been heard and felt inside the pub. Now Charles' cry for help brought folks running.

Charles stood back as some others knelt down beside Mick. "What happened?" Dargan asked, not looking up.

"I didn't see it," Charles replied semi-mendaciously. "I guess he tripped and his head went straight into the bricks." Charles' sense of honor told him not to make Mick out to be the villain that he was. He'd already humiliated him enough in the dart game.

"Kitty!" Dargan shouted out. "We *need* you." She was calling out for her friend Kitty MacNaughton, who was a nurse at the local hospital. She was the one who'd kept the score on the chalkboard during the game.

"Clean towels," Kitty shouted, looking down at Mick's bleeding scalp. "Call 999. We need the EMTs."

Jack pulled Charles aside. "You okay?" he asked.

"Jesus," Charles said. "He really whammed into those bricks."

"But you? Are *you* okay?"

"Maybe a bit in shock. But, yeah, I should be okay in a minute."

"Maybe we'd better get ourselves out of here, Charlie."

"No, we can't do that. Not until we're sure Mick's in good hands."

They could hear the *WA-wa, WA-wa* of the ambulance that was now on its way. And then just a minute later the professionals were on the scene. A couple of them were checking Mick out, while two others prepared a stretcher to take him to their vehicle.

By then a local constable had arrived, too. He pulled Charles aside to ask him a few questions. Charles said he couldn't say exactly what happened. He guessed that Mick must've tripped while making a dash for the loo. Charles was loath to say that Mick had attacked him. It was a matter of honor between guys.

Charles noticed the policeman eyeing his hands and clothing. There wasn't anything amiss for the guy to see, since in his charge Mick had merely brushed Charles' chest before slamming into the wall. And Charles had stepped away quick enough to have avoided any of Mick's blood splattering on him. The constable wrote down in his notebook where Charles was staying, then said, "Come to the station in the morning and make a statement, eh?"

"I will," said Charles. "No problem." The policeman nodded, and indicated that it was okay for him to leave.

As Ally, Jack, and Charles exited through the front door of the pub, Jack paused to glance at the sign with its depiction of Saint George slaying the toothy dragon. "Tonight the blighter did it again," he murmured softly. "I told you, Ally, that someone would be playing for blood." His soft words registered on neither Charles nor Ally.

They helped Jack into the back seat of Ally's car and then set out for home.

"Well, Jack," Charles said, "Ally really showed what she's made of tonight, didn't she?"

"Sugar and spice and all things nice . . . ," came Jack's slurred voice from the back seat.

Ten minutes later they drove through the familiar entranceway, with the pair of choughs silently standing guard atop their tall plinths.

At the house, Ally and Charles had to assist the quickly fading Jackson Lockhart up the steep staircase and into his room. Jack was definitely the worse for drink.

For a moment, Charles and Ally stood together looking into each other's face on the little landing just outside the door to Charles' room.

"You're one terrific darts player," Charles finally managed to say.

Ally smiled at him. "Charlie," she said, "how about giving a girl a goodnight hug?"

"An excellent suggestion," he said. And the two of them clung together for a long moment. Ally broke free and took a step back. Then she leaned forward and placed a small kiss on Charles' lips.

"Umm, nice," Charles murmured.

"That's what a mermaid tastes like," she said. "Just so you don't forget."

Charles stood there listening as Ally's footsteps retreated down the staircase to her second-floor bedroom.

27

It was a quiet morning. Charles roused himself at 7:30. He planned to spend the whole day working on the poem after Ally left for St. Ives. Jack was likely to be out of commission for a while and the professor would probably be enjoying a lazy lie-in. Rhys Tremayne, no doubt, was already off on his morning constitutional, and Ailish already on her way to Truro.

It was 8:30 when Maria placed two steaming mugs of coffee on the breakfast table for Charles and Ally. Maria busied herself about the kitchen preparing a hearty breakfast for them.

Charles and Ally sat quietly sipping their coffee and exchanging shy smiles. Charles thought back to the day he first saw her, almost two weeks ago now, when she was leaning into the refrigerator, her back to him. He'd liked what he saw then, and he liked it now even more.

"Guess we showed them a thing or two, didn't we?" she finally said, grinning.

"Guess we did," Charles replied.

"I'll be back late afternoon or early evening tomorrow," Ally said. "You'll have you two whole days for editing and annotating without me being a bother."

"You a bother?" Charles replied. "Well, maybe a distraction but never a bother. But being here this past week and a half has been great. What a good thing your father took the professor's advice and invited me along."

"Yes, a very good thing. Well, have fun with your musty old manuscripts. It's obvious how much you care about them."

"I care about them a lot . . . though they're not all I care about."

"Oh yes? What else do you care about?" she asked, eyebrows lifted, a hopeful look in her eye.

Charles reached out and placed a hand atop one of hers. "I'm pretty sure you know what else."

"Say it, Charlie. Put it into words. What else do you care about?"

He sat quietly for a moment, then said, "Cornish mermaids. I've developed quite a fancy for them – and the taste of their sweet lips."

Ally leaned over to Charles and planted a very soft kiss on his lips. "You'd better not forget that sweet taste, mister."

"Not likely." Then after a little pause Charles added, "But I've heard that mermaids can be dangerous to mortal men."

"Absolutely true," she said. "Well, I'd best be on my way. Don't want to be too much of a bother to you and your precious manuscript."

"I'm glad you'll be driving us to Yeovil on Saturday," Charles said.

"Makes two of us," she replied. Then she snatched her bag and departed.

Charles walked her out and watched as her car trundled down the graveled drive. When he saw her give a little wave in her rearview mirror, he waved also.

Twenty minutes later, Charles Bascombe had all his materials neatly laid out on the long table in their host's library: laptop, typescript of his transcription of the poem, pad of lined paper, and the Riverside edition of Chaucer's poetry. Later he would want to consult the physical manuscript, though at the moment Rhys Tremayne had secreted it off someplace in the house. For his immediate purposes, the typescript of the text would suffice.

He'd spent an hour annotating the text when Maria appeared to say he had a phone call. Charles took the call out in the hallway and listened as the policeman on the other end of the line told him he wouldn't need to come and make a statement. Mick had regained consciousness and told them his fall had been purely accidental; that Charles had been an innocent bystander. Mick had sustained a serious concussion, Charles learned, and the gash in his head had required several stitches; but he should be more-or-less fine in a couple of days. Charles was glad it hadn't been worse. He harbored *almost* no ill will toward Mick, though he doubted the same was true of Mick.

Rhys Tremayne, back from his walk, was the next one to

poke his head into the library. "All good in here?" he asked.

"Yes, sir, all good."

"Morning, Charlie," came the professor's voice from behind Rhys Tremayne.

"Good morning, sir," Charles replied.

"Making progress?"

"Yes, definitely. And some interesting discoveries, too."

"Wonderful," their host said. "We'll leave you to it, but we'll want to hear everything over lunch."

"Where's Jackson this morning?" the professor asked.

"We may not see much of him today. He kind of tied one on last night."

"Oh, dear," Rhys said. "Maybe Maria can be of assistance. Knows a few special remedies, she does. Ally can attest to that."

"Sounds good. Well, I'll get back to it," Charles said, and turned his attention back to Chaucer.

But even Chaucer didn't totally absorb his attentions, he discovered, for the interruption had broken his concentration on the great medieval poet. Now Charles found his mind drifting back to an email message he'd read first thing that morning. From Clare Reilly. It was clear that Clare wanted to see him; she'd suggested coming to Oxford for lunch. That sounded good to Charles, and he'd felt a frisson of excitement at reading her words. In all honesty, he wasn't sure how wise it was for them to reopen their relationship; but knowing how poorly he'd handled its abrupt ending, he felt a need to make amends. Clare didn't seem to harbor any deep resentments. The truth was, the responsibility for the way they'd left things didn't totally belong to either one of them, and Charles knew he owned a fair share of it. He'd been far too quick to judge and far too harsh in that judgment. He regretted never giving her the opportunity to explain. He'd owed her that much.

✠✠✠

Jack Lockhart felt like hell. He wondered if Thick Mick felt as bad as he did? Probably worse. He hoped so.

Mick's head-butt of the brick wall had been a mighty blow. Everyone in the pub had felt it. Damned good thing for Charlie Mick hadn't done what he'd intended. Otherwise it might be Charlie in the hospital instead of Mick.

With an effort, Jack climbed out of bed and stumbled toward the bathroom. He ran cold water on a washcloth for his forehead. He gulped down a small handful of ibuprofen tablets. Then he went and lay back down again on his bed, the cool washcloth in place. He'd love a mug of strong black coffee, but he didn't feel up to going down in search of it.

Jack heard a soft tap at his door.

"Yes?" he called, thinking it might be Maria.

The door swung open about a foot and Charles' head popped around it. "Thought you might like a cup," he said. He was carrying two large ceramic mugs. He held one up invitingly and Jack nodded.

"What time is it?" Jack asked.

"Eleven-thirty," Charles said.

Jack took a moment to rearrange his pillows against the headboard, then reached out for the mug. "You're a pal, Charlie," he said.

"We aim to please," Charles replied. "How's the head?" He sat down in the room's single chair and sipped from the mug he was holding.

"Umm, just what the doctor ordered. Man, Charlie, I haven't felt like this since our olden golden days. You're a bad influence on a guy. Ally gone to work?"

"Yep. I've been at it too."

"Doing any good?"

"I think so, yes."

"Major discoveries?"

"Probably not *major* major. But some pretty interesting things."

"Do you think the poem is really Chaucer's?"

"I'm almost certain of it."

"Great. I hope so. Want my friend to become a famous scholar."

"Giving it my best shot, pal."

"Just like you did in that game of darts." Jack looked across at his friend, a smile on his face. "That dude last night, Charlie, he thought he was the biggest, baddest lion in the valley. He wasn't. It was you. Man, you and Ally were amazing."

"She really came through, didn't she?"

"Charlie, in case you have noticed, she's a gem."

"I've noticed. Well, Jack, anything else I can do?" Jack shook his head. "Maria will come up and let you know when lunch is ready, probably in about an hour, if you feel up to it."

"Let's see what the coffee and ibuprofen do. Thanks for checking on me, amigo."

Charles nodded, then closed the door gently behind him.

✢✢✢

Jack didn't come down for lunch. When Maria went up with soup and a sandwich, she found that he'd fallen asleep.

"So, Charles," Rhys Tremayne said, "let's hear it. What wonders have you discovered?"

"The most interesting thing so far is that the text offers a few glimpses into the narrator's personal life – during a time period about which we know very little."

"Goodness," the professor said, "glimpses into his personal life. Chaucer doesn't often do that. Just the odd little tantalizing hint here and there."

"What period, Charles?" Rhys asked.

"Late 1350s, during his experiences in France. He was still just a teenager."

"Ah, when he was captured and ransomed?" the professor asked.

"Yes. He gives few specifics about himself, since his primary purpose is to celebrate the martial prowess and knightly virtues of Prince Lionel, in keeping with his larger intention to valorize and glorify his lord and patron. But yes, after he's been captured, he comments on his treatment by the French, lauding them for their honorable handling of noble captives. Apparently that included the narrator, though young Geoffrey wasn't really of the noble class. The fact that he was Prince Lionel's personal valet probably had something to do with that."

"Does he say how he came to be captured?"

"Not explicitly, just that he and some others had been on a foraging expedition when they'd been taken. Prince Lionel hadn't been with them. He makes a point of exonerating him."

"It makes sense that Lionel's valet would have received honorable treatment," the professor said. "According to the *Life Records*, Chaucer commanded a rather hefty ransom – sixteen pounds, if I'm remembering correctly, quite a tidy sum in those days."

"Yes," Charles said, "twice the amount of the ransom paid for a chaplain and only four pounds less than what was paid for the knight named William de Graunson. The *Records* also mention an archer named Richard Dulle; that fellow's ransom was a mere forty shillings. I've wondered if Richard Dulle might've been the model for Chaucer's Yeoman in the *General Prologue*."

"All quite fascinating, Charlie," their host said. "Encounter anything else especially notable?"

"He briefly describes the façade of a building he could see from the room in which they were held. Sounds a lot like the Maison des Musiciens in Rheims."

"Ah," the professor said, "the building that's been suggested as providing the model for Chaucer's description of Fame's palace in *The Hous of Fame*. That will help to pin down that speculation."

"Keep at it, my boy," Rhys said, beaming. "Anything more you need?"

"Yes. Tomorrow I'd like to have access to the manuscript. Want to double check it against the transcription of the parts I've already worked on."

Rhys Tremayne nodded his agreement. "Happy to bring it to you when you want it," he said.

✠✠✠

By four on Friday afternoon, Charles was running out of steam. He hated to break it off, but the last two days of intense concentration had been mentally draining. Time to call a halt.

He carefully packed away all of his materials, then left the library. In the ground floor sitting room, he found Professor Wentworth sitting alone reading a book. It was Somerset Maugham's *The Moon & Sixpence*.

"Any good?" Charles asked. The professor raised one hand and tilted it back and forth.

"That good, huh?" Charles said.

"Charlie," the professor said, "we need to talk."

"I was thinking that, too. Why don't we go out in the back garden," Charles said. "Give us some privacy. There's a bench just beyond the rose garden where we can sit."

A few minutes later they were perched side by side on the bench, alone and safely away from the ears of Maria or Rhys Tremayne. Charles could hear distant sea sounds and the raucous cries of seagulls.

"You go first," Charles said.

"Two things, Charlie. I had a call today from the solicitor who's handling matters pertaining to Neville Smallwood's estate. He said I could have access to Neville's study and wondered if I'd like to come and pick up the materials I'd wanted from the project the two of us had been working on."

"Ah, he heard the tale you fed that crotchety woman at the Minster Church."

"Quite right. So on our way to Yeovil on Saturday, why don't we stop by there and do that. That be okay?"

Charles smiled. "So it will look like you were telling the

truth?"

"Ah . . . well . . . yes. But also to give us a chance to take another look at everything in Neville's study, especially those manuscripts we noticed in the curtained-off alcove where we found the Polminster Manuscript – or what we *thought* was the Polminster Manuscript. We were too rushed the other night to look at everything properly. I'd really like to do that."

"Sure. Why not? I wouldn't mind seeing the vicar's study by the light of day myself."

"Okay, then. Well, that's one thing."

"And the other?"

"That manuscript we brought back with us, Charlie, which we thought – and Rhys believes – to be the Polminster Manuscript. What are we going to do about it? We can't let him continue to think it's the real thing."

"No, we can't."

They both sat there without speaking for a short while before the professor finally said, "And then, Charlie, what's going to happen when you've finished working on the poem? What did you have in mind doing, Charlie?"

"I've assumed that we'd try to publish a monograph edition of it: introduction, text, critical and textual notes, and glossary. Maybe, as an appendix, a photographic facsimile of the manuscript text. And perhaps, sir, with a short introductory headnote written by you, if you'd be willing?"

"Publish it where? Rhys will have strong views about that. I doubt he'll want you to publish it with any of the British academic presses, given his feelings about British academics. Maybe we could try one of the more prestigious academic presses in the U.S."

"Yes. Let's give that some further thought. And maybe take his suggestions into account."

"Okay, I'll ask him. But when it comes to the manuscript itself, Charlie, what do you think you'd say about it? Of course you'd have to provide a thorough description of it and its entire contents. No problems there, really. But you'd also have to say where it is and how you came by it. And people won't be satisfied with just your description or even by the photographs. They'll insist upon seeing the actual thing. That's where things are likely to get dicey."

"Yes, you're right. Maybe we could say we believe it to be a copy of a copy. After all, many of the extant manuscripts of Chaucer's poems were made after his lifetime, in the fifteenth century. What matters most is that the text itself will stand up to close scrutiny, isn't it?"

"But Charlie, people will want to know how Rhys got it. They will ask the very questions we asked him that first night. He didn't convince us, did he? You yourself were immediately suspicious. And rightly so. We can't have him trying to palm off the copy, good as it is, as an authentic medieval manuscript."

"No, sir, we can't."

"We don't want him to be revealed as a fraud. That would destroy him. Do you think that's what someone wants? And if so, who might that be?"

"I don't know, sir. Mad Meg, perhaps?"

"Mad Meg?"

"Ally's mother? Aided and abetted by the loyal Maria?"

"Goodness," the professor said. "Hell hath no fury? That

what you mean?"

"You remember last Sunday afternoon, when we briefly crossed paths with her?"

"Yes, of course."

"As she was leaving, Maria placed a large bag into the back seat of the car, a bag big enough to have held the manuscript. I don't know if that's what it was she was doing, but the possibility crossed my mind."

"Goodness," the professor said again. "Mad Meg. Lowenna Tremayne. And Maria in on it as well. A possibility, I suppose.

"But Charlie, if you're assuming that Lowenna was bitter because she's a woman scorned, that Rhys dumped her for a beautiful and sophisticated woman fifteen years her junior, you'd be wrong. It was Lowenna who forced the split-up. She was the one who insisted upon it. I never really understood why, just supposed she'd had her fill of living with a boring old scholar who loved his books more than her.

"At the time, I did pick up on the fact that there was some additional grievance, one involving a dear friend of hers who'd suddenly died, a woman who made Lowenna promise to provide for her daughter after her death. I don't know all the intricacies of that business, though."

"Would that daughter happen to be Dargan Owens?"

"Why yes, Charlie, that would be her. How did you know?"

"From things Ally has said."

"I've never met the girl," the professor said, "but I believe that Lowenna has generously provided for her, paid for her schooling and living expenses for several years, and has taken an interest in her beyond that."

"Well," Charles said, "maybe we're jumping to conclusions about the former Mrs. Tremayne. Maybe Mad Meg isn't the one behind all of this."

"Yes. But maybe she is. If not her, who? Anyway, Charlie, the big thing is to prevent Rhys from declaring to the world that the manuscript copy he now has is truly legit. He surely has his own suspicions about that, though he just doesn't want to admit it. All that business about the manuscript's cover being different must have given him an inkling of the truth."

"Yes," Charles said, "but what would really be best would be for him to discover the truth for himself. We need to figure out how to make that happen."

"I agree. Well, we'll think of something, won't we?"

28

Maria was supposed to call Lowenna Tremayne if there were any new or unexpected developments. Now Maria punched in the number of Mrs. Tremayne's mobile phone.

"Hello, Maria," the woman said, when she recognized the caller's number. "You have news?"

"Missus, I just thought you might like to know. The professor and the lads will be leaving in the morning. And I overheard them say they plan to stop on their way north at that old church up near Boscastle. The professor has permission to go into the vicar's study. That's why they're going there. Don't know if it's important, missus, but just in case, I thought you should know."

"Oh, Maria, I do appreciate your call. You were absolutely

right to tell me this. Thank you so much. About what time do you reckon they'll be leaving?"

"Right after breakfast is what they said. Probably about nine."

"Okay, good. But call me on my mobile if they leave earlier. Actually, Maria, why don't you call me on my mobile just as soon as they leave, at whatever time that turns out to be."

"I will. Please be careful, missus," Maria cautioned, though she had no idea what Lowenna Tremayne might be intending to do or what she might need to be careful about.

✦✦✦

Charles stood looking out his open window, watching and listening for signs of Ally's car. Nothing so far, and it was moving toward six. She must've been held up at the gallery, he thought.

This would be their last evening in Cornwall, and the plan was for them to have a very informal final meal. Charles felt regretful about leaving the Lizard, a place which up until two weeks ago he'd never even known about. He'd grown quite fond of the Tremaynes, Ally especially, but also Ailish and Rhys, who wasn't really such a difficult person, once you got used to his ways.

Charles had never liked goodbyes, and he knew saying goodbye to Ally would be specially hard. At least seh would still e with them for much of the day.

After a few minutes, Charles gave up watching for Ally and went on down to the main floor to check on the others. The sitting room was empty – the two older men were probably still out on their late afternoon walk. Who knew where Jack might be? But when Charles heard music coming from Ailish Tremayne's study, it told him where she was.

Charles had seen Ailish's car come up the driveway around four. Now, having changed into more casual clothing, she'd probably begun her weekend ritual of relaxing in her study with music and a drink, just what she'd been doing on that first evening, a week and a half ago.

Ailish's study door was partway open, and hearing footsteps outside her study, she called out a cheery "hello."

When Charles stuck his head around it, she motioned him in.

"Please come and join me, Charles," she said. "I'm just having a little nip of whisky. You'll have one too?"

"I will. But only a very little nip, please. Actually, why don't I pour it myself?" he asked, recalling the large dose of whisky she'd given him on that first night.

"And while you're at it, you can freshen mine," she said, holding out her glass to him. Charles stepped over to the sideboard where he found an opened bottle of Glenfiddich. Going for the good stuff tonight, he thought. As he poured the celebrated single malt into their glasses, a small one for him, a larger one for her, he tuned in to the orchestral music filling the room with a swell of strings and woodwinds. He struggled to identify it.

"Ah," he said with a grin, "Beethoven's Tenth. Took me a sec to recognize it."

"Ha, ha. Yes, I've heard people refer to Brahms's First Symphony as that," she replied. "Do you like it?"

"I do, though I have to admit his Second is my favorite."

"No surprise there. Most discerning music lovers prefer

the Second. I like each of the four just about same."

"So Charles," she went on, "you and the professor and Jackson will be departing in the morning? Back to Oxford and those dear old Dreaming Spires?"

"Yes, back to my cozy little flat in Summertown, those dear old spires, and the musty old Bodleian."

"Well, let me tell you something. Rhys is really going to miss you. He's loved having you and the professor here. And it's been so good for him, too. Helped to bring him out of that shell he tends to retreat into." She took a sip of her whisky and smiled at Charles over the rim of her glass. What striking, deep blue eyes, what a wonderful smile, Charles thought. Rhys Tremayne is one very lucky devil.

As Charles was thinking that, Jackson Lockhart poked his head around the door jam. "There you are. I was wondering where everyone was," he said. "Hey, nice music."

"Beethoven's Tenth," Charles said with a straight face. Jack just nodded, Charles' witticism lost on him.

"Come in, Jackson," she said, motioning with her arm. "Join us for a drink?"

"Nope, I'd better not. But thanks all the same. I'm still drying out from the other night."

"Ally didn't lead you fellas astray, did she?"

"Not a bit. What happened was entirely my own fault. Charlie wisely made his pint of ale last about two hours – all the way through their epic game of darts – and I did just the opposite. Slugged down way too many doubles of Jameson."

"Ouch," she said.

"The price I pay for not sharing Charlie's abstemious predilections."

"What's this about an epic darts game?" she asked, her eyebrows raised. "This I want to hear."

They took turns filling her in. Jack's recollections of the actual game were rather hazy, but Charles remembered every scintilla of it.

"So you and Ally took down Dargan and the mighty Mick. Well done, Charles! I wonder if Rhys knows. I'm sure he would be proud of you both. You may have noticed that he rather dotes on his daughter.

"And you, Charles, are a fellow after his own heart. If you do succeed in establishing that this poem he cares so much about was truly written by Chaucer, he'll be in your debt for life. You know that, don't you?"

"Well, the poem is almost certainly Chaucer's. There's a lot of evidence to support that conclusion. But Mrs. Tremayne, the professor and I have some serious concerns about the manuscript. You wouldn't happen to know how your husband came by it, would you?"

She shrugged. "Not my area," she said. She obviously wasn't going to go there, even if she knew anything about it.

"Hello, hello, hello," boomed the voice of Rhys Tremayne from outside the room.

"We're in here, darling," Ailish called out. "Come join us."

The professor and their host stepped into her small study, sherry glasses already in hand. Ailish came over to her husband, embraced him, and kissed his cheek. No embraces for the professor, who looked a little left out.

"Any sign of Ally?" Charles asked.

"On her way," Rhys said. "She's stopped off to pick up

the pasties. Should be here in just a bit."

"Pasties?" Jack said. "That's terrific. The perfect choice for our final evening."

✤✤✤

Maria had laid out a variety of dishes out on the kitchen table – tossed salad, Branston Pickle, potato salad, a large bowl of homemade chips, slices of several different cheeses, and all the pasties Ally had brought – along with plates and cutlery. They filled their plates and carried them into the sitting room, where Maria had placed wooden trays close to the sofas. She'd looked none too pleased at the arrangement, but it was what Ailish and Ally had both insisted on. They wanted this last meal to be very casual.

People seated themselves randomly on the sofas.

"I'm ravenous," Jack said. "These pasties smell scrumptious."

"Then tuck in, lad," Ailish said, "tuck in."

"No, no, not just yet," Rhys insisted. "First we must have a toast."

In his raised right hand, Jack paused his loaded fork above his plate. With his left, he reached for his wine glass.

"To new friends, an old friend, a lost friend, and an ancient friend," Rhys Tremayne intoned. He raised his glass and the others did likewise.

"Hear, hear," the professor said.

"Well, yes," Jack said. "And if you'll permit me to offer a toast, I'd like to drink to new friends," nodding in turn at Ally, Ailish, and Rhys Tremanyne, "an old friend," nodding at Charles, "and a not-so-ancient friend," nodding at Professor Wentworth. Again everyone raised their glasses.

Ally, thinking quickly, realized that her father's toast may have given her an opening to a topic she knew had to be broached.

"Daddy," she said, "you had us drink a toast to new friends, an old friend, and a lost friend – I can follow all of that – but also to an *ancient* friend. What ancient friend were you referring to?'

"William, I'm sure you got my meaning," Rhys said.

"Ally, I think the ancient friend he was referring to was one Master Geoffrey Chaucer."

"Oh, right. The poem in the manuscript Charlie has been sweating over, the manuscript I found the other day in my linen closet. Daddy, I need to confess something to you about that manuscript. When you saw it, you suspected it had been rebound and found that perplexing. Daddy, I think Charlie might be able to clear that little matter up."

"Can you Charles?" Rhys asked.

Like everyone else, Charles was caught off guard by the sudden and unexpected emergence of this subject.

"Well, sort of, I guess." He paused for a long moment, wondering just how he should phrase things and wondering how far he should go. "Sir, you were quite right. It's not the same binding, as similar as it is. In fact, sir," he said, deciding to go ahead and take the plunge, "it's not even the same manuscript – although both of them look *almost* the same."

Rhys Tremayne's lips tightened into a fierce smile. Then he began nodding his head slowly. "Yes," he finally said, "I agree. I hadn't wanted to accept that conclusion. But yes, I've really known all along that it isn't the same manuscript." All of them remained silent for several beats before he went on. "So William, Charles – why don't you level with me and tell me how you got this one? Then, perhaps, I will level with you also."

"Yes," the professor said, "it's time for us all to do that. There've been too many secrets."

"Sir," Charles explained, "on our little trip earlier this week we stopped off at the Minster Church near Boscastle. We had hoped to talk to Neville Smallwood. But of course that was no longer possible. But when we were there, we stumbled upon this manuscript in the vicar's study. And right away we believed that what we'd found was the missing Polminster Manuscript. It was only later we realized it wasn't."

"What you stumbled upon, as you put it – and I'm not going to ask you how you happened to stumble upon it – was Neville's own copy," Rhys said. "Before he sent me the Polminster Manuscript, he would have made a personal copy, as painstaking an endeavor as that must surely have been. That's what Neville always did when he'd gained access to something new, made himself his own copy. He's been doing that for decades. From time to time, he'd send me one of them – I have several in the glass-fronted bookcase in the library – but up till now, never one as potentially earth-shaking as this one. This time, instead of sharing a *copy* with me, he wanted me to have the original. That's because this time he knew it was something we couldn't keep to ourselves. It was something we had to share with the world. And Neville wanted me to have the honor of being the one to do it."

"Wait," Jack said. "What are these things he's been

copying for decades and how did he come by them?"

"William will remember how fascinated Neville became with medieval manuscripts, back when we were under-graduates at Oxford. During the ensuing years, although he'd chosen to pursue a different calling, his love of the old things never loosened its grip on him. Over time Neville cultivated friendships with many others who shared his enthusiasms, and some of them went on become archivists or to hold various kinds of librarian positions at major institutions. From time to time he prevailed upon them to lend him this obscure manuscript or that. The things he got his hands on were never very important, never items of great interest to scholars. As I'm sure William and Charles know, there are lots of ancient manuscripts buried in libraries that hold little interest to scholars. They mostly just lie there in obscurity collecting dust. But such things were always of interest to Neville. So whenever he managed to get hold of one of them, he made a copy of it, strictly for his own pleasure.

"Whenever he finished copying one of them, he always returned the original; then, through one source or another, he'd acquire something new to copy. Occasionally Nev would get wind of something for sale that interested him and then he would purchase a manuscript from a dealer – *usually* from someone with scruples, but not always. Even then, after he made his own personal copy, he would anonymously donate the original item to a library or museum. All he ever kept were the copies he made for himself in his ever-growing personal library of medieval manuscripts. I'm probably the only person who has ever seen any of them.

"Anyway, now you have seen his work, too," Rhys said,

looking at Charles and then at the professor. "You know how good he'd become. His copies are works of art in their own right." Charles and the professor nodded their agreement.

"In all that he did, the only ethical line he ever came close to crossing was the sometimes unauthorized borrowing of manuscripts. But when he did that, he never failed to return them. Until this one, that is. But this one didn't come from an institution; he bought it from a dealer, a rather dubious one at that, and a fellow who had no idea that the manuscript he'd cobbled together and was offering for sale might actually contain something truly notable.

"So, Neville bought it and copied it. When he was done, he passed the original on to me. Neville felt certain it contained a truly rare poem. He knew I had friends with the skills and knowledge to determine if that was really so – one of those friends being William. So that's when I contacted William in Oxford. And that's how you all came to be here."

"When it disappeared last week," the professor said, "you didn't want anyone to investigate. Was that because you were protecting Neville?" Rhys nodded. "But he hadn't really done anything illegal, had he?"

"Well," Charles said, joining the discussion, "That might depend on where and how the fellow from whom he bought it came to have it."

"Exactly right," Rhys said. "I know that fellow. He's offered me things before. I've never dealt with him; others who share my passions sometimes do."

"But Neville," the professor said, "having a good notion of the momentousness of the manuscript's contents, couldn't resist the rascal's offer. Yes, even Neville – as morally upright as they come – couldn't resist the siren's call. We all have our frailties, don't we?"

"We do. *All* of us. Even . . . ," and he tilted his head in Charles' direction and grinned.

"So," Ailish said, "if what you now have is Neville's *copy*, where is the *original* Polminster Manuscript?"

No one responded.

Finally Rhys said, "That's the unanswered question."

But Charles, remembering the heavy bag Maria had placed in the back seat of Lowenna Tremayne's car several days earlier, had his suspicions.

29

Clare Reilly awoke at eight on Saturday morning, which for her was late. She slipped into her jogging clothes, slugged down half a cup of coffee, munched a couple of bites from a granola bar, then set off on her morning run.

After crossing the Bayswater Road she headed into the park. She passed to the right of the Serpentine and angled toward Kensington Gardens. Her route then took her to just behind the Albert Memorial where she swung to the left and jogged along a path parallel to Rotten Row.

Clare treasured her weekend runs. It was the one time when she could release all the tensions of the week and just let her mind run free. Usually her mind – having a mind of its own – wandered where it would. Today, though, thoughts of Charlie Bascombe forced their way in. Clare found herself imagining what her visit to him in Oxford would be like; then she imagined him coming to visit her in London. She envisioned them walking companionably through Regent's Park, passing the zoo, and climbing Primrose Hill, where they spread out a blanket and unpacked a picnic lunch. Later they lay close beside each other in the sun reading books, dozing, watching kite-fliers. She didn't picture them sharing any physical intimacies, just drinking in the comfort of being together. It seemed idyllic. Maybe that was how it would be. One could always hope.

Then her thoughts skipped back to that fateful night – the night in which she did the dumbest thing she'd done in her entire life. The thing for which Charlie, not knowing the full truth of the matter, had judged her so harshly. She bitterly regretted both what she had done, and the fact that her actions had caused her dearest friend to turn his back on her without giving her a chance to explain.

Clare had been so lost in her thoughts, she'd nearly reached Hyde Park Corner before she realized it. She veered to the left, cut behind the bandstand, and jogged parallel to Park Lane in the direction of Marble Arch.

Last night she'd received a text from Jackson. He'd said he hoped she would be available to have lunch with him on Sunday. So, the Cornwall adventure was apparently coming to its end. This morning she would text him back and say yes. She was eager to hear all about Cornwall and eager to get Jack's read on Charlie. She would try to discern from him what Charlie's feelings toward her might be. Jack would surely have some sense of that.

As usual, Clare walked the final few blocks as a cool down. She felt the sweat on her chest soaking through the front of her T-shirt.

✢✢✢

The road through the middle of Cornwall seemed quite familiar to Charles; it was his fourth trip on it in less than two weeks. Jack must've felt familiar with it too, since he'd driven it twice earlier that week.

Despite the Saturday morning traffic being fairly heavy, they made good time, reaching Launceton by ten – leaving only half an hour till they reached the Minster Church.

As soon as they'd gotten on the road, a little after eight-thirty, Ally had plugged her iPod into the car's sound system and assumed the role of music selector. Knowing the professor's preference for American music, she'd served up an eclectic mixture that included Jackson Browne ("Running on Empty" and "Stay"), Crosby, Stills & Nash ("Love the One You're With"), and the Talking Heads ("Love Comes to Town" and "Burning Down the House").

Charles couldn't help wondering if there were messages, conscious or unconscious, in Ally's choices.

✢✢✢

It usually took Anna fifteen minutes to walk the three-quarters of a mile from her parents' house in the village to the Minster Church, and on this Saturday morning she arrived at the church at 9:30. On a normal Saturday, she would use the next two hours to complete her preparations for the Sunday morning church services, and she'd be back home by noon. Today would not be a normal Saturday and she wouldn't be home by noon.

In the vestry Anna took off her sweater and draped it over the back of a chair, then put on her oversized work shirt. She stepped across to the closet where the cleaning supplies were stored. By force of habit she ran her eyes over the row of pegs holding their various sets of keys. One peg was empty – the one for the vicarage.

She had a moment's trepidation before remembering that Mrs. Brashler – or the dragon-lady, as she now thought of her, courtesy of that young man's remark earlier in the week – had said the old gentleman who'd been with the young man wanted access to the vicarage this morning. Had he come already? Had he found the keys on his own?

As she was pondering that, her nose registered a faint smell of smoke. What in the world? It didn't seem to her that it was coming from within the church. But from where? She knew she'd better find out.

Exiting through a side door, Anna stepped out beside the graveyard. Here the smell of the smoke was a good bit stronger. Then she noticed wisps of it drifting through the trees; they were coming from the direction of the vicarage. Anna dashed back inside and snatched her mobile phone from her handbag, then retraced her steps and set off at a run for the vicarage. She ascended the steps to the little lane just above the east end of the church two at a time, then dashed past a green car that was parked in the lane.

As Anna neared the vicarage, the smoke had become thicker. It had an acrid, rather revolting smell. Anna paused for a moment to stab 999 into her mobile phone. She informed the operator of her location, then sprinted on toward the vicarage.

Outside the door, she paused to suck in several deep breaths. She pulled the loose bottom of her work shirt up over her nose and mouth, and then she rushed through the partially open door and into the pall of gray smoke that filled the sitting room.

Peering through the occluded air, she could see that the door to the study was open. That was where the smoke seemed to be coming from. Anna willed her body to cross the sitting room and enter the study. The air inside the room was nearly impenetrable. The smoke, she felt sure, was coming from the grate in the fireplace – a fireplace she knew hadn't been used in years. The flue was probably closed, the chimney blocked by leaves and birds' nests.

As Anna attempted to cross the room, she nearly tripped on something lying in the middle of floor. She caught herself just in time. With the hand not holding her shirt's hem, she reached down and felt the object on the floor. It was a body. Of a woman. Mrs. Brashler? Next to the body Anna's hand touched something else. A small stack of books? Or were they the vicar's precious manuscripts? Had the woman been trying to burn them? Well, no time to worry about them now. Anna had to do what she could for the woman.

"I'll have you out of here in two shakes of a lamb's tail," she murmured.

Reluctantly, she dropped her shirt hem and pulled the woman's arms above her head and began dragging her toward the study doorway. The woman's body was heavy.

Not being able to hold her breath any longer, Anna gulped in a breath of the acrid air. She nearly gagged. It was awful. Still, she persevered. Now she had the woman out of the study. Now she was dragging her across the sitting room. Her lungs burning, her arms aching, Anna reached the open door of the vicarage with her heavy burden. She stumbled out into the less turgid air.

Once more Anna took hold of the woman's arms. She lugged the body several additional paces away from the building, then finally let go. Anna crumpled to her knees. She panted for air – she knew she'd come quite close to losing consciousness.

After a moment of resting and deep breathing, Anna felt somewhat restored. She bent down to check on the woman. It wasn't Mrs. Brashler. It was Mrs. Tremayne. What was *she* doing here? Anna was hugely relieved to see small up-and-down movements of the woman's chest. She was alive and breathing.

Then Anna remembered what she'd seen inside, the pile of things the woman apparently had been trying to destroy. And she knew what she had to do. She didn't want to but she had to – she had to go back in there, because that woman had been trying to destroy things precious to the vicar, a man who had been precious to her. She had to do it for the vicar.

Anna drew in several slow, deep breaths, lifted her shirttail to her face, and willed herself to re-enter the vicarage. She dashed across the floor of the sitting room and re-entered the smoke-filled study. Yes, she could just make out a stack of the vicar's manuscripts lying on the floor. In the fireplace grate, one or two others smoldered. That was where all the evil smoke was coming from. She could do little about those, but she could try to rescue these. She let loose of her shirt's hem, bent down and scooped them up. My, they were heavy. Clutching them to her chest, she staggered back through the building.

As she stumbled through the vicarage door a second time,

she saw that the firemen and the EMTs had now arrived on the scene.

⁂

Jackson swung the Jaguar off the main road and into the narrow lane that descended toward the Minster Church. He drove slowly through the tunnel of arching trees, creeping past the entryway to the long flight of steps that led down to the church, and then on up to the open area just above the east end of the church, an area which today was far from open. It was packed with vehicles: an ambulance, a fire engine, another official-looking car, and a small green Ford. Tendrils of smoke swirled about the vehicles.

"Holy moly!" Ally shouted. She was out of the car and running even before Jack had brought it to a full stop.

The others piled out, too. Charles and Jack sprinted after Ally, who already had a good twenty yards on them.

At the vicarage, the EMTs were attending to someone lying on the ground. Close by, Charles saw the shy young woman who helped out at the church. Her name, he remembered, was Anna. Sounds came from within the building. Several firemen were inside, dealing with matters in there. One of them suddenly emerged through the vicarage door. He held a charred and still smoldering bundle wrapped in a fireproof blanket. He placed the bundle on the ground at a safe distance from where the others were gathered.

"Geez, what a stench!" Jack said.

"Animal hides," the professor said. "They don't make a pleasant smell when they burn."

"And they don't burn so good, either," the fireman said, "not even when they've been doused with paraffin." The fireman who'd come out of the building after him held up the can he'd taken from inside.

"Paraffin?" said Jack.

"Kerosene," the professor explained.

"She musta thought they'd burn like paper," the first fireman said. "Well, she were quite wrong. And o' course she didn't know that that old fireplace hadn't been used since who-knows-when. Room musta filled with smoke in a matter o' seconds after she lit the bleedin' thing. It's a miracle she didn't die from smoke inhalation."

"And a miracle the whole place wasn't burnt to a crisp, all the books and papers and whatnot that were in there," the second fireman said.

Ally was on her knees beside the body of her mother. "Mum? Can you hear me? Mum, it's me, Ally." The woman's eyes were just narrow slits. Her eyelids flickered a moment, but she looked very out of it.

"We'll take her to the infirmary in Wadebridge," one of the EMTs said. "They'll probably want to keep her overnight. Check her out good, see how her lungs are doing and such like."

"I'm her daughter," Ally told them. "Tell her I'll come and see her later today."

Ally provided the EMTs with the all the bits of inform- ation they wanted. Then they lifted Mrs. Tremayne onto a rolling stretcher and began wheeling her along the lane toward their vehicle.

"Miss," Ally said to Anna, "are you going to be okay? Why don't we go somewhere and get you a nice cup of tea?"

Anna nodded. She was shaking. She looked very green

around the gills. Ally put her arm around her and pulled her close.

"You saved my mum," Ally said. "You are a hero." The young woman mustered up a smile.

The professor, who'd picked up a stick, started poking through the still smoldering pile the fireman had brought from the vicar's study. He glanced toward Charles and shook his head sadly.

Charles had been looking through the manuscripts Anna had rescued. He, too, shook his head. "It isn't one of these," he said. "It was probably a long shot, anyway. But why don't we hang on to them, see what they are."

"Yes, why don't we," the professor agreed. "Neville put in a lot of work on them, and they surely meant a great deal to him. After we've satisfied our curiosity, we can pass them on to Rhys. He'll treasure them."

The professor glanced toward Anna. "We have the solicitor's permission," he said, extracting a letter from his coat pocket and holding it up. Anna, still very shaken by the whole experience, just nodded. But it was probably a good thing the dragon-lady hadn't been about this morning.

In the small office just off the vestry, Ally brewed the tea, then served it to Anna and the professor, Charles and Jack having declined the invitation. Anna had been much shaken by the morning's events. But she was a resilient young woman, and after twenty-five minutes, having been fortified by two cups of tea and several McVities digestive biscuits, the color in her face had returned to normal.

"It's very odd," she said to the others.

"What is?" asked the professor.

"Mrs. Tremayne's actions. She'd stopped by here earlier in the week. It was the day after you were here, sir. And Mrs. Brashler actually allowed her to go into the vicar's study, a real rarity. She'd claimed she needed to retrieve something. But I kept a close eye on her, and I'm quite sure that rather than retrieving something, she left something."

"She *left* something?"

"Yes, sir, she did. I think it may have been one of the manuscripts she was trying to destroy."

"Hmm," the professor said, "that's odd indeed. Thank you for pointing that out."

"Can you make any sense of it, sir?"

"Yes, I think maybe I can." He glanced over at Charles, who gave him a tight-lipped nod of agreement.

Ally and Anna waited for the professor to go on and explain, but he didn't.

An hour later, after Ally's mother had been taken off to the infirmary in Wadebridge, Anna returned to her morning's chores. The firemen were still wrapping things up at the vicarage.

For Charles and company, it was time to head for Somerset. So after bidding Anna adieu, the four of them piled back into the Jag, Jack still behind the wheel. They returned to the A30 and set off in the direction of Okehampton. For the first half an hour, they rode without speaking, each of them seemingly lost in his or her own thoughts; or in the professor's case, in his dreams, since he'd nodded off soon after they'd returned to the main road.

As they skirted the western slopes of Dartmoor, Jack broke the silence by intoning ominously, "The Hound of the Baskervilles." Charles and Ally ignored him.

"What on earth did she think she was doing?" Ally said, giving voice to her thoughts for the first time. For several beats, no one responded.

"Destroying the evidence?" Jack said. "Covering her tracks?"

"What tracks? What evidence?"

"That smoldering mass they recovered from the fireplace?" Charles said. "It's quite likely the original Polminster Manuscript was in there."

"Hmm," Ally said. "Well, I guess. But there's a lot I just don't understand. If it was, why in the world would she want to destroy it? And how did she know it was at the vicarage?"

"It appeared to me," the professor said, who'd been awakened by their voices, "that there were two manuscripts in the fireplace, both destroyed beyond recognition. It might have been one of them. Charles says it's not among the ones that Anna saved, the ones we have here with us."

"Which means the original Polminster Manuscript is now toast, so to speak," Jack said.

"Ally's father has Neville's copy of it, anyway," Charles said. "As for the edition of the Chaucer poem, we'll have to make the best case we can, without having the original. That's what we were going to have to do anyway, so it doesn't really change anything."

"No," Professor Wentworth said, "but it removes any hope we might've had that the original could still turn up."

"Yes," Charles agreed, "it does do that."

"But why?" Ally muttered. "Why destroy the manuscript? Why would she do that?"

For a long moment her question remained unanswered.

It was Charles who finally muttered softly, "Maybe just a case of Mad Meg."

"Mad *who*?" Jack asked.

"Meg," Charles replied.

"Mad Meg?" Ally asked. "Are you referring to *Dulle Griet*? The Bruegel painting?"

"Yes," Charles said. "That would be the one. Neville Smallwood had a poster of that dreadful thing on a wall in his study. A pretty weird choice for a gentle, kindly old clergyman. Though maybe a bit prescient, given your mother's behavior."

"Charlie," the professor said, "maybe not such a weird choice. Not given how stuck Neville was in the Middle Ages. A fellow who devotes decades of his life to recreating medieval manuscripts has to be a very peculiar man."

"Not like Charlie," Jack said. "He just transcribes them and edits them like a totally normal man."

"Hey, watch it, dude," Charles said.

"Mother as Mad Meg?" Ally mused. "Hmm. I've certainly never associated my mother with Mad Meg. But . . . maybe. My mother is an odd woman, no doubt about that. And she definitely has a store of pent-up anger at Daddy. But an out-and-out crusade to undermine his scholarly reputation? I wouldn't have thought she'd go as far as that."

"Neville Smallwood and Lowenna Tremayne, a pair of true eccentrics," the professor said.

"The madwoman in the attic," Jack said.

"Hey, watch it, dude," Ally said, echoing Charles' earlier words. "She's still my mum, you know."

✢✢✢

After they'd driven beyond Exeter, Jack pulled off at a service area for a petrol stop and bathroom break.

"Only half an hour to go," the professor said. "Lunch here, or wait till we get to Yeovil?"

"Here," Jack said. "I be famished."

The service area wasn't the one where they'd been accosted by Robbie Stevenson, but to Charles they seemed interchangeable. Fortunately, rather than eating inside, there was a pasty kiosk attached to the place, so they ordered there and then sat outside at a picnic table.

"Yum," Jack said. "This final pasty will have to last me for who-knows-how long."

When they'd disposed of their trash, Ally said, "I'd better take it from here. Town driving can be trickier, and the streets in Yeovil are a bit of a rat's nest. That okay by you, Jack?" She climbed in behind the wheel before he'd had a chance to answer.

"Okay by me," Jack said, belatedly.

Charles sat in front beside Ally, Jack in back beside the professor.

"Home, James," Jack said, from the back seat, "and don't spare the horses."

Ally didn't. They reached Yeovil in less than twenty-five minutes.

30

"First stop," Ally said, "train station."

"Oh, man, you guys are booting me?" Jack expostulated.

"All good things must come to an end," Charles said.

"Sending me back to my boring life, huh? No more mysterious manuscripts, no more spooky late-night adventures, no more wild dart games in noisy, crowded pubs, no more lovely, sophisticated ladies, no more delectable Cornish pasties?"

"There will be lovely ladies in your future, Jackson, I feel certain of that," Ally said. "Perhaps even a redhead or two."

"Now there's a hope I'll cling to," Jack replied.

Jack retrieved his bag from the boot of the car and set it down on the curb. He gave the professor a final handshake, then gave Ally a vigorous hug. Lastly, he hugged Charles.

"You take care, amigo," Charles said.

Jack, his lips compressed, nodded. "You too," he said. "Really hope to see you again, Ally."

"I'd like that," she replied, smiling.

Jack stood and watched as his friends drove away. He had an empty, forlorn feeling. Well, at least he'd get to see Clare tomorrow. Then it would be back to work in Charlotte. He couldn't help sighing.

Police Constable Martin Goodrich stood on the sidewalk next to the professor's sparkling, light-green Morris Minor, which was parked on the street outside the police station. Ally pulled in behind it, and they piled out and greeted the policeman. After the professor had produced suitable identification, PC Goodrich handed him the keys. He'd already placed a large box containing all the CDs they'd been able to recover on the back seat.

"Oh, splendid," the professor said, glancing in at the box. "And do you think there's any chance the Stevensons might still have the CD player they removed from the car? It would be wonderful to have it back."

"I'll give 'em a jingle and find out," Constable Goodrich replied. "Only take a second."

"We're in luck," he said, returning a minute later. "Normally they're closed on Saturday afternoon, but today the brothers are both still there, working on a car they bought yesterday. Colin said they do still have the CD player and will be happy to return it. So, if you'll follow me, I'll lead you there."

The professor climbed into the spiffed-up Morris Minor, Ally and Charles popped back into the Jag, and they both followed the constable's old Ford Cortina. Five minutes later the little three-car caravan came to a halt in front of the Stevenson & Sons Auto Repair and Recovery shop.

"They said to come 'round the back," PC Goodrich told them, "so leave your cars here and we'll walk 'round."

The first thing Charles saw was the hulking figure of Robbie Stevenson. His back was to them and he was peering into an opened hood. He looked exactly as Charles remembered him – hair a wild tangle, back broad as the trunk of an oak tree – and Charles couldn't help a little nervous frisson at the sight of Mr. Half-Hyde. The car Robbie was tinkering with was an old black Morris Minor, about the same vintage as the professor's car. It appeared that the brothers were getting ready to repaint it.

Colin Stevenson came around the car from inside the body shop. When he saw the visitors he waved them a greeting.

"Hey there, Marty," he called out to the policeman. "Robbie, go and see if you can track down the CD player we took out, eh? It's probably in amongst that jumble of odd parts on the shelves in the far back."

Robbie turned about and stared at their visitors. He glanced for a moment at Charles and the professor. Then his attention *fixed* on Ally.

Finally wrenching his eyes from Ally and shifting them back to Charles and the professor, he said, "I remember yous – bought a car from yous, I did."

"Robbie, get a move on it," Colin said. Robbie shrugged, then dutifully shambled off.

Colin stepped forward, extending his hand to the professor.

"Hello, sir," he said. "Terribly sorry about the little misunderstanding about your car. Really appreciate that you were willin' to go easy on my brother. Robbie's thoughts sometimes get a bit muddled. We don't normally let him handle business matters. But sometimes, when he sees a car that grabs his fancy, he gets so excited he can't help himself. That was the case with yours. Robbie?" he shouted out. "I'd better go and see what's keeping him." Then he disappeared into the back of the shop also.

"Sometimes gets a bit muddled," Charles scoffed. "Yeah, right."

"Charlie," the professor said, "all's well that ends well."

Then Robbie reappeared from around the side of the building. He was cradling the CD player in his hands. "Weren't where Colin said it were. Well," he said, a big grin on his face, "how ya like the car? Turned out real good, yeah?"

"Yes, very nice," the professor replied. "What's the one you're working on now?" he pointed to the car in the bay.

"Ah. Just brought 'er in. Bought 'er yesterday, we did. Gettin' all set ta work on 'er."

"What sort of shape is it in?"

"Real good. Don't hardly need no bodywork. I likes doin' body work. We just hafta paint 'er up good. Gonna make 'er the same color as yors. Folks seem ta like that color."

"How does it run?"

"Runs like a top, sor. Even better'n yors."

"You sell it?" the professor said. His words sounded to Charles very much like ones Robbie had used at the service area two weeks ago.

"Sell 'er? Nah, just bought 'er."

"How much for?"

"Thirty-five hundred quid, it were." Charles had a sense of déjà vu.

"Well, if you won't sell it, how about exchanging it?"

Robbie had a confused look on his face. "Exchangin' it?"

"Yes. This one for mine."

Things were moving too quickly for Robbie's brain. "Exchangin' it?" he said again, looking perplexed. He glanced toward his brother Colin, who had just emerged from the body shop where he'd been looking for Robbie and the CD player.

"What's this about an exchange?" Colin asked.

"My car for the one you have there in the bay," the professor said.

"Swap 'em?"

"Yes, straight up swap." Charles, Ally, and PC Goodrich stood silently by, all three of them rather nonplussed by this curious negotiation.

"Well, goodness," Colin said. "Whatta ya think, Robbie? I hafta say I kinda like the idea. We put in a helleva lot of work on the professor's car. If we keep it and sell it, we'll surely turn a hefty profit. And if he'll take this one as is, we won't have ta do a blessed thing to it. Robbie, we could have the afternoon off."

"I really likes workin' on 'em," Robbie said. "But yeah, I see yor point."

"Do we have a deal, then?" the professor asked. Colin nodded his agreement, Robbie grunted his.

"That's super," the professor said, handing the keys to Robbie.

"I assume you have all the proper papers for this one?" Constable Goodrich asked. Colin nodded again. "Then, Professor, why don't you and me and Colin go inside and look 'em over, eh?"

When the other three had disappeared inside to the office Robbie said to Charles and Ally, "Be okay for me ta have another look at the other car?"

"Sure," Charles said, "it's out front. Why don't you just pull it around?"

"I really love this car," Robbie declared, after he'd

returned and clambered out. "I really does. It sure did come out good."

"It sure did," Ally said. Robbie beamed at her. He was ogling her shyly, Charles thought, if such a thing was possible.

"Colin did the painting," Robbie said, "but I did all the body work."

"You both did a super job," Ally said. A blush suffused Robbie's cheeks.

"Hey, listen," Robbie said. "There's somethin' in the shop you might like ta have."

"The CD player?"

"Nah, nah, not the CD player. I give you that a'ready. Back in a moment." He disappeared into the body shop.

"What do you suppose he means?' Ally asked.

"With Robbie Stevenson, there's no telling."

PC Goodrich, Colin Stevenson, and the professor came back out through the door of the front office and moved toward them. The professor was clutching an envelope.

"Got it all worked out?" Charles asked.

"Yes indeed. So, I guess we just need to shift our things from the Jag into my new car, and my box of CDs from this one, and we'll be ready to hit the road." He jingled a set of car keys and started toward the black Morris still parked in the bay.

"Hang on a minute, sir," Charles said. "Robbie says he's got something for us."

Then there he came, holding a plastic carrying bag. It said "Tesco" on it.

"This were in the car," he said. "Just some ratty old book,

seems like. So here ya are, if you want it. We got no use for it." He paused for a moment and looked hopefully at Ally. "Miss, think mebbe you'd like it back?"

As he handed it to her, Charles pictured a humble supplicant doing his obeisance to a noble lady.

Ally peeked into the plastic bag and beamed a blinding smile at Robbie. "Yes, Robbie, you're right, it is just some ratty old book. But it is ours, and we'd be delighted to have it back. This ratty old book holds a lot of sentimental value for us. Thank you so very much for returning it, extremely kind of you." Charles thought Robbie's blush deepened even more, which seemed hardly possible.

Charles peeked in and nodded. "Yes, it's just some ratty old book all right. But a real family treasure. Thank you, Robbie."

Ally stepped over to Robbie and gave him a small kiss on the cheek.

Robbie Stevenson, his face all aglow, looked down and studied his toes.

Charles walked Ally back out to the front of the Stevenson & Sons auto repair shop. They stood beside the Jaguar, neither of them speaking. They were still trying to take in the astonishing thing that had just occurred.

"Well," Charles said at last, "how about that?"

"Daddy will be so pleased," she said.

"I guess the professor and I had better hang onto the manuscript until the editing is all wrapped up. Tell your father we'll get it back to him just as soon as we can," Charles said. "Tell him we have it and that it's safe and sound. That will be a big relief to him."

"Of course I will," she replied. "But when you do return it, Charlie, I hope you will do it in person. That would be the only safe way, right? You wouldn't want to entrust so valuable a thing to the mails." She gave him a meaningful look. "Promise me you'll do that."

"I promise."

"And Charlie Bascombe is a fella who keeps his promises."

"He tries, anyway." Charles held the driver's door open for Ally.

"Thank you, kind sir," she said. Then she made a beckoning gesture with her finger. "Please to step over here, kind sir." She leaned back against the open door.

Charles obliged. Ally reached out her arms and pulled him close. She held him in a tight embrace for a long moment, reluctant to release him. Finally, she did.

She looked into his eyes. "You won't forget, right?" she said.

"No, I won't. Though a little reminder wouldn't hurt."

Ally smiled. She leaned forward and kissed Charles on the lips, a kiss which Charles fully reciprocated. Ally finally broke it off. She swung about and climbed into the car. She turned her head towards him for a final look.

"See ya," Charles said.

"See ya," she replied. And then Ally drove away. And as she did, Charles felt that a little piece of his heart had gone with her.

31

Ten minutes later, having shifted their bags and the professor's CD collection to the professor's new old car, William Wentworth and Charles Bascombe were ready to hit the road for Oxford.

"So, why don't we just get the hell out of Deadwood," Charles said with a straight face.

"Charlie," the professor responded, "I think it's Dodge people get the hell out of."

"Dodge it is, sir – so, let's do it."

"Why don't we not backtrack to the M5," the professor said as he started the engine. "Take us twenty-five minutes just to get there. Why don't we push straight up the A303? Much more direct, and it's mostly dual carriageway anyway. Time-wise should be about the same."

"Entirely up to you, sir."

"Wish we could have asked those fellas to put in the CD player, but that probably would have been asking too much. Anyway, let's put this old buggy through her paces, eh what?"

"You're the driver, sir."

"Really quite astonishing, Charlie, that Robbie simply handed the manuscript over to us. My word. What a jolt that gave me. And how extremely fortuitous."

"I don't think it would have happened if Ally hadn't been with us. He seemed quite taken by her. Wanted to do anything he could think of to please her."

"Very understandable," the professor said. "I'm quite

taken by her, too." He glanced at Charles, who didn't give him his expected response.

"Gabrielle-Suzanne Barbot de Villeneuve," the professor said.

"Say what?" Charles replied.

"Beauty and the Beast."

"Ah, I get you. Yes, quite possibly. But let's not push that idea too far."

"So, Charlie, I guess the blasted manuscript must've been in the car all along."

"That's how it appears."

"But then what were all those shenanigans at the vicarage about? All just much ado about nothing? Really hard for this old brain to sort out."

"I can only speculate, sir. But if you want, I'll give you my best guess."

"Yes, do, Charlie. Your best guesses often have a habit of turning out very well."

"Here's what I'm thinking, sir. The night your car was carted off by the Stevenson brothers, the manuscript was stolen also. That much seems clear."

"But Charlie, how did it come to even be in the car?"

"When I came downstairs that night around midnight, Maria had just come back in from being outside. She said she'd been making a final check on things. But my guess is she had just nabbed the manuscript from Rhys's study. When she suddenly became aware of me, she needed to find some place quick where she could hide the manuscript, so she slipped outside to avoid me, then decided to leave it on the back seat of your car just until the coast was clear. Anyway, when she came back in, she was empty-handed. I'm guessing that before she had a chance to retrieve it, the Stevensons nicked the car. That's my hypothesis, anyway."

"But if she'd lost the manuscript, what did she give to Lowenna Tremayne?"

"Again, I can only speculate. But we know that Neville had given Rhys copies of several of his manuscripts. Maria, having lost the original, must've substituted one of those for it, passing one of them on to Mrs. Tremayne in hopes she wouldn't know the difference. Apparently she didn't. After all, most people wouldn't. To the uninitiated, one medieval manuscript is a lot like another."

"But, Charlie, how did Lowenna know we would break into the vicar's study, find the copy, and assume it was the original manuscript?"

"Yes, that's a tougher one, isn't it?" They drove in silence for a moment before Charles continued with his theories. "Maybe she just knew you too well, sir. Maybe she knew that once you'd gotten so close to Neville's secret cache of goodies, you wouldn't be able to contain your curiosity. Maybe she just guessed right.

"Perhaps," Charles continued, "if we hadn't stumbled upon the copy and taken it, as she hoped we'd do, she would have had to try another means of tricking us into finding it. But, as it turned out, she didn't have to. We took the bait."

"Charlie, my head is spinning. This is all just a little bit too much for me to take in at one time."

"We may never know the answers to these questions, sir. But we do finally have the actual Polminster Manuscript back. That's the thing that really matters."

"Thanks to Ally. And to Robbie."

They drove on for another ten miles without speaking.

"How do you think your wife will like the new car? Or do you think she'll even realize it's not the same one? Sir, that wouldn't be why you wanted to make the exchange, would it? To stay in your wife's good graces?"

The professor gave Charles a sidelong glance. "Never a bad idea to stay in one's spouse's good graces, Charlie. Tuck that bit of advice away. Maybe someday you'll need it. But, Charlie, I do wish we had some music," he said, steering the conversation away from his protégé's discomfiting questions.

"Music? Well, sir, I suppose I could sing."

"Umm . . . yes . . . I suppose you could. But why don't you not. Why don't you give the radio a try? But please, find something other than Adele or Lady Gaga. I'm really not up for any pop crap."

Charles did give the radio a try, and he didn't find any pop crap. On BBC 3, he found an opera. And so, William Wentworth and Charles Bascombe rode all the rest of the way to Oxford with Mozart's *Don Giovanni* washing over them.

By the time they pulled up in front of Charles' flat in Summertown, it was almost five o'clock.

"Well, Charlie," the professor said, "that was a wonderfully exhilarating trip. Just what I'd hoped it might be. So glad I decided to join you."

"Me too, sir. Wouldn't have been the same without you. Oh, if it's okay with you, I'd better hang on to the manuscript for a couple of weeks. "

"Of course, Charlie. You'll want to have it at your elbow

as you work. But why don't I hang on to the ones from Neville's study. Should be fun seeing what they contain."

"Sir, why don't we get together for coffee around mid-week?"

"Yes, let's do that. Well, Charlie, for me it's back to home and hearth."

"Sir, I really hope your wife likes her new car."

"Yes . . . well . . . I'll let you know how that turns out." Then he fired up the engine and headed for home and hearth.

"Charlie!" cried Mrs. Hawkins, who was just returning from walking Agnes. "You're home. And just in time for tea."

32

Charles Bascombe sat at his desk in the front room of his Oxford flat. He was just finishing a final proofread of his work on the edition of the Middle English poem that had totally occupied his life for the last two weeks. He planned to present a completed copy to Professor Wentworth tomorrow morning when they met for coffee at Brown's Café.

During the fourteen days since his return to Oxford, Charles had hardly come up for air – no trips to the local pub, no long walks in Port Meadow, no bicycle rides out to the Trout, not even a visit to the dear old dusty, musty Bodleian. It had been all work and no play – and it had been good work, he felt sure of it, even if it did make him a dull boy. His critical edition of the poem was going to cause quite a stir in the world of Chaucer scholarship, no doubt about it. It would create a good bit of controversy; but at the same time, it would almost certainly assure him of promotion to the rank of associate professor. It might even establish him as something of a name in the field of Medieval Studies – but he tried not to think about that.

A movement from outside the flat's front window caught his eye. The postman was just coming up the drive. A minute later, Mrs. Hawkins sang out from downstairs, "Charlie! You have a letter! A big thick one!"

She stood at the foot of the stairs, holding a large cream-colored envelope. "It's from the U.S. – from your friend Jack," she declared, eyeing the return address. She held it out to him, seeming as eager to discover its contents as he was.

Charles tore open the envelope and extracted a single page of writing, along with a smaller envelope containing several photos. He pulled out the photos and flipped through them, one by one. The first one was taken from high up above the graveyard at the Minster Church; the second one showed a pub sign, the pub where he and Ally had done battle with Dargan and Mick. The third showed Charles, Jack, and the professor, looking very wind-blown, out on the craggy cliffs at Tintagel where they'd asked another tourist to take a shot of them. All really nice photos. But it was the last one that was special. It showed two people standing at the end of a long causeway, a castle looming dramatically behind them. It was Charles and Ally. He didn't remember Jack having taken that one.

"Ooh, I like that," said Mrs. Hawkins, peering over his shoulder. "That's Saint Michael's Mount, isn't it? And who's your friend, Charlie? My, she's quite lovely."

"That's Alwyn," Charles said. "She's Rhys Tremayne's daughter."

"A lovely Cornish maiden," Mrs. Hawkins said, a twinkle in her eye. "You make a handsome pair, Charlie." She gave Charles a meaningful glance. Charles smiled, tilted his head to one side, and gave a noncommittal shrug of his shoulders.

"Actual photographs," he finally said. "Not so common in this digital age."

"I'm sorry I didn't get to meet your friend Jack," Mrs. Hawkins said. "So thoughtful of him to send the photographs."

Charles ran his eyes over the words of the thank-you note. They sounded a bit wistful. The only contact he'd had with Jack was their brief exchange of emails on the Monday evening after Charles got back to Oxford. Jack said he'd had a safe and uneventful flight back to the U.S. After that Charlie had immersed himself totally in his scholarship; he hadn't attempted any further contact. Now, he thought, once he'd turned over the draft of his edition of the poem to the professor, he'd write Jack a long message.

After he'd seen the professor tomorrow and given him the draft copy of his work, the rest of Charles' week was open – open, that is, until Saturday, when Clare would be coming for her visit. While he'd been working, Charles had shelved all thoughts of Clare far back in his mind. Now maybe he should shift the matter more into the front of his mind.

As for Ally, staring at the photo and seeing the two of them together like that had stirred Charles' emotions. While he'd worked, he'd done his best to keep all thoughts of her from intruding on his mind. He had called her on the Sunday night of his return, wanting to check on her mother, but since then they'd had no contact. Now, looking at the photo of the two of them standing together, he realized how much he missed her. He wondered if Jack had sent her a copy. If he did, did the photo have a similar effect on her? He hoped so.

✠ ✠ ✠

On Tuesday morning, Charles Bascombe, his manuscript snug inside his shoulder bag, set off down the Woodstock Road toward the center of Oxford. It was 8:30. He would walk the two-mile trek at his leisure. It was a slightly longer route than going down the Banbury Road, but even so it would only take him about an hour. The morning was cool and misty, typical summer weather for Oxford, and he should reach Brown's Café in the covered market well in advance of his 10:15 meeting, giving him time to enjoy a solitary cup of coffee before the professor arrived.

As he walked, cars and bicyclists zipped by him heading toward the center. He passed St. Edwards College on his left, a rather posh public school almost on a par with Eton in status. Across the road on his right were several sports fields attached to various Oxford colleges. Eventually he reached the sprawling complex of the Radcliffe Infirmary, also across the road to his right, and then there opening up before him was the broad expanse of St. Giles; at the end of it stood the Martyrs Monument. It was pushing 9:30, and the sun was just now beginning to dispel the morning mists.

Brown's Café, at mid-morning, was only sparsely occupied. Charles always loved the homey atmosphere of Brown's. One of Oxford's most venerable establishments, it had been a favorite haunt of students and faculty for decades. The fare they served was basic, no-frills English cooking – reasonably good, for what it was, and quite inexpensive.

Twenty-five minutes early for his meeting with the professor, Charles took a seat at an empty table and ordered coffee. He also gave the waitress a special order for later on. Seated at a nearby table were a pair of Oxford undergraduates, drinking tea and apparently arguing about the novels of Vladimir Nabokov. Seated at the table just beyond them were a couple of old graybeards, men Charles assumed were retired professors. Occupying a large table in a far corner was a family of what Charles thought were probably tourists; maybe they'd read about Brown's in a guidebook.

After shoving the bottles of HP Sauce, malt vinegar, and Lea & Perrins down to its far end, Charles gave the table a careful wipe with a napkin, then extracted his manuscript from his shoulder bag and placed it down on the tabletop by his right-hand side. He would keep his coffee cup well off to his left. It was only a draft, but still, no need for extraneous coffee stains at this point. It would surely have enough of them by the time he got it back from the professor.

It was just then that Charles became aware of the figure of a woman who had suddenly materialized just across from him. She was a slender brunette of medium height; her arms were folded across the front of her light-blue sweater; her face wore a scowl.

She stood there in silence for several beats staring at Charles icily. Finally she spoke: "Well, hello there, stranger."

"Oh, hi, Sophie . . . ," Charles replied, glancing up.

"Been avoiding your erstwhile friends?"

"Uh . . . no . . . no, not at all, at least not intentionally. No, I was away for a couple of weeks, down in Cornwall. I left you a note, didn't I? Since I've been back, I've been up to my ears in the project I brought back with me. Been working like a fiend. I've just come up for air, actually. This is my first trip down to the center. Here," he said, pointing to the stack of pages on the table as if he needed to offer proof. "Here's the result of my labors." He placed his hand atop the thick draft of the manuscript he'd brought for Professor Wentworth. "Um, you did get my note, didn't you get it?"

"Yeah, I got it. You said you'd probably be away for a few days. Charlie, that was a month ago. And now you tell me you've been in Oxford for the last two weeks. You couldn't even be bothered to come and say hello?"

"Hey, wait. No fair. Look, Sophie, why don't we go for coffee tomorrow? About the usual time? That sound okay? We could do it right now if I didn't have a meeting with Professor Wentworth this morning. He'll be arriving any moment."

"Coffee tomorrow? Usual time?" she scoffed, not sounding at all mollified. "No Charlie, I don't think so." Shifting her hands down onto her hips she declaimed in a firm voice, " 'he who would not when he could, shall not when he would.'"

"Ah, a line from a Robert Henryson poem, if I'm not mistaken," said William Wentworth, who'd just come into the café and now stood close beside the angry young woman. "That line has always been a favorite of mine."

"Sophie," Charles said, doing his best to remedy the situation, "have you met Professor Wentworth? Professor, this is my friend Sophia Sinclair."

"A pleasure to meet you, Sophia," said Professor Wentworth, extending his hand. Sophie took it shyly.

In the presence of the esteemed holder of the Bosworth

Chair of Medieval Literature, Sophie's hostile demeanor had quickly dissipated.

"It's an honor, Professor," she said, shaking his hand. "Charlie says the two of you have important matters to discuss, so I guess I'd better take myself off and leave you to it."

"You won't join us for a cup?" the professor asked graciously.

"Very kind of you, sir, but not today," she replied. "Charlie, nice to see you once again – finally. A real honor to meet you, Professor." And Sophie, giving Charles a departing black look, took herself out through the door.

" 'He who would not when he could, shall not when he would,' eh Charlie?" the professor quoted. He couldn't help grinning. "It sounds like you might've burned your bridges with that one."

"Sir, I have been very hard at work. A simple matter of priorities."

"Charlie, you and your abstemious ways. You need to learn to strike when the iron is hot...hmm...a blacksmithing metaphor, I suppose," he mused. "Attractive young woman, nice shoulders, lovely dark eyes, had a sweet smile for me if not for you – improbably white teeth, though. Well, your loss, lad."

"Sir, we are, or were, only acquaintances."

"I think she was hoping it would be more than that. Well, c'est la vie."

The professor dropped himself down into a chair across from Charles.

"Sir, here's my progress." Charles shoved the typescript

of the manuscript over in front of the professor. The waitress came over to their table, poured the professor a cup of coffee and topped up Charles'. "Oh, lovely, my dear," the professor said to her. He helped himself to a little packet of creamer.

"Speaking of women," Charles said, "I've been wondering what your wife thought of the car. Could she tell it wasn't the same one?"

"Oh my, Charlie, listen to this. Here's what she said: 'Billy – that's what she calls me – Billy, did you have work done on the car while you were down in Cornwall? Seems to have fewer dents than before.' 'Well, yes Martha, something like that.' 'Well, thank you, Billy, it does look quite nice. And I've been wondering whether we might want to get it repainted. There's a lovely shade of green that's become quite fashionable lately. How would you feel about doing that?' "

Charles laughed. "Sir, I know a couple of follows who just might be willing to do the job for you."

"Yes, so do I. But I think I'll have it done locally. And Charlie, speaking of women, what's the latest on Ally's mother."

"Turned out they needed to do a blood transfusion. Tricky business. Had to call in a famous herpetologist from the London Zoo to handle it."

"A what? A herpetologist? . . . Oh, Charlie, you're having me on again. What am I ever going to do with you?"

"Actually, sir, the truth is, she's made a full recovery."

"Well, I'm very glad to hear it. A herpetologist indeed," he muttered.

"Anything of special interest in the other manuscript

copies that brave Anna rescued from the vicarage fire?" Charles asked.

"Not a whole lot. Though one of them has a section from *Piers Plowman*."

"Wow, that's cool."

"Yes, I guess it is. I have a grad student working on Langland. He'll be interested."

"Nothing else?"

"They are lovely things, all impressive, in their own way. But nothing of great literary consequence."

"Well, Rhys will treasure them."

"As well he should. So, then," the professor said, pointing to the stack of manuscript pages by Charles' right elbow, "that's it, is it?"

"That's it," Charles replied.

The professor picked it up and turned to the final paragraph of the introduction. Then he read aloud:

> Can we attribute this poem to Geoffrey Chaucer with a high degree of confidence? And if we can, can we also assert that this poem is the work Chaucer refers to in his *Retraction* as *The Book of the Lion*? The answer to each of those questions would appear to be yes. It will, however, be incumbent upon Chaucer scholars to determine if that is truly the case.

"Charlie . . . that last sentence makes you sound a bit uncertain? Is that how you truly feel? I thought you'd become convinced the poem was most certainly Chaucer's. Now you sound somewhat diffident."

Charles chewed his lips for a moment.

"Charlie, what's the problem?"

"Well, sir," he finally said, "everything fits. Everything

looks totally perfect. And frankly, that's what's begun to nag at me. Everything looks a little too perfect, a little too pat."

"Explain what you mean, Charlie."

"For one thing, there isn't a single word in the poem that isn't already in the *Chaucer Concordance*. That may not seem terribly surprising until you consider the fact every one of the poems in the Chaucer canon has a few words or phrases that are unique to it."

"That bothers you?"

"Yes, it does."

"Sometimes those unique words are truly unique words, like the famous hapax legomenon *cankedort* in the *Troilus*?"

"That's an extreme example, but yes. But you see what I mean. In addition, how about this, Professor? Every pair of rhyming words in this poem also occurs in a rhyming couplet elsewhere in Chaucer's poetry. That's another thing that isn't true for any of his other poems."

"You actually went to the trouble to check that?"

"I did."

"Goodness, lad. Must've taken you hours."

"These days, sir, there's a thing called a database."

"Ah ha. I've heard of them. Never actually used one, self-confessed Luddite that I am."

"And sir, although the quality of the verse in this poem isn't great – not surprising if it's the work of a novice poet – the poem appears to be tricked out with a small number of Chaucerian flourishes and allusions, things like a reference to May 3rd as a day of unfortunate occurrences; or an alusion to Alcione as a faithful wife; or a passing reference to a character who's described as 'a slender choleric man'– "

"– like the Reeve in the *General Prologue*."

"Precisely."

"Or with phrases such as 'Dun is in the mire'?" asked the professor.

"Yes, though that one isn't in the work. The poem isn't loaded with such things, there's really just a light scattering of them. But I can't help wondering if someone slid them in there to make us go, 'Yes, there's a Chaucerian phrase, one he uses in such and such.' "

"So Charlie, what is it that your scholarly intuition is telling you?"

"It's telling me that we should tread lightly – that some clever rascal might be leading us down the garden path."

"So the poem strikes you as being too good to be true? You smell a rat?"

"Just a faint whiff of one. And it alarms me."

Noticing that the young waitress was looking in their direction, Charles lifted a hand signalling to her. She'd already placed two servings of apple pie on the countertop, ready to be served; now she added a scoop of vanilla ice cream to each one. It was the order Charles had placed earlier, knowing how much the professor liked pie á la mode with his mid-morning coffee.

"Oh, thank you, my dear," he said to her when she arrived and unloaded her carrying tray. "Well done, Charles, just the thing, eh?" He spooned a large bite into his mouth and took his time savoring it. "Umm, yes, just the thing."

Finally swallowing he said, "But do go on about the poem, lad."

"Sir, if it is a fake, it's a masterful one. If it is a fake, it has to be the work of someone with considerable knowledge of Chaucer." Charles cocked his head and pursed his lips.

"Charlie, you surely aren't suspecting *me*?"

"No, sir, of course not. I really don't know if it was anybody; but if it was someone, it certainly wasn't you. You would never compromise the integrity of your entire scholarly career, or do something to profane the works of Geoffrey Chaucer. And if you had done it, you would have done it with greater subtlety. But if someone has, they have to be fairly knowledgeable about Chaucer's poetry."

"Oh my, oh my," he said. "Well, Charlie, I will look over all you've done most carefully, and I'll bear your suspicions in mind. I don't for a moment think that Neville or Rhys, or both of them working in concert, could have brought off such a thing, even had they wanted to, which they wouldn't have. But, I suppose it's possible they could have been duped.

"Speaking of Rhys," the professor went on, "he says he wants the monograph to be published by a Canadian university press. Perhaps the University of Toronto Press. Turns out the editor there is an old friend of his."

"Sounds like the perfect choice," Charles said, nodding his approval. "But whoever publishes, they'd had better be prepared to take some flak."

"Which is true for you, too, Charlie. And for me as well, if I write the preface you've committed me to write."

"Sir, you aren't thinking of backing out?"

"Never in life, Charlie."

After their meeting ended, the two men walked together back to Broad Street. There they parted, the professor turning to the left, Charles to the right. Charles walked on down the Broad toward the Bodleian, thinking he might pop in for an hour or two. As he strolled, he glanced across the wide thoroughfare toward Blackwell's Bookstore and the White Horse Pub. It was there in that little pub, just over four weeks ago, that this whole adventure had begun.

What a four weeks it had been, Charles mused, the most eventful four weeks of his relatively young life.

32

At 10:30 on Saturday morning, a nervous but excited Clare Reilly stepped from the coach at the Oxford train station into a lightly falling rain. She ran her eyes across the faces of the many people standing behind the barrier. It took only a moment for her to spot the familiar, grinning countenance of Charles Bascombe. He saw her at the same time and lifted a hand in greeting.

As Clare approached, Charles felt slightly trepidatious. Had inviting her here been such a good idea? Her warm embrace helped to ease his mind. Neither made any attempt at a kiss. Charles stepped back, his hands atop her shoulders, and studied her at arm's length. She was definitely Clare, a woman he had once known very well. She wasn't twenty-one any more, but this still youthful, vibrant-looking professional woman was easily recognizable as Clare Reilly.

"You look familiar to me," he said, narrowing his smiling eyes slightly. "Are you Clare Reilly, the young London barrister we've been hearing so much about?" Clare couldn't help smiling at his words. They reassured her that this visit might not be entirely painful.

"Yes, I must confess, my name is Clare Reilly," she said. "But I have my doubts about the up-and-coming barrister bit."

"Well, Miss Reilly," Charles went on, "could I talk you into joining me for a little stroll about the fine City of Oxford – if that wouldn't be too forward?"

"Sir, I believe you could."

When they exited the station, Charles opened his large umbrella against the morning's gray drizzle. Clare threaded her arm through his, and they soon walked across Friedeswide Square and then up the road that led toward the city center.

"How are you, Clare?" he asked.

"Aside from being extremely nervous about visiting a fella I haven't seen in a decade, I think I'm doing pretty well. How about you, Charlie?"

"I'm a bit nervous myself, but all in all, I've been doing great."

They walked the next half a block in silence. "So this is Oxford. Looks rather nondescript so far, pretty much like any other English town."

"So far. But appearances can be deceiving."

"Yes, they can," she said, giving his arm a squeeze. "It's really good to see you, Charlie. Good to see you and to hear your voice again. It's been quite a long time."

"Much too long, Clare. So, how's life in London treating you?"

As they walked toward the town center, Clare told Charles about her law firm and her various activities there.

She explained that her work had little to do with British legal matters, barristers or solicitors and what you might pick up from *Masterpiece Theatre*, since she worked for an American company that dealt primarily with international business affairs. Though Charles knew virtually nothing about legal matters, her remarks were lucid enough for him to be able to follow them.

When they reached Cornmarket Street, they swung to the right into what had once been a major thoroughfare and was now a jam-packed pedestrian mall. Charles thought they might stop at The Cup & Chaucer, a coffee shop with used books, down toward the far end of the Cornmarket close to Carfax.

When they arrived it wasn't too crowded so they went in, snagged a booth, and ordered coffee. Now Clare's talk had moved on from her work to all the things she loved about London, her favorite places to eat, shop, and walk – New Oxford Street, Green Park, the Victoria & Albert, Fortnum & Mason, the National Film Theatre – mostly places Charles knew by name but had never visited.

"It was such a delightful surprise to run into Jackson that day at the British Museum," she said, "quite an unexpected pleasure."

"If you hadn't run into him, I wouldn't have known you were in England."

"And I wouldn't have known you were in England." She looked across the table and studied Charles Bascombe's face. It was slightly fuller now than it had been a decade ago, but it still largely preserved his look of boyish innocence. Above his light-blue eyes, the frown lines that ran across his fore-head seemed etched a little deeper, as did the smile lines at the corners of his eyes. Charlie was finally approaching the end of his first youth, Clare reflected.

To Charles, Clare looked lovelier than ever, her complexion clear and glowing, her dark hair thick and lustrous. She still wore a minimum of makeup, as she'd always done, with only a hint of lipstick. He detected a subtle fragrance, which he had no hope of identifying.

Suddenly the bells of Oxford began chiming the hour.

"How wonderful," she said, counting off the eleven bongs. "The tintintabulation of the bells. You know what I really love? I love hearing the church bells in London ringing the changes on Sunday mornings."

"Me too, here in Oxford. Always makes me think of a Dorothy Sayers novel when I hear that," Charles said.

"*The Nine Tailors*," she replied.

"That's the one. Her college, Somerville, is only about three blocks from where we now sit."

Five minutes later, another loud and sonorous bell began chiming out the hour of eleven.

"A straggler?" Clare asked.

"That's the Great Tom, the bell in Tom Tower at Christ Church, just a few steps from here," Charles said. "It always rings five minutes after the other ones."

"Why is that?"

"It's set to old Oxford time, not to Greenwich Mean Time like the others. Makes Tom unique. It's housed in the entrance tower at Christ Church College, a beautiful tower designed, no surprise, by Wren. I'll show it to you when you get the grand tour."

Clare looked pensive. "Charlie, a rather odd thing happened on the train. Since this is my first visit to Oxford, I wanted to be extra sure I was getting off at the right stop. So as the train was approaching the city I looked over at a tall, cadaverous-looking fellow in the next seat and asked him if this was Oxford we were coming to. I thought it was, but I wanted to be sure.

"Charlie, the guy literally looked down his nose at me. And then, after a pause, he declared rather scornfully, 'It *couldn't* be anywhere else.' Condescending bastard!"

"Ouch. Well, I suppose one gets inured to it after a bit, but that's rather typical of the snobbiness frequently encountered in this city. It's why the fellow we went to see in Cornwall despises Oxford so much."

"Tell me more."

"Rhys Tremayne – our host down there – has a passionate dislike of Oxford, ever since he was an undergraduate here. Claims the place is filled with nothing but frauds, posers, and perverts."

"Is he right?"

"No, not really – though there's a grain of truth to his claim. But Clare, not to excuse the rudeness of that guy on the train, he's right in his belief that this could only be Oxford. It's true that there isn't any other place like it."

"Really? What about Cambridge?"

"Cambridge, as charming as it is, isn't like Oxford. Cambridge is a wondrous and unique place in its own right, but it has quite a different character. More picture-postcard.

The Backs along the River Cam are stunningly beautiful. But the city isn't as vibrant and alive as Oxford. People here – true to form – when they deign to speak of Cambridge, usually refer to it simply as 'the Other Place.' "

"Charlie, I really hope there are at least a few perfectly normal people living in Oxford," she said, half-seriously.

"I can affirm that there are at least two," he said.

"And who would that be?"

"Me, and my friend and mentor, Professor William Wentworth, the celebrated medieval scholar."

"You?" Clare said with a grin. "Normal?"

"Well, how about semi-normal?'

"That I'll buy." She raised her coffee mug to him, he raised his, and they clinked them.

"So tell me about your trip to Cornwall. I got some of it from Jack the day before he left."

Charles did tell her about their adventures in Cornwall, though not all about it. Certain parts he chose to leave out.

By the time they finished their coffee, the drizzle had dissipated. Charles took Clare on an abbreviated tour of the center of the city, starting with Christ Church and ending up at the Radcliffe Camera and the Bodleian Library. Clare spent fifteen minutes in the library gift shop, picking out postcards like a typical tourist.

Charles had planned to take her to lunch at the Turf Tavern, but with the weather improving, a different idea came to him.

"Ever been punting?" he asked her.

"Punting? No, but I've heard of it."

"Are you game?"

"I'm not sure, actually."

"Why don't we grab some sandwiches and a bottle of vino. We can either picnic in the boat, or if you prefer not to go punting, we can wander out into Christ Church Meadows and find us a shady spot of grass somewhere."

"Sounds good to me."

They stopped in a small shop and picked up sandwiches, then walked down to the far end of the High Street to Magdalen College and Magdalen Bridge where people, mostly tourists, were renting punts.

After watching the proceedings for a couple of minutes, Clare voted for walking out into Christ Church meadows rather than punting.

"If I were wearing shorts and a T-shirt, I would feel differently about it," she said.

"Fair enough," Charles agreed.

So they cut down a path beside the Botanic Gardens, a path that soon took them out into the Meadows.

Charles led them down a shady lane that ran close to the river and after ten minutes they were deep into the Meadows. They found a place where they could have a good bit of privacy, and spread out their coats on the grass, damp side down.

"Welcome to Fangorn Forest," Charles said.

"Really?"

"No. But this *was* one of Tolkien's favorite places to walk. He may have picnicked on this exact spot."

"Well, I say he did!" Clare declared.

He filled their plastic cups from the bottle of Beaujolais

he'd bought. They sipped the wine and ate their ham and cheese sandwiches without speaking. It was pleasant in the shade. A gentle breeze rippled the surface of the river and whispered through the tree leaves.

"This is a truly lovely place," Clare said. "Is this the River Thames?"

"Well, almost. Actually, it's the Cherwell, a tributary of the Thames. In Oxford the Thames is known as the Isis. It and the Cherwell are the two main streams that flow through the city. Just below Oxford they unite and form the mighty Thames."

"Charlie," Clare said after ten minutes, "picnicking here with you like this is a delight. But listen – we have yet to touch on the one thing we really have to touch on."

"I know, Clare." He breathed out a big sigh. "I know, but I haven't been eager to do that." He stared glumly into his wine, then swallowed down a large gulp of it.

"Charlie . . . I think that ten years ago you judged me very harshly," Clare said. "And you never even gave me a chance to explain. That wasn't at all like you. And I think that was really unfair."

"I never gave you a chance to explain? No, I guess I didn't. But Clare . . . I know what I saw."

"You know what you saw? And what was it that you saw?"

Charles didn't reply for a long moment. He wasn't eager to say what he was about to say. "Well . . . okay . . . here's what I saw. It was you, Clare, climbing into a car with René Bouchard at one in the morning. And then it was you, Clare, returning to your dormitory almost three hours later, climbing back out of the same car. And saying good night to that arrogant prick. René Bouchard, good old GG."

"GG," said Clare with a tight smile, almost a grimace. "I remember we used to call him that – 'God's Gift to the undergraduettes.' Was it you who came up with that very apt phrase? He really did think he was God's Gift, didn't he?"

"Clare, I always believed you despised that serial abuser of co-eds as much as I did."

She nodded her agreement. "I did, Charlie. I always considered him to be slime."

Charles took another sip of wine. "Then how could you have done that?" he said softly.

"But, Charlie, you saw all that?"

"I was half a block away when you and good old GG came ambling down the walk from the party."

Clare remained silent a long moment before saying, "Charlie, I don't deny that you saw what you saw. But sometimes, Charlie, appearances can be deceiving – as you told me just a little while ago. Anyway, what were you doing? Spying on me?"

"I decided to look in on the party after all. I'd finished the paper I was writing and figured I could still make a brief appearance, late as it was. Thought it might please you, since you'd been so irked when I'd chosen not to come."

"Clare, I couldn't believe my eyes. You, of all people, leaving the party with that smug bastard and getting into the car with him. Did I really see that? Even now, it's hard for me to believe . . . but . . . I know that I really did."

"Yes," she said after another long moment of hesitation, "you did see that. I guess you also saw me returning later.

What were you doing, lurking around outside the dorm like some pathetic stalker? Were you jealous, Charlie?"

"I was feeling a welter of emotions – jealousy was probably one of them – but the main one was disillusionment. What I'd seen had knocked me sideways. If I had only heard the next-day rumors – that you had spent the night with him – I wouldn't have believed them. But I knew what I'd seen."

Neither of them spoke for a long moment. They each brooded in silence.

"You say I never gave you a chance to explain. Would you like that chance now?"

It was Clare's turn to take a big drink of wine. Then she set the plastic cup down by her knee, her legs tucked back beneath her.

"After an interval of ten years you are finally offering me a chance to explain? Well, yes, I suppose I should do that. Better late than never."

Again a silence briefly enveloped them. Now Charles poured himself some more wine and Clare breathed out a great sigh.

"Charlie, the truth is, I've never fully understood why I agreed to leave the party with him. Probably a combination of things. For one, I'd had more to drink than usual, which is certainly no excuse. For another, I was still miffed at you for not coming when you knew I really wanted you to. Thought maybe you didn't care much about what I wanted. And for another – probably the biggest reason – I was actually quite flattered by the fact that it was me he'd chosen when he could have had his pick of any girl there.

I'll confess that I relished seeing the disappointed looks on the faces of those snotty sorority girls when they realized it was me he'd chosen, not any of them. *He'd* chosen me, and *you'd* chosen to write a paper!

"Anyway, as soon as I'd gotten into his car, he gave me a slimy smile and reached over and patted my thigh. I knew I'd made a horrible mistake. 'What the hell am I doing?' I said to myself. So, I told him what I wanted him to do was give me a ride back to the dorm. At first he was livid. I told him to return to the party and find himself someone more compliant. He said no. He said he'd been surprised and delighted that I had even agreed to leave with him. He said that he'd always known that I was impervious to his charms. Then he asked what I might like to do instead of going to his apartment or back to the dorm. I suggested coffee. So, we ended up at Denny's."

"At Denny's?"

"About the only place that's open at two in the morning."

"And then what?"

"We talked. And I slowly sobered up."

"You talked about what?"

"He tried to talk me out of going to law school. Said it would be a terrible waste of my talents. He said he'd heard that the paper I'd written on Trollope was virtually publishable. He nattered on about how I could have a truly brilliant academic career, that that's what I was cut out for. I think he was buttering me up, maybe in hopes he could still seduce me."

"Your paper on Trollope *was* terrific, as I remember,"

Charles said. "Clare, was he right about telling you not to go to law school?"

"He was one hundred percent wrong. It was one of the smartest things I've ever done. But Charlie, one of the stupidest things I've ever done was go with him that night. And the second stupidest was not explaining it all to you. But the next day, when I saw you get up and leave the Caf just as I was coming in, I felt that you had judged me and chosen to spurn me. So, I climbed up onto my moral high horse and spurned you right back. I never imagined we'd finish out those last two weeks without even speaking."

Charles just nodded glumly.

"You've just put your finger on my stupidest thing, Clare. But you can't imagine how much the events of that night hurt me. I felt totally let down, disillusioned really. I couldn't believe that you would spend the night with GG, in violation of what had always been one of your most cherished beliefs."

They both took deep sips of wine. Then Charles replenished their glasses, emptying the bottle.

"I was young and stupid, Clare. I didn't know how to react, what to think, or what to do. So I simply retreated into my shell. You know why I didn't talk to you? I was afraid to have all my fears confirmed."

"Come here," she said. Charles scooched across the space between them, and then she reached out put her arms about him. "Do you remember how good we were together? All these years ago?

"Charlie, can you forgive me now?"

"Can you forgive *me*, Clare?"

"I can and I do. But Charlie, tell me you forgive me?"

"Yes. Absolutely."

They sat there clutching each other for nearly a full minute.

"How could two otherwise intelligent and sensitive people who cared deeply for each other have been so obstinate and pigheaded?" Charles asked.

"I don't know," she said. "But . . . that was us."

They arrived back at the train station a few minutes before the 5:15 train to Paddington. On the long walk back, they had only engaged in desultory conversation. They were both emotionally spent.

"Will you come and visit me in London?" Clare asked. "I'd love to share my favorite places with you."

"Sounds good to me. And there are manuscripts in the British Library I'd like to see, too."

"That's you, Charlie, always combining work with pleasure."

"Hey, my work is my pleasure. But Clare, spending some time with you would be an even greater pleasure."

She smiled at his words. "Do let me know when you can come. You're welcome any weekend. Weekdays, too, if you want to work in the library while I'm at the office. We could have dinner and see a show or go to a concert."

"I'll let you know."

"Great. Soon, I hope."

The train pulled in, and Clare gave Charles a final embrace. She kissed his cheek, then turned away. After climbing into the coach, she gave him a last wave. He waved back and mouthed, "Take care."

"You, too, Charlie," she mouthed back at him.

As Clare watched the City of Oxford recede behind the train, she felt a palpable sense of relief. She'd seen Charlie! It had been *hard* – for him as well as for her, she felt sure – but they'd said their *mea culpas*. Now, maybe, the old wounds could finally heal. She knew she would like to see him again – but as a true and dear friend, not as a lover. And yet . . . one never knew for sure.

Charles really hadn't known what to expect from Clare's visit – mutual recriminations and irremediable enmity; or a rekindling of amorous passions. As it turned out, it had been neither. And at Clare's parting words, Charles felt a profound sense of relief.

33

The following Friday, when Charles Bascombe returned to his flat after a long day in the Bodleian, he discovered a large package leaning against his door. His name was on the front of it, but there was no other writing.

He unlocked the door, lifted the package, and carried it in. As he began to unwrap it, he realized it was a painting. It was a painting that he himself had commissioned. It was Ally's painting. He set it atop a bookcase and examined it closely. He found himself grinning from ear to ear. The painting was a true delight. It certainly wasn't a Kandinsky. To Charles it was something far better. And it was his.

"Charlie!" came Mrs. Hawkins' voice from downstairs. "You have a visitor. From Cornwall, I believe. Why don't you invite her up?"

Charles looked down the stairs, and there stood Ally Tremayne.

"Invite her up, Charlie."

"Ally, you brought the painting in person."

"I did. I really wanted to see your reaction to it."

"It's fabulous."

"Charlie! Invite her up!"

"Ally, would you like to come up?"

"Yes, I would. I would very much."

Charles watched as Ally glided gracefully up the short flight of stairs to his flat. He stepped back through the opened door, and when she reached the landing, he motioned for her to come inside. When she did, he scooped her up in his arms and then holding her in a tight embrace, he backpedaled toward the sofa. Clinging together fiercely, they tumbled on to it.

Ally turned her face toward him, her mouth soft and inviting. Charles leaned his head forward and placed his lips upon hers. Electricity sparked in their kiss.

When it was ended, they stared into each other's eyes without speaking. Words weren't needed.

Finally Ally said, "You do know, Charlie, that Cornish mermaids can be dangerous to mortal men."

"Yes, that's what I've heard. But Ally, I think I'm willing to take my chances."

✤ ✤ ✤

www.ingramcontent.com/pod-product-compliance
Lightning Source LLC
Chambersburg PA
CBHW021455240626
47154CB00002B/386